Misthaven
of Maine

Volume 1

of Maine

Loretta Boyer McClellan

mcclellan
creative
Los Gatos, California

Misthaven of Maine
Copyright ©2012 by Loretta McClellan
All rights reserved. Published 2012

This book is a work of fiction. Names, characters, places and incidents are either products of the author's imagination, or are used fictitiously. Any resemblance to events, locales or persons living or dead is entirely coincidental.

"Fair Winds, Tanka," Poem, ©2012, Loretta McClellan;
all rights reserved.
"Family, Haiku," Poem, ©2012, Loretta McClellan; all rights reserved
"Author's Ridge," Poem, ©2001, 2012, Loretta McClellan;
all rights reserved.

ISBN: 978-0-9856496-0-9

Published by McClellan Creative
P.O. Box 1201, Los Gatos, California
95031-1201 U.S.A.
First Edition, 2012
McClellanCreative.com

When the sun goes down,
family stands beside you—
in spirit, in truth.

For My Husband:

Forever is what we have.
I rejoice in our match made in heaven—
a partnership of unequaled triumph.
Together, it transcends all time and imagination.

Thank you for being the constant in my life.

Journey to beyond
Skirts the surface winds of fair
Billowed, blessed sky
Snared enchantment wields the air
Scented sounds, whispers the deep

Preface

Many human beings choose travel—vacations, specifically—to meander the planet in search of respite, or a change of pace. Contemplation, adventure and wide-eyed wonder are likely to prevail during the temporary sojourn. For me, somehow relocation became a primary opportunity for self-discovery over the years, providing a fuller immersion in the places and people.

One location in particular I have lived, loved, toiled and thrived in is New England. For several years my family and I lived and worked in the Boston area of Massachusetts and coastal Maine—the setting for these characters who have become an indelible cast of unswerving possibilities. As a writer and artist, I lingered between the layers of history and the ever-presence of these locales. It was an experience that will always be a part of me and who I hope to become.

Moving from the west coast to New England was the first of many journeys of truth for me and my family. The region did and does continue to inspire me, providing a gravitational pull with considerable reach. It is fitting that this should be the first setting for this inaugural novel, as just as the pages of this book reflect a permanent connection to love, loyalty and home, so too is New England forever home in my heart. Its voice offers a resounding clarity, one that for me, will always ring true.

—Loretta Boyer McClellan
California, May 2012

Acknowledgments

Editing, logo, photo, book covers, layout and wave ornament design:
©2012, Loretta McClellan; all rights reserved.
McClellanCreative.com
Facebook.com/McClellanCreative

Cover design includes a detail from the original watercolor painting:

"Misthaven," ©2011, 2012, Loretta McClellan; all rights reserved.

Chapter 1

It's not every day that a person turns sixteen, I thought to myself, wondering what Father had waiting to surprise me with at *Misthaven.* The e-mail he sent was vague regarding my birthday party. It was even signed with his legal name: Benjamin P. Hales, *Esq.*, as if I was some sort of client. That gave me the heads-up that something was in the works for a rather substantial endeavor. With my return text message I responded, confirming my arrival time on the Portland ferry around six thirty in the evening on Friday. That gave me a week to finish up the semester at Hawthorne Academy and pack up my belongings.

All week long I kept myself busy with cramming for finals. Trig was so indelibly etched in my brain that I could ace the next test, even in my sleep. Keeping a hectic pace was good for me; it helped to keep my mind off of my imminent soiree, the one that I knew Father had been planning for me for quite some time.

As Friday came and it was time to leave, I took one last look around my dorm room and glanced in the mirror, as is customary for a teenager to do. *One can never go out in public without one last glance in the mirror,* I championed myself, echoing my mother's poised instruction. As I took a longer stare at my reflection, I began to notice how much of a resemblance I had of my mother: I had the same long, naturally-light blonde hair with flecks of gold, alternating with a richer, deeper blonde, and expressively warm, brown eyes that were easily read; hiding my emotions or earnest feelings was impossible. My high cheekbones and aquiline nose were traits from Father's side of the family. My skin was of a light olive complexion, quite clear and tanned easily. I was grateful for a five-foot seven, slim, but athletic build that was still quite feminine, with long, lean legs and agility to complete the package. I never thought of myself as anything spectacular, but it had been said by others that I was growing up to be a true beauty—a "heart-breaker" by some. *Eliza Seelye Hales was not capable of intentionally hurting anyone's heart, or anything else for that matter*, I firmly assured myself.

So many of my friends were regularly anguishing over their appearance. With our school uniforms of a deep scarlet, boiled wool blazer with the Hawthorne emblem and pewter-like, crested, shank buttons; a pleated, plaid skirt of black, red and cream for girls and black slacks for boys; as well as white, oxford shirts and black, diamond-patterned ties for all, at least fashion was not a source of debate during school hours.

These unique, but beautiful good looks I'd been told I was blessed with was a tremendous compliment; however, a strong sense of self-confidence and awareness of my potential—of what I could *do*, could *be*—was my true source of self assurance. I had my parents to thank for that. They took an in-depth approach to teaching me that if I had the desire to do something, that my ambition should know no bounds—truly limitless. I lingered at the mirror not for my own reflection, but for the memories of my cherished family and the many, happy times we'd shared.

After I changed into my favorite, well-worn jeans, faded, red, *Harvard* t-shirt and olive cargo jacket for travel, I grabbed my luggage and left through the main entrance of Hales Hall. Stone-faced with high, arched, stained glass windows and imposing porticos, ivy-clad balustrades and exterior walls shrouded in rich, velvet moss, the expansive, historic building was named after my great-great-Great Grandfather, William Hales; he was one of the founders and a major benefactor of the academy. The school name originated from a Hawthorn tree, or *Crataegus,* a sentinel that once stood on the pasture land the campus was built upon. My ancestor liked the idea of providing for a prep school that prided itself on instilling tradition. He was a very wealthy and successful shipping magnate who loved the ocean and marveled at the world and all its gifts. He once had a spacious sea captain's estate in Thomaston, Maine, but on one of his trips to the Pacific, he contracted Leprosy and settled Hales Island, the isle that I now call my authentic home, as it is there where I feel the most free.

This island has become a chorus of destination and journey, bringing forth abundant fruit in both life and in the healing of death. Hales Isle is only a handful of miles in length; the pounding surf—a gift, and yet, an equal bane—has threatened to erode it further still. Maine Balsam trees are everywhere; their aroma wafts across the island like a cherished memory. Sailboats pass by often, with a distant wave of their passengers always expected. Some moor off the shoreline and venture aground for a change of pace, which is always provided in grand example by our unique society of multifaceted locals. Lobster buoys adorn many sides of the weathered, clapboard houses, as well as covered waterfront buildings in abundance. Red and white, blue and yellow, black and gold, green and white—the buoys grant a variety of unique color combinations representative of their lobstermen owners, to help them find their traps off shore.

The center of the island has a dirt road that branches-off to the northeastern, the northwestern, the southeastern and the southwestern points of the island, like a giant "X." Several off-shoots of driveways and tertiary roads split from the central vein. Cars are infrequently used on the island, but scooters, bicycles and meandering on foot are the norm. Hales Isle offers a peaceful way of life, but is never boring.

I caught a cab outside the campus gates to Boston and took the comfortable, coach bus ride to the ferry terminal in Portland. As I sunk into my seat and leaned my head against the window, I bid farewell to student life for the time being. As I closed my eyes and imagined soon breathing in deeply the scents of my path to familiar, I looked forward to the one and a half hour excursion to Hales Isle, via Casco Bay. I knew the gentle rolling of the waves beneath the boat would lull me to sleep under normal conditions, but today was different. It was my birthday!

What a gift it truly is when a person gets to spend a large portion of their life in the most picturesque spot on Earth. Picturesque is only the beginning of how I would describe *My Island*. Hales Island, Maine, had a year-round population of seventy-five. During the summer months the isle marginally swells with people from all walks of life. Doctors, lobstermen, lawyers, software professionals, artists and writers, among others, all coexist together in blissful, seaside harmony. Mingled with these folks—some of whom drift in and leave with the tide—are several, year-round characters who add to the comprehensive flavor of our domain. Their genuine approach to living taught me how to be more industrious and live life more fully.

On the northeastern point of Hales Island sits a magnificent lighthouse along the craggy shoreline. It is stately Colonial in architecture—not just a nod, but a full embrace of another century is offered in earnest. The front of this maritime icon has twelve windows: four, "four-over-four" sash windows on the first floor and four more on the second. The dormers have four, half-moon, eyebrow windows at the base of the roof with "orange peel" mullions. Centered on the roof is a grand, octagonal cupola, complete with an ornamental railing at the peak, similar to a widow's walk. This cupola served the island and its ships' passers-by well, as it had a handmade, crystal beacon within its walls. It was the only lighthouse of its kind in all of Maine. It had passed the test of time, withstanding all the changes in lighthouse technology, from coal, oil, gas and electricity, to being electronically controlled with no lighthouse keeper required.

My great-great-Great Grandfather Hales chose his architect well. He also was very generous in specifying in his will that this family home must forever remain in the family and be willed from father to firstborn son. Being the firstborn and only son, my father was blessed with a handsome treasure in *Misthaven*. Being an only child and a daughter, I often wonder if it will be called my own someday.

Sightseers from all over the country would witness this beacon of light emblazoned across the pages of all the famous New England lighthouse publications. Surprisingly, very few would actually come to see it in all its majestic splendor. That was fine with me, because I valued my island sanctuary. There was, however, one strategic vantage point from which to view *Misthaven* on the island, and that was from the Longfellow's family boathouse. The Longfellow clan resided on Hales Island for almost as long as my ancestors. They were hardworking with many talents; they were not just our neighbors, but close family friends.

Hales Island would become a refuge for me and for Father as well. Mother died in May when I was eight, leaving me with a man who initially could barely cope with his loss. Mother was everything to him; she was the air he breathed, the sweetest sound of singing birds. She was a phenomenal artist who painted on location all throughout New England. She sang while she painted—not a concert performer, but a lilting voice, nonetheless. In fact, my parents met while she was painting the House of Seven Gables in Salem. They were madly in love long after I came along, remaining so, always.

When she passed away, Father wasn't prepared for this monumental grief. For at least a week he would spend the majority of each day following her funeral at her gravesite, running his fingers over the engravings on her tombstone, which read, "Catherine Seelye Hales: Wife, Mother, Painter of Life. Her life touched so many—so deeply, never to be forgotten." A month after her death, we left our townhouse on Beacon Hill in Boston and moved to *Misthaven* indefinitely. I don't remember my birthday that June, but I do remember that was when the healing started for Father and a love of Maine island life began for me.

As long as I can remember, I loved to comb the beaches for shells, sea glass and jasper. Shells of any kind were a prize in my little hands. I would put them in bottles to always admire. In my room up on the shelf at *Misthaven* were all kinds of these gifts from the sea. I would also select a nosegay of lupines, in memory of my mother, as they were her favorite. I always placed them in a little mason jar of water next to the shells. Nearby on another wall were two of my mother's paintings: a matched pair, depicting the pond at Boston Common, both in summer and in winter. I vaguely remember trying to ice skate along with my parents when I was barely three. The few paintings that I had of hers were kept for multiple reasons: artistic expertise, sentimental locations and reminiscent of the family; a piece of her life was preserved in each one.

What a tragic waste of talent it was for Mother to die at such a young age. She was teaching at the School of the Museum of Fine Arts in Boston and had exhibited her works locally and nationally. She was about to ascend to the next level of international exhibition, when she was run down by a taxi right out in front of the MFA. Her short life that had so much promise was taken away so quickly. The taxi was car-jacked by a high-profile criminal trying to outrun the police. He succeeded to escape, initially. The incident provided media fodder for weeks. If only my mother had successfully responded to the EMTs.

I can recollect about this all now freely, as much time has passed. Time does help heal my wounds; however, "A girl's loss of a mother while still young, may stifle emotional progression," my guidance counselor at Hawthorne keeps repeating. I try not to focus on the fact that my mother is no longer living on this earth, but that I know I'll see her again, one day. The only consolation about the tragedy was that the felon was eventually caught before he could hurt anyone else, so her death was not completely in vain.

The first summer we lived at *Misthaven* was quiet, but packed full of excitement. Father had hired a nanny, the effervescent red-head,

Charlotte Fitzgerald, age twenty-three, from County Cork in Ireland. Her job was to take care of me while he shuttled back and forth to Boston, where his law firm, *Hales, Whitehead, Mayhew and Olmstead* was located. At the age of nine, I thought I didn't need supervision, but luckily, parental wisdom prevailed and Father won in securing someone to keep me out of trouble. On the weekends he would be there to share with me in my many recollections of weekday adventures that he had missed. Only later did I discover just how much he did miss my escapades. It wasn't long after that summer that he left one of his senior partners to take charge of the firm so that he could reap the blessings of business ownership and be a more present father at the same time. As I look back, giving the reins of his firm to someone other than himself was very therapeutic in Father's recovery over Mother's death. It was also a permanent seal on a father-daughter alliance that would never be broken.

Christmas that year took some getting used to. After three months of private, home tutoring for school, we attempted to spend it on the island, but found that Boston was a little more of what we needed in holiday fare at the time. Since all the limousines were spoken for, from the ferry landing in Portland we directly taxied to the townhouse on Beacon Hill. It was the first time we had been there in six months. I didn't think Father could set foot in any taxi at all, but he surprised me tremendously with that quantum leap. Our trusted housekeeper, Emmeline Smith, a New York Yankees fan from Connecticut—a team allegiance we didn't hold against her—was in perfect form for the holidays; the house was not only pristine, but decorated to the hilt! There were Christmas trees in every major room, including a few, "themed" trees that I absolutely adored. My favorite tree was the "Northwoods" one. It depicted moose, canoes, loons and snowshoes for a remarkably woodsy feel. The front parlor was decked-out in formal attire, including antique glass ornaments on the tree in the bay window, facing the street.

On Christmas morning, just before heading back to the island, we opened presents. I was expecting the normal type of gifts for a young girl: dolls in grand estates, dress-up clothes, etc., but this time was memorably different. Father gave me a family heirloom: an antique sea captain's telescope made of solid brass, with a single lens. It was engraved with, "For Eliza, With Love, Father," on it. He told me that this particular gift represented his hope that I would always keep on a straight course in life and to always know where I should go and how I should get there. I didn't quite understand the magnitude of the gift at the time, but I kept it all these years. It has been very dear to me.

In fact, I could have used it right now to "scope out" the greeters on the landing waiting there for my arrival for the big, Sweet Sixteen, "surprise" party. That was not the case; as I got off the ferry, Father was there with no one else. He wanted to spend a few moments with me alone, I suppose. Before I gave him a big hug, I quickly studied him to always remember this moment by. The rich, dark brown hair, cut short with layers and subtle bronze highlights from spending so much time in the sun, accented his tan, distinguished, facial features and darkest brown eyes. At six-feet four inches in height, he was a man of considerable presence, who instantly commanded respect.

Thanks to genetic strengths, he was still blessed with a trim physique as well—for a *Dad* that is. Surprisingly, he was sporting a mustache and close-cut goatee this visit; he alternated between a mustache, a mustache and goatee and clean-shaven, every time I saw him. One never knew what to expect—well almost never. One thing that was for sure was that he spent some considerable time in another part of the country other than New England, based on his accent. Father was born in Boston, but moved to San Francisco at the age of two. He summered in Maine, but didn't return to Boston permanently, until college. The Bay Area in Northern California would produce an accent that was clipped and considerably pin-pointable if you could recognize dialects. Most just thought we were from "out west."

People often couldn't understand why I didn't have a more "Bostonian" accent, until they met my father.

He asked how finals went and if I expected to make the Dean's list. I wanted to get down to the real business at hand: my party, and who was coming. Being the straight-faced man that he was, Father wasn't going to give away any surprise—not for such a significant achievement of turning sixteen.

We drove in the station wagon taxi that Rusty Copper—part lobsterman, part taxi driver—owned down the dirt road in the center of the island, out to our point on the rocky peninsula. Seeing our lighthouse standing there amongst the pines, firs and the rocky shore made me remember when my mother had given our island home its name: *Misthaven*. For generations it had been known simply as the "Hales' Estate," but a name with a more ethereal quality was required, to make it truly ours.

The name came about one summer day when there was some fog about the point that quickly turned into a misty shroud. The dew in the air was so light and soft. I remember it touching my face like thousands of tiny drops of moisture dancing in a whirl. Mother completed the experience by swinging me by my hands around and around and around, until I couldn't stand it anymore. I squealed in delight. She was singing a beautiful rendition of, "Singing in the Rain," all the while she was spinning me. After we were finished with our rain dance, Mother explained to me the importance of special moments like this one, between parents and their children, moments that you never forget. She told me of the significance of the home being a haven from the world and how you should always feel safe there and secure. The name *Misthaven* came to her lips and she mumbled it over and over a few times, until she had the name solidified in her mind as the perfect emblem for our lighthouse home on the point. What Mother didn't get to see, was that year after year, *Misthaven* stayed true to its name, even in idyllic weather, as moisture

9

would collect under the canopy of the nearby stand of trees from the sea.

As Father and I got out of the island taxi to walk down the path toward our humble abode, he gave me another big hug and a smile. He told me how he had been waiting for this day to come, so that he could show me just how much he still loved his little girl. He always made it a point to remind me that fathers' daughters will always be their "little girls," even when they grow up. He made no exception that June seventh.

Chapter 2

Before Father and I walked inside of *Misthaven*, I took a moment to gaze out toward the horizon and be thankful for the life I had been able to lead thus far. I turned and walked inside the main entrance hall, wondering who would be there to give their best wishes for me on the other side. Normally, I would not be so me-centric, but there was something epic about this particular milestone.

As I approached the door, someone came up behind me and covered my eyes with their hands. I grabbed the hands and detected a sinewy, muscular feel to them, like those of a sculptor, mechanic, or guitarist. I spun around, and to my amazement, found my Uncle Seth standing there before me. Tears began to well up within my eyes to see him there after all the years that had passed. Seth Seelye was my favorite uncle, even if he was my only uncle. He was my mother's baby brother, also an accomplished artist and world-renowned, who traveled the globe as he painted, or perhaps it was the other way around. Like Paul Gauguin, you wouldn't be surprised to hear that Seth spent a year living in Tahiti enjoying himself with the people, while at the same time, exhibiting his work amongst the royal elite of the Pacific, Asia and elsewhere. He was well-loved by the local people wherever he hung his canvas.

After my tears quickly dried, the three of us crossed the threshold one by one, to meet my special guests. A quick glance directed to the inlaid compass rose gracing the foyer floor. It was still there, in its rightful place, welcoming all who pass over it. It offered an iconic sense of comfort and familiarity to me.

Father gently tugged my arm, gesturing that we needed to go to the parlor, which was on the first floor, opposite from the foyer. The grand space was clad in polished oak floors with a one-inch, mahogany strip along the edge of the room; it was also centered by a large, formal brick fireplace, with a hand-carved, mahogany mantel facing the rear. The fireplace replaced the original, center chimney that was removed when the lighthouse was installed—a major architectural feat, per the story passed through the family. The only first-floor evidence remaining of the center chimney was the entry hall, which passed from the front of the house, to the rear. This gracious entertaining room also offered two expansive, oval picture windows on either side of the fireplace, each with an ocean view so breathtaking, it was an other-worldly experience, like being outside the house taking in an aerial perspective, spinning around and around, until you collapse from the breathlessness of it all.

While the parlor was a favorite gathering spot, guests would always eventually gravitate to the finished attic, which housed the lighthouse cupola. It was the one room all visitors wished to see. In this lengthy expanse, the exposed, bottom portion of the lens housing cast a shimmering light that created such a gossamer effect, it felt like one was in some sort of dreamlike state. I was reminded how the room looked at night, the darkness bathed in crystal beams when the beacon was in full swing, monitoring the point for all at sea. I especially appreciated those moments alone, when the sparkle was like the sky, burdened with stars.

As Father and I joined the party, there were about one hundred people there applauding, as if I were some famous mezzo-soprano who just gave an encore performance. After initial embarrassment, I immediately felt assured that everyone present knew my flaws and liked me anyway. When I regained my visual perspective of the whole celebration, I began to recognize each individual, standing side by side. Some were friends of the family who knew my father for years from various business dealings with the firm. Some were state representatives, congressmen, senators and judges, from both Maine and Massachusetts. Two of my favorite professors from Hawthorne

Academy, who were old family friends and Harvard alumni from Father's graduating class were present, as well as several attorney colleagues of his and cherished neighbors. As I was combing the wall of people, my eyes drew me to the center of the crowd. As if we were the only two people in the room, our gazes were set upon each other and locked in-place.

"Caleb?" the name came out barely as a whisper. We moved closer to one another, and the gathering temporarily gave way for us to meet face to face for the first time in almost a year. I was looking into the eyes of a person who knew my soul better than most—a true friend in every sense of the word—my oldest friend. Caleb Daniel Longfellow was a native son of Maine, born and bred from island soil. He left for Japan with his family for a job of a lifetime for his father, then returned and made up for lost time with fervent dedication. I loved Maine from the start, but Caleb's perspective heightened my awareness of so much more to offer in the Pine Tree State.

His father was a master shipbuilder, as his ancestors were before him; they took advantage of their property's deep water access and boat yard on Hales Island to mesh maritime tradition with creative skill and engineering prowess. During their time abroad, his father honed his craft at a waterfront tourist attraction in Nagoya, in Aichi Prefecture on the main island of Honshu, Japan. Nagoya was deemed the largest shipping port in the country. They had recruited Caleb's father to individually build several, traditional, American-made, double-ended dories—a distinctive boat of Maine. His contract expanded to build several more—all by hand. It was a boutique operation and cultural exchange that promoted quality over quantity for a boat design that heralded home.

Now seventeen, staring at me with his ocean-blues, I studied Caleb's dark brown lashes and eyebrows that set off his spellbinding, sapphire eyes even more so, and layered, sandy blonde hair that was casually swept away from his sun-kissed face, looking slightly windblown, in a pleasing way. His jaw line was firm and unwavering, which partnered flawlessly with the chiseled planes of his photogenic face. His full lips were pleasantly reserved. An effortless ease in appearance, the dimple on one side of his face—his left—caused ladies of all ages to swoon whenever he smiled.

He stood there in front of me with his khaki-colored, twill slacks and apple green polo shirt, busily shifting his position, from one foot back to the other. His trademark boat shoes were as well-worn as ever, the same as his weathered, red and white dinghy. If it wasn't in use, it would be found run aground, along the wisps of shoreline grass about the island. He left it outside, year-round, never stored indoors. It had an odd, "043" painted on its bow, from when it was briefly owned by a northern yacht club. It was Caleb's first example of boat building, so his sentimental side got the best of him; he bought it back as soon as he earned the money.

Compared to the Longfellow family, I guess we Hales' babied all of our vessels. Caleb insisted to his father that upon arrival back home to Maine, the two of them would embark on a boat building endeavor of their own, hence the dinghy he was so attached to. It was a reminder of his return home to Maine, as well as a special time with his father, Jacob—a quiet man of tremendous design and engineering talent, who liberally passed on his knowledge to his eager-to-learn son.

"Eliza Seelye Hales, well isn't this a nice occasion, and such an intimate group of friends and dignitaries," Caleb wryly announced, as the party guests stepped aside. His sarcasm was sorely missed. I was comfortable with this resuming of our predictable, friendly banter. This same, jovial interaction transpired at a wonderful reunion three years ago, after his return to the island from Japan after two years of infrequent, "via air mail" letters. When they did happen to grace my mailbox, they were plastered with "scenes from Japan" stamps. It was even a rarity to receive an email message from him. What Caleb didn't know was how very much I looked forward to his letters. I saved all of them.

We went on to briefly reminisce about the last couple of summers we both lived on the island and how we enjoyed those simpler times. We agreed to get together the next day and would pick up our conversation then.

Father had another surprise—I could tell by the way he came up behind Caleb and me, poised with this grin on his face. "Eliza, you have another special guest to greet," Father anxiously proclaimed. He seemed far too excited for this to be just *anyone*. As he and I worked our way through the sea of guests, I came to the southern picture window and saw my best friend from Hawthorne: Ashleigh Bennington.

Her hair looked even more of a deep and gorgeous red than I left her with at our dorm yesterday. *Yet another trip to the salon*, I suspected. Between her frequent hair coloring, weekly facials and her bi-monthly French manicures, she kept that salon in business. Her eyes were a cross between a light hazel and a rich brocade of gold, giving her a stare that would mesmerize even at great distances. With her pouty lips, striking good looks and five-foot, ten-inch wispy frame, it made her a frequent choice of the local modeling agencies in Boston. Because of her industry ties, Ashleigh always came dressed to kill in designer everything—right down to her purse, shoes and keychain.

"Father, you must have gone to great lengths to get Ashleigh here, because she was supposed to be cruising the Caribbean with her parents right about now; it's an undisputed family tradition."
"It really wasn't that difficult to arrange, because your father has had this party in the works since last fall; my parents were happy to oblige with such an unusually long notice," Ashleigh confirmed. "By the way, why such a grand affair for your sixteenth, that isn't even technically presenting you to society?" she asked in a pseudo-aloof tone.

"Oh we have a tradition here at *Misthaven*, to not obligate ourselves to social norms—especially when it comes to birthdays," informed Father, with a wisp of a smile.

"I rather like this nonconformist attitude we have, but it applies strictly to birthdays; everything else is pretty much standard, Yankee Method," I proudly stated.

After a few more introductions of business associates of Father's, we got to the festivities at hand. Appetizers included the traditional, New England fare of smoked Atlantic salmon, crab legs, crab cakes and other assorted sea treasures. Dessert—chocolate mousse torte, my favorite—was then served, along with white grape juice punch, animated with the bubbles of mineral water. During dessert, everyone had the opportunity to share some funny stories about me, in between mouthfuls of decadent, chocolate dreamery. It was a little uncomfortable for the associates of Father's who didn't know me well enough to quip, but they enjoyed the camaraderie just as well. Father was able to catch-up on business news, in between his hosting duties, so it was a double-win for him.

The funniest story of all was actually a triple-tie between one from Ashleigh about my "adventures in science," where I grabbed the wrong beaker of chemicals and made, "quite a show" for my class; the next one from Caleb, where he and I had gone sailing when I was ten and ended up capsizing in shallow water, with me coming up with a giant coil of seaweed on my head; and last but not least, Father's. He stated rather proudly how when I was but a few months old, I threw up so heavily on Mother in a helicopter ride over Kauai, that he had to literally hose her off when we disembarked. The pilot kept handing my mother tissues while he narrated the journey, as if a small swatch of fragile paper could clean up the massive destruction I had spewed all over the place. Thank goodness Father waited until after everyone was finished eating to tell his horror story!

After all the humor, it was time for me to really reap the rewards of being roasted on a skewer—opening the presents! I began to unwrap the gifts that were nearest to me. They were all extremely generous: a lady's mariner's watch, complete with my name engraved on it; several gifts of money in varying denominations from diverse people who didn't know what to bring me—I was grateful that they thought of me at all; and a unique gift of requesting my presence at the upcoming filming of the latest, coastal, Maine-based movie, complete with my favorite actor—compliments of Warren Creighton, my father's old dorm mate from Harvard and currently the most in-demand film Director in the U.S. It was too bad that he couldn't attend in person, as I knew that Father was missing his comrade in arms.

These fabulous gifts, along with many others were ceremoniously overshadowed by the gift from the three most important men in my life: Father, Uncle Seth and Caleb. Caleb had everyone come outside to the tip of the peninsula to see what was in store for me. Neatly up against the dock, down behind the house at twilight, was the most magnificent, wooden sailboat I had ever seen. There, in all her numerous, hand-sanded coats of marine-grade varnish and gleaming, teak glory was *Eliza's Wake,* a twenty-eight foot, handmade sloop of the finest, Maine-made craftsmanship. What a sight to behold! Caleb couldn't wait for me to board her. As I approached this magnificent craft, Caleb sped ahead of me and with great agility, jumped on deck to assist. I called ahead, "Permission to come aboard?"
"My lady, but you are the owner and captain of this mighty vessel, and thus do not need to request permission!" Caleb answered in his most seaworthy brogue. I came aboard and surveyed my maritime acquisition, drafting my fingertip along the black canvas sail cover. What beautiful lines she had!

What did I do to deserve this? I thought to myself. Beyond the familiar, welcoming fragrance of sea spray, I could still sense the faint aroma of the many finishes, as I gazed up at the crisp, white sail, looking like a brand new bed sheet, soon to be snapped taut. An amber-weave picnic basket with gold buckle was stowed neatly in the cockpit—*a nice touch,* I surmised, raising my eyebrow.

"Caleb, where did you find the time to *do* this?" I asked in astonishment.
"My Dad had completed most of the hull a while ago. I also had a little help from a mighty fine lawyer from Boston and a globe-trotting painter who had a great interest in making you happy," he resounded gleefully. I still couldn't figure out how they all worked on this together with their negligible free time, and Seth's global meanderings. I gave up trying to figure out the mystery and enjoyed her miraculous beauty.

It was all pretty evident by now that their surprise was a complete success, because I had made great strides to ready her for sail, by barking preliminary orders at Caleb immediately. I was the Captain and I was in charge of my destiny!

We had guests that I needed to attend to, plus arrange the christening ceremony before we sailed her anywhere, so I quickly postponed our voyage for the next morning, as the weather was projected to be optimal.

After the guests had all left for the mainland—with the exception of Ashleigh and Uncle Seth, as they were staying the night—I took one more look out that magnificent window, out to the point of the peninsula to watch the last of the sun's rays set behind the horizon. I thought to myself with a wide smile: *this was a day I'll never forget.*

Chapter 3

The next day Uncle Seth—the quintessential, night owl artist that he is—didn't surprise any of us and slept in. Father didn't want him to miss the early morning festivities, so he beckoned him to hurry along so he could be a witness of this momentous occasion. Ashleigh and I got shipshape in a hurry to join Caleb and his parents on the dock. Each person who played a role in the reason for this event was present. All gathered around to witness this tradition and to wish us a bon voyage on our maiden voyage of *Eliza's Wake*.

Thankfully, good weather did indeed prevail. Caleb had let me know last night after the party that he had written a fitting tribute, as words were a token of good luck and must be spoken. After his recitation ended and the naming words of *Eliza's Wake* were uttered, we broke out the fancy reserve and christened her—more like doused her—with the best, native water money could buy from our very own island. It was a most appropriate sentiment, fulfilling the sage requirements of nautical lore. We got under way around a quarter past seven to a solid gust of wind. Bidding farewell from the dock, Father shouted that dinner would be ready at six thirty and steamers would be on the menu.

As we headed around the island and *Misthaven* was out of sight, we picked up some wicked wind and the *'Wake* showed what she was really made of. Caleb didn't need to scrutinize her seaworthiness, as generations of ship building expertise had led the way.

Sea birds chased us for a bit, then vanished as quickly as they came. Rocky shorelines were fading in the distance, as we whisked through the course of the bay at a brisk pace. No motor to deafen the experience—just speed, with just the sound of the wind—was pure, joyous exhilaration. The sun was shining so brightly, that everything white—including the sail—was intensified, three-fold.

I watched as Caleb trimmed the sail, seemingly happy in his thoughts. He caught himself squinting as he turned his direction toward me, immediately softening his expression into a warm, broad smile. The ocean was competing in brilliance to the elation on Caleb's face. I too felt completely peaceful and at home on the sea.

After a short while, I gave the helm to Caleb and Ashleigh and I began to catch up on the latest news of our classmates from the academy. Caleb, wanting to be included in our conversation, interrupted us with something to the effect of, "Nothing can compete with this..." as his words trailed off.
"What was that?" I said.
"Oh, just that nothing can compete with a steadfast ship, good company and a hearty wind," Caleb answered in his best, pirate-like accent.
"Aye-aye Captain!" Ashleigh approved.
"Hey, *I'm* the Captain here—just taking a break while the crew takes over for a bit, aye Swabby?" I interjected with an impish smile. It was so nice to be amongst friends who knew me so well.

Caleb asked me if I remembered that first summer when I was nine and we met that old salt who hung out at the general store regularly. His name was Captain Campbell, we both recalled, and remembered that his boat was called the *Scottish Lass*. Captain Campbell was of Scottish descent and his ancestors had made their way to Maine, via Nova Scotia. He was a lobsterman and prided himself on bringing in the biggest catch, each time he set out from Hales Island.

Captain Campbell had reeled us both in one day by spinning a yarn about a mermaid named "Matilda," who dwelled a quarter mile southeast off the coast of the island. He had told us that he visited her each time he headed out that way and she always had a message for him to bring to us. Most often it was, "Mind your parents," or "Mind your manners," or something of that sort. We figured later on that this was his way to creatively keep us behaving well, out of trouble, and give him something he could laugh about from time to time.

Just then we saw an alarming sight: another sailboat approached us so quickly and so closely, as if it was on a death wish. It startled us so much that we all stopped talking for a while, just to catch our breath. Nothing but the salt spray whispering in the air was all we heard for what seemed like several minutes.

To break up the silence, Ashleigh brought up a subject that I never thought she'd mention in front of Caleb, so soon after the party: "So Eliza, when are you going to leave for your study abroad program this summer?"
I caught my breath and answered, "Hey Ashleigh, I thought you were going to let me mention this at the *right* time?"
"*Hey*, what's this about leaving the island already? You *just got here!*" Caleb exclaimed, rather irritated.
"I was going to tell you tomorrow, after we had a picture-perfect sail day and had a chance to get our land legs back," I jokingly, yet timidly defended myself.

I could tell that Caleb was not pleased that his oldest friend was contemplating halting their summer plans before they even started.
"What about the boat? Aren't you going to get some use out of her, after all the hard work we did building her?" Caleb asked, clearly annoyed. *With all that painstaking effort he was certainly justified, but I didn't know. How could I?*
"I had no idea this maritime gift was in store for me when I made my plans to go to England," I stated, matter-of-factly. "Seeing that my oldest friend is rather upset with me at this point and I really was looking for any excuse to not have to be apart for a time, I think you win—I will spend the summer on the island!" was my diplomatic addition.

"Whatever you wish, my lady!" was Caleb's reply, patently victorious.

After a day of fine sailing, which included a brief, shore excursion to Big Diamond Island for a pickup of cream puffs from Caleb's favorite chef, we headed back to Hales Island. We were windblown, but invigorated by the bay and all its natural splendor.

Uncle Seth was sitting on the dock in his bare feet painting in watercolor, when we returned. He got up and assisted us with the boat, when Caleb jumped off and ran farther down the shore to pick up something. He immediately came back to the dock and gave both Ashleigh and me each our own, beautiful shell. "Something to remember this day by," was his way of saying that all was well.

Caleb headed off to his place on the other side of the island, which wasn't much of a hike, since the area was so tiny. Ashleigh and I went inside the house, while Uncle Seth finished up his session of *plein air* painting, which was just a fancy way of labeling painting outdoors.

Dinner was on the table in the dining room, which was quite a large area for lighthouse quarters. Father had converted one of the parlors into an addition to the dining room to allow for larger company at the dinner table.

The steamers were there, along with clam chowder flown to Portland and ferried in from our favorite Boston seafood restaurant. We also had the pleasure of feasting our eyes and later our appetites on homemade blueberry pie from Mrs. Godfrey. She was a retired schoolteacher from the island who taught in the one-room schoolhouse for forty years. I often regretted not attending that school and living here consistently year-round.

"So how was your sail today? Was the wind favorable?" asked Father.
"We had a nice sail, but had a close call with some tourist with a

vengeance out of Annapolis—a forty-foot ketch I think, named '*Annabelle*,'" was my reply.

"Yes, Mr. Hales, we aimed to bring your daughter back in one piece," Ashleigh added with a twinkle in her eye.

A few moments later Uncle Seth joined us and we all enjoyed our meal with lighthearted conversation. After dinner, Ashleigh excused herself so she would be well-rested for her big travel day tomorrow. She would take the ferry back to Portland, a shuttle flight to Logan and another flight to Miami, where she would join her parents before they headed out to the Caribbean, on-board their usual, luxury cruise liner. It would be a full day, so I said goodnight to her and let her get her beauty rest.

It's amazing how much travel alone we each survived at tender ages. My father trusted the ferry and bus captains and flight stewards tremendously, to allow me to leave his sight as a young girl. I was grateful for the independence I had achieved and the trust in me to get from point A to point B safely, under watchful care.

Upstairs in my room I looked out my window with my antique spyglass, trying to "see" if that mermaid was making an appearance off the point. Actually, I rather enjoyed watching the moonlight dance upon the water as the waves lapped along the shore. Stretching and yawning, I climbed into bed thinking about what a picture-perfect day I had shared with Caleb and Ashleigh. "This is living…" I mumbled to myself, as I drifted off to sleep.

Chapter 4

When I awoke the next morning, I threw on some clothes and ate breakfast. I accompanied Ashleigh to the ferry landing and saw her off with a wave. It was a fun time to share, and I took comfort knowing that I'd see her again in a couple of months when school resumed in the fall.

On the way home, I decided to walk instead of taxi back and savored each and every sight, sound and smell of the island. Summer is the season when the world is teeming with life, reveling in sunshine. On our Atlantic oasis, one can never cease to find interesting creatures, flora or fauna to observe. Along with spending time with friends, studying nature was a favorite pastime for me and just about everyone who lived here.

Taking the dirt road down the center of the island, I made a few detours to encompass the shore along my trek back to *Misthaven*. I made my way by the one-room schoolhouse and noticed that no children were playing on the playground equipment—not even tourists. I kept plodding along, when I noticed some unusual noises coming from the Hampton place. I crossed the road to get a closer listen, when all of a sudden there was a big crash! About one hundred feet from their faded, brown and white, clapboard house in the back along the shore was their artist's studio in the process of being demolished. Mr. Hampton had finally removed his wife's retreat, clad with lobster traps and wooden buoys. After a year of it reminding him daily of being a widower, it finally met its demise. It broke my heart to see him still grieving. I guess that was to be expected when you had been married for forty-seven years and the love of your life dies, leaving you left behind, alone in your thoughts. "One day someone will be in love with me like that," I vowed to myself.

Continuing on my way back home, I stopped to sit on a rock along the water's edge. I loved to peer out to the other islands in Casco Bay. It made for feeling less isolated, so far off the shore from the mainland. While the harbor buoys were gently clanging at repeated intervals, birds were flying overhead, trying to figure out if I had any treats for them or not. Pulling a small bag of bread out of my pocket, I began to see what good retrievers these aviators were. Sitting there feeding them, my mind wandered off to the summer the year before Caleb had left for Japan.

We had been inseparable friends—better than family, with fewer arguments. Summer truly began the minute school got out at Hawthorne and Father and I would head off to the island every June. Caleb and I would be the famous twosome who palled around all season long, while the adults vicariously lived through our adventures.

That particular summer was especially memorable. Caleb had come by the house to spend the day with me venturing about, and while we were out on our excursion on foot, tragedy struck. We made our way to the ferry landing where some tourists were waiting for the next transport. Their two, small children were playing near the edge of the pier, when one of them fell off into the water. The husband had taken a restroom break, so the wife was there with their three children alone. As quickly as the child fell, Caleb had leapt into the water to save the little boy, while his mother shrieked in panic. Caleb was an accomplished swimmer and reached the toddler before he even had a chance to start to sink. It was a perfectly choreographed maneuver, only he had no time for a trial run under these exacting conditions.

He swam the little boy toward the shore, who was coughing and sputtering, and continued to wade closer toward the mother, who was by this time at the waters' edge on the rocks. With her older child in tow and a baby in her arms, she quickly moved to calf-deep water to meet up with Caleb and claim her precious cargo.

The father finally emerged from the public restroom to find that all his family was still intact. I was amazed that he hadn't heard all the commotion and came out sooner. Later I found out that the creaking of the landing pylons, combined with the echo of the bathroom interior made for bad acoustics to hear outside the facility.

Caleb emerged a hero that day and soon after was given a medal from the Portland, Maine Fire Department, who monitored the island. It was the talk of the area for the entire summer. After that episode, we were treated with the utmost respect from all the islanders, and even some prominent tourists.

All the locals made it a point to give credit to the Portland, Maine Boy Scout Troop 580 for the Lifesaving merit badge training. Caleb would ferry to the mainland every week to have his patrol meetings, even though it was an additional trip from his already scheduled, mainland, school ferry trip. "Above and beyond the call of duty," was a fitting description of Caleb's scouting dedication and Eagle Scout rank.

Suddenly there was a soft pelting of pebbles on my back. "I knew I'd find you here," Caleb heralded. I was suddenly back in reality and turned around to see a perfect smile of epic proportions.
"I was just thinking about the time you saved that little boy off the ferry launch," I recollected, sitting upon my roadside rock.
"You know how I don't like attention called to myself; can we reminisce about *your* glory days?" I took the hint and stood up, stretching myself in a rather large, sweeping motion, side to side.
"Let's take a walk, Caleb; I need to work the kinks out of my legs."
"You're too young to have kinks," was his immediate response. We both got up and moved on, despite my friend's reluctance to leave an ideal vantage spot for viewing the water.

We kept a leisurely pace along the dusty road while we talked some more about summers gone-by. As I listened to Caleb's voice calmly itemizing each and every facet of a particular journey we once set out on, I recalled that his comforting tone brought me out of a very scary situation once, one that I had forgotten about—until now.

I remembered that there was a time that we were hiking in the woods on the southern tip of our isle a couple of years ago, where the tall pine trees whistled so loudly in the wind that you got chills up your spine from the eeriness. Creating a sense of adventure, I decided to scale one of those trees to almost the top branches, as I imagined that a lightweight girl would be of no consequence to the stature of that tree. Caleb was not amused and demanded that I begin my descent immediately. Not wanting to be labeled as a girl who didn't have a mind of her own, I laughed at his vehement request!

The wind picked up. Due to the slim nature of the tree, my perch began to sway tremendously. A storm approached out of nowhere and began to rain heavily, with wind speed later estimated on the news as rather substantial. Hanging on with all the strength I could muster, I screamed and began to white-knuckle my clasp around the circumference. Caleb sensed that I had mentally "vapor-locked," and climbed his way up to me immediately, sensing I was quickly losing my grip. In between the rustling sounds of the storm, in a soothing pitch, he asked me to trust him. Knowing that I was still not with him mentally, he started talking about my mother to quickly get my attention.

"Eliza, your mother would really appreciate you returning safely home to your father...*do you hear me?*" he had said. I was temporarily snapped out of my altered state and paid attention to him. "Hey, there you are!" he beamed. That smile and tranquil voice brought me back to the task at hand. "We need to get you down from here, okay?" my climbing buddy exclaimed.

By this time, my hands were pretty raw from clinging to that trunk with all my might. Caleb coached me down with extreme repose and I responded by obeying his every word. Audibly grasping at each word he uttered, I made my way back down to the ground, safe and unharmed, but quite damp.

"Eliza? Are you with me here?" Caleb nudged me from the side. I hadn't heard a single word he said since we left my perch near Mr. Hampton's.

"I guess I was off somewhere in another place," I answered remorsefully. "I was concentrating on your voice as you were speaking and totally veered-off into remembering the time you begged me to come down from that pine tree on that stormy day."

"Begged you?" he refuted with raised eyebrows. "If I recall, you were so scared that you couldn't have heard my voice if I had told you that you had won a million dollars!" he firmly corrected. "I had to climb up that sliver of a conifer and make total eye contact with you to persuade you to focus your attention! Even then, I still had to resort to emergency tactics to get you to listen to me!"

Laughing, I think Caleb realized that I was just teasing.

"You sure know how to get to me Eliza," Caleb conceded, and then, while ceremoniously grabbing at his heart, he fell dramatically to the ground. He picked a nice, grassy knoll to demonstrate his acting abilities, I surmised, as did a few onlookers, who rolled their eyes as they stood watching from across the road. The one constancy on the island was plenty of supervision, due to people who liked to make it their sworn duty to monitor our every move. Despite the nosiness, I admit I liked the comfort of knowing everyone here, and everyone here knowing me. It was a big sense of security for me.

While lying there on the rolling sod, I was informed that today was the last day I'd see Caleb for a while. "I have to go to the mainland for a few days," he informed me.

"Whatever for?"

"Can't I ever remain mysterious in your eyes?"

"Fine, I won't press you anymore, Caleb." So I helped him to his feet and we were off again on our roundabout trek toward *Misthaven*.

Without saying any words for a great distance, we both took in the vast beauty that surrounded us. A blue heron flew overhead and several wild blueberry patches were in our midst. We continued along and came upon Maddie Kennedy's lemonade stand. She was a precocious, towheaded six year-old, and quite the young entrepreneur.

"Would you like to buy a cup of nice, cool, fresh, tasty lemonade for twenty-five cents?" she inquired in her most salesman-like, tiny voice.

"After that vivid description of the beverage, why of course—we'll take two cups," I replied, while handing her a one-dollar bill. "Keep the change," I added. Maddie was so excited with her tip that she almost abandoned her strategically positioned sales post.

"Thank you both, very much!" she gleefully cheered, pocketing the money in her miniature-sized, embroidered jeans.

By this time of the day, the lemonade was a refreshing treat, so we leaned against a nearby fence post and savored each drop of the heavenly liquid. Our presence remained unnoticed only for a short time, when there was a shout from the front porch behind the fence. "Good day to you two!" was Mrs. Emily Stanfield's standard greeting. She was sweeping off the sand from the stoop of her cottage. While she kept fussing with this one, gray curl of hair that kept making its way across her field of vision, she finally completed her task.

Her home was New England farmhouse style with two, gothic windows flanking each side of the door; a low roofline slung over the front porch, with two dormers above. The multi-gabled roof afforded well against the bright, blue sky, adorned with big, billowy clouds. The path leading up to the house was fieldstone, sandwiched by tiny tufts of bright, green moss. Beautiful roses and hydrangeas adorned the railings of the porch, completing the quintessential cottage look.

Mrs. Stanfield was for a time, sort of a mystery around the island. She came to live in our society of island dwellers after a terrible tragedy in her family. She had lived in Cape Elizabeth, Maine for most of her adult life, when her entire family: her husband, two daughters, her son and all three of her grandchildren were in a pond skating accident. They were all skating when the ice cracked; while her husband tried to save their son, daughters and grandchildren, he fell in as well, and no other adult was around to help them to safety.

It was too much to bear living amongst familiar sights, sounds and smells, yet Emily couldn't give up living in Maine. So she told me one day as the two of us were swinging on her Adirondack porch swing a few years ago, that she came to Hales Island for solace, peace and a desperately needed change.

She definitely got the change part, because each person on this expanse of rock was prone to individuality to the fullest extent. She was determined to, "live *by herself*, taking care *of herself*," until she died. She was the best example of how I imagined any of my grandmothers might be like, as they, along with their respective partners in life had all passed on, long before I was born, with similar reputations of self-sufficiency and fortitude. I admired Emily's determination to live in a place where an occasional ice storm hits, and also where there was no doctor on the island, save a vacationing practitioner during the summer season. The nearest hospital, fire department and police were on the mainland in Portland.

"Well, well, well, Master Caleb and Miss Eliza," Emily Stanfield surveyed, with her hands on her hips after she tossed her broom aside. "What are you two up to this fine day?" Emily peered through her thick, wire-rimmed glasses, framed by her silver curls, still intact, despite the wind.
"We're just studying nature and the like," Caleb said matter-of-factly.
"And the like?" What an odd turn of phrase for him, I thought to myself, stifling a chuckle.

30

"If you two don't mind, I'd like to show you something I found yesterday along the shore; it's out back," Emily said, as she wiped her hands on her apron and made her way around the side of her hazy-gray and black-trimmed cottage. "What exactly is it?" I asked cautiously, wondering what was in store for us.

As we approached her back yard, we both advanced our leisurely stroll to a full-out run toward an Atlantic surprise! Standing there with her expressive, green eyes—that had surely seen her share of life experiences—wearing a small, yellow print, floral apron covering her favorite gardening dress, was Emily Stanfield, holding up a small shark in all its glory! With her last bit of strength she collected, she hoisted up the sleek creature of the sea for us to marvel at.

"How did you catch this?" I asked, not sure how this elderly lady could reel in one that big. "With heavy gauge fishing line, and a wicked resolve!" she boldly answered back, mighty proud of herself. I was impressed that a lady in her eighties could have done such a thing. She made me realize that when I get old, I too want to live my life like I was young, despite what other people thought or expected of me. I knew that day that I might get old, but I was determined to *never grow up!* Emily always made me feel like I was her peer—someone her equal, not some silly child who didn't have anything much to offer in a conversation, deemed invalid by their youth. I think she fully understood what it was like to be misjudged due to misperceptions of age. In this respect, we were both in the same boat.

Mrs. Stanfield was my surrogate, "Nana." Throughout the years, she would spend hours with me teaching me to crochet, letting me listen to her play the piano (her favorite repertoire consisted of plenty of Scott Joplin and many, many hymns), and telling me all about her family. Her ancestors were as present in her life as her own, immediate family. She taught me a sense of connection to our roots that I will always remember.

Caleb and I finished our conversation with our "heroine of the seas," and headed out toward the island beacon I like to call home. He reminded me of his pending trip to the mainland, and I reminded myself of plenty of boredom in the few days ahead. We said, "So long," for the next little while. As I climbed the stairs to the front entrance of my house, I paused and looked behind me to watch Caleb, his muscled arms swinging to and fro along the shoreline, as he headed toward his place.

For the next three days I bided my time with saying goodbye to Uncle Seth. He always amazed me with his choice of funky attire. Today he was wearing a vintage Hawaiian shirt, torn jeans and Birkenstock sandals with glaring, white tube socks. His pinky ring of garnet and gold my mother gave him years ago as a graduation present was still on his finger, despite his globetrotting. Uncle Seth had to go paint on location in Giverny, France, kind of like a "return to Monet's stomping grounds." I was impressed with his choices of places to travel. He even asked me this time if I'd like to come along, but I kindly refused the offer; after all, I was waiting for one of my best friends to tell me what he had been up to on the Mainland.

Chapter 5

Morning came, and along with the grand sunshine, the ferry had arrived with Caleb on board. He and his parents had taken the trip together, making it a family affair. After they went home to unpack, I got a phone call from "Mister Mainland" himself.

"Eliza, can you meet me on your boat in fifteen minutes?" Caleb asked, almost out of breath.

"You don't want to take her for a sail, do you?" I asked reluctantly, half asleep, as I had stayed awake reading late into the night.

"Just meet me there and I'll tell you the whole story, okay?" was the only answer I got.

I threw on a light sweater and some jeans, put my hair up in a ponytail and grabbed a scone on the way out the door. As I approached the water, Caleb waved to me in one direction, and Father in another. Father was already downwind from us doing some maintenance on the other dock he built years ago.

"Hey," I said.

"Hey back at ya!" Caleb mocked in a parrot-like tone.

"So what is the big secret?" I pursued.

"I took a placement test and I passed."

"What kind of placement test?" I asked, nervously.

"Remember how you thought about going to school in the U.K?" he asked shyly.

"Yes, what about it?" was my hesitant reply.

"Well, I am going to be going to college a little early, Eliza."

"WHAT?" I shouted in total disbelief.

"Eliza, one of the benefits of attending school on the island for my elementary years, was to give me a big head start toward middle school and high school on the mainland; in addition, school in Japan for those two years pushed the envelope in academic advantage," his folded arms emphasized his pride.

"Yes, so what," I retorted angrily, knowing what he was about to say.

"Evidently, I have a gift of being an insatiable learner and tested quite highly—so highly, in fact, that I am attending HARVARD in the fall!"

I was stunned. "Caleb, how can you stand there telling me you're going away to college for several years, when you wreaked havoc on me for even contemplating a brief, summer abroad in jolly ole England?"

"Eliza, this is a great opportunity for me, especially for someone of a more meager pay source for my future education." Caleb stated, confidently. "I even have a special scholarship awarded to pay for my tuition until I am nineteen; by then, I can pick up another one maybe, if I need it."

"And just what kind of scholarship is this?" I demanded.

"It's based on testing scores and long-standing, New England heritage. Isn't that unbelievable?" Caleb asked, with a proper smile befitting an award recipient.

I had to feel joy for him. I had to share in his gladness and success. That smile would melt anyone's heart—even a heart as hurt as mine. Friends share in each other's achievements, and I was going to be happy for him, despite my own, selfish wants.

"By the way, when did you get so intelligent, Caleb?" I joked. I knew the answer. I only spent the summers with Caleb for the majority of my life; the school year was pretty much an issue we never much discussed before, including his birthday on the seventh of March, exactly three months before mine. After a deliberate smirk came across his face, Caleb went on to explain that he would be leaving in mid-August for a new student orientation.

I knew in my heart that once he left the island for Harvard, that I would lose him for the next few years at least—*maybe forever*. A sense of sadness welled-up deep within me, for I hadn't prepared myself for such a life-changing event as Caleb's premature departure from our normal, summer routine. This affected me in a most profound way. Why would he ever want to maintain a friendship with me once he meets all these adults with adult ideas and adult aspirations? I still was just trying to figure out what dress to wear to the next dance. It all seemed sort of trivial now.

Caleb interrupted my downward spiral of self-pity with a nudge and his trademark, dimpled grin that always made any type of difficult situation seem not so difficult. "Eliza, don't you think that perhaps the close proximity to Hawthorne during the school year might be a little on the advantageous side?" Caleb beamed optimistically. *Hmmm...he had a point.*
"I suppose that we might be able to arrange some visits—*if* my schedule *will allow*," I added in my most aloof-like tone. Caleb looked at me suspiciously, then knew that reason had prevailed.

After a while of hashing out all the logistics of the move, we decided to see each other in a few days after Caleb got back from a weekend, dorm supply trip to Portland.

As I watched Caleb walk away from me this time, I had a sense of, "this is a time for my personal growth" come over me, to the point of it almost echoing in my head. I needed to prepare myself for lots of quick changes, alternate plans and expected unknowns in the years ahead. I tried to cheer myself up with hopeful thoughts of Thanksgiving with Father and Caleb in Boston. If I really wanted to get greedy, Christmas and New Year's Eve with my dearest friend wouldn't be a bad plan, either. As the day progressed, I helped Father at the dock for a while. After a quick bite for dinner, I retired to bed to sleep away my anxiety.

Chapter 6

When Caleb returned from his trip to become a full-fledged, college-bound guy—complete with all the stuff a dorm-dweller could carry—I was surprised at the change in his demeanor already. It was as if he matured overnight. He didn't seem like a seventeen year-old going away to college. He seemed like an older adult going away to study with other grown-ups. It was a side of him I'd never seen before. It really caught me off-guard. I wasn't prepared for such a drastic change in attitude. I felt the need to reevaluate my own maturity level, and search for ways of improvement and ridding myself of all childish, selfish thoughts.

For our parting outing, we decided to walk through the woods of the notorious, "spindly pine tree" of stormy fame, and head out toward our favorite beach with the sun shining so brightly, as if it was saying, "All is not lost." I was extremely uncomfortable with the thought that this might be the last time I ever see him here—*ever*. I felt like climbing up that wispy tree, just to have him rescue me again and have everything return to normal.

We hiked out to the beach and picked a nice location to throw down our picnic gear. After laying out our towels to sit on, he handed me a sandwich and an aluminum thermos of spring water. I hastily ate most of my sandwich, while deep in my own thoughts of impending separation from my friend.

The beach had a lot of jasper rocks, so I took a quick round to see if I could find a "lucky rock" as a parting gift for Caleb, a black, jasper rock with a white band around its circumference. To no avail; there were no lucky rocks for me today. I looked around and determined that it couldn't have been a more beautiful day. The blissful, seventy-five degrees, gentle breeze and deep azure sky, dappled with streaks of white clouds were divine. The smell of the sea was mesmerizing, primed to sustain a tranquil mood.

"Hey there, my friend," was Caleb's attempt to bring me into the conversation. "Eliza, *are you in there?*" was his second attempt. By the third time around, his language got a little more urgent: "Eliza— EARTH TO ELIZA!"
"Yes, I hear you loud and clear," was my dazed reply.
"I don't think you heard me until the last greeting, he answered, a little bothered.
"Okay, we've established that I am on another planet for the moment, but do you blame me?" I said, with slight exasperation.
"No, I suppose not, but please realize that I am making a big adjustment here too," he gently reminded.

We both sat there, staring up at the heavens, not really saying much. We had been friends for seven years or so; we sought each other out when there were very few children to play with; we had an instant connection and have remained loyal to each other, ever since.

"Caleb, promise me you'll keep in touch, okay?" I asked, trying not to plead.
"Of course I'll keep in touch. School will be tough, but I think I'll eventually get to the point where I can have a life outside of studies."
"Plan on spending Thanksgiving Dinner with Father and me at the townhouse, and maybe even *pencil me in* for New Year's Eve?" I encouraged, offering my most coy expression.
"I have penciled you in, Eliza, my dear," Caleb assured, quickly glancing away.

Secretly, I had hoped he would pick up on the fact that I didn't mention Christmas, and graciously include that in our future plans as well.

August was quickly coming to a close. Caleb's day of departure was fast approaching. I considered accompanying him and his parents to Cambridge for the orientation, but I decided that it was a family thing and I should step aside.

D-Day, or rather, *Departure Day* had arrived. I stood there at the ferry launch with my bravest facade and said farewell to my truest friend. My heart ached, knowing that my sentences wouldn't be finished by him anymore, or for him to be there to catch me if I should fall, or to know that things would always be the same. As I stood there, watching him "sail into the sunset," I came to the realization that our paths were about to diverge. I had to create my own destiny, and live life to the fullest.

Chapter 7

The telltale signs of autumn were in the air, and nothing evoked the changing of the seasons quite like Boston in the fall. Temperatures were dropping steadily. The maples were ablaze with a riot of crimson. I had fully immersed myself with my studies during my junior school year at Hawthorne, barely coming up for air for at least two months. I received a couple of obligatory emails from Caleb, but I could tell that he was quite engrossed in his new life at college. I still couldn't believe that Caleb Longfellow was a "Harvard Man" at seventeen.

Thanksgiving was fast approaching. I had toyed with the idea of popping-in on Caleb on campus to personally invite him to Thanksgiving dinner. As quickly as the idea entered my mind, I dismissed it. I didn't want to appear as if my life was on hold, or that I was clingy. He was now living closer than ever to me for a larger portion of the year! How silly would that appear?

I decided to send him a formal invitation on Hales letterhead, postal mail, complete with RSVP, with a, "pleasure of your company requested," type of correspondence. This would be the most independent-looking, I thought. I absolutely did not want to convey any sleep lost over this change in our lives. It was, after all, a change in *our* lives. He was now in the big leagues, with the big players, in the big ocean of academia. I had to get over my aversion to this particular change. I needed to appear stronger for it, and well on my way to achieving my own, academic recognition.

I had just been put on the Dean's list at Hawthorne and was also voted Class President. I hadn't done too shabbily this semester after all! This will be of interest to Caleb, hearing that I had continued to move forward, despite our paths diverging quite distinctly. *I wonder what he has been doing for the last two months?* I thought to myself.

Moments later, someone showed up at our townhouse and was barraging the front door with repeated knocks, the noise permeating up the stairs to my room. I wondered where Gibson, our butler had run off to, since it appeared no one was ever going to answer the door. I ran downstairs, and through the beveled glass entryway, could plainly see it was Ashleigh, despite the light refractions from the windows. She seemed agitated, so I flung open the door and let her in.

"What took you so long?" she gasped, her voice winded.
"I thought Gibson was here and when the knocking got so annoying and no one was answering it, I came down to investigate for myself," I explained. "What is so urgent, *Miss Bennington?*" I toyed, as Ashleigh came into the foyer, kicked off her shoes, and immediately sat down in the front parlor, making herself at home.
"Eliza, how long ago did you send that invitation to Caleb?"
"I suppose about two weeks ago," I calculated off the top of my head. "Why do you ask?"
"I was just told by Laurel Mayhew that her father, who is, as you know, *partner* at your Dad's firm—*Hales, Whitehead, Mayhew and Olmstead*—that their firm is the 'mysterious benefactor' who paid for Caleb's tuition at Harvard," Ash' belted out in one, long breath.
"I thought it was a basic scholarship situation," I murmured in disbelief. *Does Caleb know this?* I wondered.
"Laurel told me that some tuition documentation inadvertently arrived in Caleb's mailbox that had the firm's name and address on it, and he immediately called the school financial department," Ashleigh reported. "The school validated that the firm was paying his tuition through this scholarship set up in his name," she added.
"This could be bad if Caleb's pride is running away with him," I answered in a voice of concern.

"Well, I better get going; you can thank me later!" Ashleigh stated, as she hurriedly put on her shoes and coat and ran out the door before I could even say goodbye. I immediately called Father on his cell phone to ask him what was he thinking when he set up that scholarship.

"Eliza, young men like Caleb don't grow on trees, and neither does money," was Father's pat answer over the phone. "I felt very strongly about contributing to his bright future, in a way that his parents could not at this time."

"Well, that's very noble of you Father and very generous, but Caleb didn't know you were the benefactor when he accepted the scholarship," I countered.

"I take it his *pride* is a bit wounded?" Father inquired, likely a sparkle gleamed in his eye.

"I don't know yet, but wanted to be prepared if this was the case," I cautioned.

"How is the best way to handle this? *Very diplomatically,* I'd suspect," was Father's verbal plan.

With my most thought-out strategy, I came up with, "Why don't I try to track down Caleb, and see if we can all get together at the townhouse for dinner. After all, it's Friday night and you *know* how Eugenie *loves* spontaneous company for dinner!" I offered in unveiled sarcasm.

I took a taxi back to Hawthorne to pick up some homework I had left in my dorm room. I figured I'd better get caught up on my schoolwork if I was going to spend the weekend at home, instead of at school. It seemed a bit silly having housing so close by at Hawthorne in Wellesley, with the townhouse on Beacon Hill moments away. Father insisted I have the "complete" academic experience. I knew he wasn't trying to be rid of me, but had my best interests in mind. I also had to admit that my friendships were much deeper and stronger, due to living on campus and not depending so much on family at home. I saw him so frequently that it was like I was living at home still, with better dialog than most teens who lived at home.

As I turned around after paying the cab driver, I saw someone leaning against the big maple tree amidst the shadows, outside Hales Hall. It gave me a bit of a scare, until I realized it was Caleb.

"Show thyself, Sir," I theatrically demanded in my most Shakespearean-like voice. Caleb was not amused. Still somewhat hidden under the shelter of the maple, I made my way toward him. Trying to lighten the moment, I told a couple of jokes, but alas, my audience was not appreciative.

Breaking his silence, Caleb announced, "I'm not accepting this scholarship any longer; it was given in the worst kind of pretenses— *false!"*
"What do you mean, *false?"* I queried in amazement. "You deserve it Caleb! There's nothing false about how much you deserve this!" I shouted, in disbelief that he thought so little of himself.
"Your father's firm is who is behind this scholarship, Eliza."
"I know Caleb; I just found out today, myself."
"Why didn't your father tell me—why the *big secret?"* Caleb asked, visibly distraught, as he paced about.
"The only guess I have, is that he anticipated your arrogant, *'Longfellow pride'* getting in the way of your future, and figured that being anonymous was the only way to go. Is it really *that big of a deal,* Caleb?

"One way you can look at it, is that Father sees a lot of potential in you, and wanted to smooth over the path toward your future in a way that he could, financially, and from a distance," I assured him.
"I suppose that could be *one* way to view the situation," he agreed, ever so slightly.
"Good! Eugenie is planning for dinner for three tonight, so let's go to the townhouse, and you can hash things out with Father until you're

satisfied." We hailed a cab and headed for Beacon Hill, *together, once again.*

How I loved New England when the leaves changed color! There is no other place like it on the whole planet! With my best friend beside me, how much better could life get? I felt completely at peace, admiring the scenery as the daylight was quickly fading outside the taxi windows. Row upon row of brownstones were blurring past my window now, as we neared our home.

We arrived at the townhouse and stepped inside to find Father already there to greet us at the door. He reached out his hand toward Caleb for a reconciliatory handshake, which was accepted, with a bit of apprehension.

"We're having salmon for dinner, with apple-cranberry pie for dessert," Father informed us. Food was always his way of a truce in our family. My mouth was watering; however, Caleb was still a bit reluctant to seem excited about the menu.

"I'll go check on what Eugenie is up to and see if I can lend a hand," Father announced, knowing full well that he was not welcome in her kitchen at any time, especially when impromptu guests were joining us. Clanging pots and pans, mixed with exaggerated and exasperated sighs were meant for our benefit. Usually she was the one employee of the family who seemed more in control than most of the rest of us. Father obviously saw that he needed to do a little "damage control" before dinner, so he left us in the front parlor to finish our conversation.

"I'm leaning toward being okay with this Eliza," Caleb assured, trying to appear calmer.
"What will it take to push you over the edge into our corner?" I inquired, batting my eyelashes, looking for negotiation possibilities.

"Well, I wouldn't mind two helpings of that pie and an extra helping of salmon for starters," he replied with a mischievous grin, slowly working its way to the corners of his mouth. I was relieved that the Caleb that I knew had returned.

During dinner, Father timidly approached the subject of the scholarship with his trademark sincerity: "Caleb, I know you've felt a little betrayed that I wasn't up-front with you about my firm backing this scholarship, but I want you to know——"
Caleb interrupted politely and finished the sentence for him, "——that you care enough about me and my future that you just wanted to help. It's okay Mr. Hales. Eliza already filled me in on my issues," he guaranteed.
"Well then, it appears we are back on track with your future," Father added with a sense of relief.
"Let's raise our glasses and make a toast: to Caleb's fine choice to continue being a Harvard Man," I announced, as our glasses of milk, spring water and tomato juice clanked.

As I looked across the table, I was looking into the eyes of not just a treasured friend, but a friend who I had just discovered I hoped would one day be more, *much, much more.*

Chapter 8

October had passed in the blink of an eye, with the famed New England weekend of Columbus Day, with all the "leaf peepers" descending upon the area like a swarm of locusts. Soon after, Halloween came and went and Thanksgiving was a complete blur. It didn't seem possible that Christmas was already upon us.

I had been enjoying my newfound celebrity as Class President at Hawthorne for a few months now, and was feeling well-adjusted to my presidential responsibilities. My classes were now more manageable this semester. To reward myself for keeping up the good work, Ash' and I had found a new pastime of private art lessons with a prominent, national artist and former graduate of The School of the Museum of Fine Arts-Boston.

This fine art instructor was actually a former classmate of my mother's. His name was James Atwell, and often would express his appreciation for my mother's talents as an artist. We started out with rudimentary drawing exercises, and within weeks, were exploring other media, such as watercolor and acrylic. I was in heaven, and actually had tapped into a talent that I thought belonged only to my mother. *Perhaps she willed it to me upon her death,* I thought to myself, wondering why after so many years, I finally discovered this ability to create. I wasn't complaining; I was now able to more fully feel like I had a purpose in life—a contribution to society—*a destiny.*

I was home for Christmas vacation and my room in the townhouse was becoming more and more like a studio, with dozens of paintings all stacked up against the wall. I even contemplated what they would look like framed and hung in someone's home. At that moment, Father peered through the door.

"Your room is looking more and more like I remembered your mother's studio, and even similar to your Uncle Seth's stash of work," Father announced observantly. "I do believe those lessons are invariably creating another artist in the family to trot the globe, far away from me, and instead, dazzling the dignitaries of the art world."
"Oh come on now. My recent aspirations to make art a focus in my life are only to help me feel more purposeful," I asserted with wisdom, as I sorted the paintings by subject as they lay against the wall.
"I'm glad to see that you are enjoying your talents. I hope you continue to magnify them," was all that Father added as he walked down the hall toward the upstairs study.

Alone in my thoughts, I considered what my life might be like as an accomplished artist, jetting around the world, enjoying the celebrity of my one-woman shows and exhibitions. I practiced shaking hands with quirky buyers in front of my oval floor mirror—identical to my mirror at Hawthorne—as well as giving a rehearsed speech to all the gallery owners on the contrasts of gouache versus watercolor as a medium.

I took a step back away from the mirror with thoughts still in my head of how I was going to "wow" the art world, when my foot caught hold of something that had worked its way out from under my bed; it was my keepsake box. I leapt over to my dresser to grab the hand-wrought, tiny key of iron from the top drawer and opened the carved container. The box was a gift from my mother on my sixth birthday. It was about twelve inches long by eight inches wide by five inches tall and was of a very rich, oiled and well-worn walnut. It had been in my mother's family for one hundred and fifty years. The box alone was valuable, let alone what I kept inside it.

As I slowly opened it, careful not to overwork the delicate hinges, I gazed upon the old photos and postcards, letters and other mementos that were once my mother's and now belonged to me. Some of the postcards were from the time my mother went to England on her study abroad program, hence my interest in following in her footsteps. These messages were to her parents, and some of the postcards were hers alone, picked up from various countries, and many, many of the states of the U.S., from family vacations. I then came across a miniature portrait of someone I hadn't recognized before and still didn't at this time, only now I was curious who it was. It appeared to be an antique painting; from the clothing on this woman, it appeared to have been done in the 1600s, based on her puritan-like dress and egg tempera-like paint.

Carrying the tiny portrait in one hand, I stepped across the display of memorabilia I had set out and retrieved from the other hand, a minute watercolor of mine to fit into this box for safekeeping. "This painting I will always keep in my private, studio collection," I whispered to myself.

Just at that moment, Father called me to come and help decorate the Christmas tree in the front parlor, a tradition since childhood. I put away my mother's memories back in the box, safely stored for another time.

Upon the fragrant and traditional balsam tree we hung up our best, antique glass ornaments—most of them Egyptian glass, along with strings of crystal beads, as garland. At the top was our showpiece: a five-pointed, cut crystal star with 18 carat gold accents. It was a magnificent sight to behold. Christmas music was lofting through the air, to complete the "picture postcard" scene of family togetherness.

"The tree is missing something over on this side," I directed Father, as I handed him another ornament. The bauble I chose was a beautiful, green and gold, frosted glass, "pinecone and tassel," made in Germany, representing our favorite state of Maine.

"Aren't you putting that one on the 'Northwoods' theme tree, as usual?" he inquired. I obviously wasn't paying too much attention to my decorating choices, and was alarmed by my mistake. "Ooops." I whispered, grinning in embarrassment.

"You seem a bit distracted, Eliza..." Father's voice trailed off in query. "As a matter of fact, I am; my mind is taking a vacation from the task at hand," was my pathetic reply. I then mentioned, "I stumbled across an antique portrait of a woman in the wooden box that used to be Mother's. Do you know who it is?"

"It's your great-great-great-great-Great Grandmother Stout I think," was Father's answer.

"You mean, the same Grandmother Penelope who helped found the New Jersey colony, who barely made it there alive, at great peril?" I asked in surprise.

"Yes, she was an example of hardy strength and inspiration, both qualities that were essential in early America," he elaborated.

Father went on to explain how this grandmother, of English descent, had come to America via Holland in the early 1600s. Her ship had capsized off the coast of New Jersey. Being one of only a handful of survivors, she made her way about on land, only to endure heinous brutality by the hand of another and left to die. He continued to share that she was later found alive—barely, was nursed back to health and later sold in New York, which was called, "New Amsterdam" at the time. Richard Stout found her there and married her. They had several children and she always showed their grandchildren her skull cap and the scars on her side, in testimony of her life that needed to be preserved, to provide for her legacy—and greatest joy—of family.

I was sure that portrait was of her and I appreciated it even more, knowing that her trials were so very tremendous. I decided that I would place it in plain view, so as to always remember her sacrifice and consider her my hero.

We got back to decorating the tree, attempting to juggle hot cups of cocoa while doing so. I was admiring the obscuring effect the street light had on the lightly falling snow, outside the parlor window. After the dozing effect the beverage had, I decided to call it a night.

In the morning, I went shopping at Fontaine's. After finding many great Christmas gifts, I went over to Boston Common to go ice skating on the Frog Pond. I no sooner got my skates on, when I heard the familiar, "Hey Eliza!" shout from the other side of the frozen, sleek surface. Caleb was there with some friends and came swooshing over quickly, not hesitating to kick up some ice fragments when he came to a perfectly executed stop.

"So what are your plans for Christmas?" I asked hopefully.
"My Great Uncle William asked for all of us to come to his house in Little Falls; my Nana is joining us there from Bangor, so we all have to go," he answered. Sensing my disappointment, Caleb threw out a quick compromise, in suggesting we get together for New Year's Eve, instead.
"You know, I really would like to spend Christmas in Maine this year; we could celebrate the holidays together!" I blurted out.
"Sounds great 'Liza," was his very atypical reply.
"Since when did you start abbreviating my name, *Sir?*"
"Come on 'Liza, don't you like to be called 'Liza?" he taunted.
I angrily glared at Caleb with a look that could melt the ice that he had just sprayed about us and skated off, as if to dare him to follow me. As expected, he did.

After a few rounds about on slivers of steel, I decided to call it quits for the day and let Caleb know when I'd be on the island. "After Christmas Day you'll have to swing back to *Misthaven* to see me, okay?" I nonchalantly reminded him. "Oh, and be sure to dig up a tuxedo for New Year's Eve; I envision a party befitting the island elite will no doubt create a stir," I laughed, but looked on with a semi-serious intent.

"See you in a few days," was all Caleb said, his voice fading away as he skated across to the other side.

"I think an island holiday is perfectly in order!" Father agreed from across the room, as he finished making arrangements for travel from Portland to Hales Isle. "I haven't spent Christmas on the island since before your mother passed away."
"Then it's high time we broke our usual routine of a Boston Christmas and headed on up to our beloved Maine," was my resounding, supportive reply. On that positive note, we got to packing our luggage and the next morning we were on our way to Portland, via limousine.

We arrived in Portland two days before Christmas. Before we took the I-295 exit from I-95 for the ferry building, we asked the limo driver for a brief detour and headed inland in search of the perfect Christmas tree. We opted for a roadside tree lot sponsored by local Boy Scout Troop 580 and brought to the terminal the most enormous Frasier Fir I had ever seen. The mailboat captain looked at us in disbelief when he saw the two of us dragging this very plump, nine-footer aboard. I was concerned he wouldn't let us bring it with us, but he just smiled and tipped his hat, then helped us load our aromatic cargo.

We arrived on the isle in record time, despite the opposing wind. Our resident taxi driver, Rusty, was already there waiting for us. The look on his face when we motioned for him to help us throw this enormous tree up on his station wagon to tie down was priceless.

Just as we got inside the taxi, it started to rain—not the usual snowfall for this time of year, but most definitely rain! The pitter-patter of the gentle drops upon the roof of our 'wagon was unforgettable. Combined with the unmistakable aroma of the tree sap on my hands and the fragrance of the sea, these sights, smells and sounds made an indelible impression of this return to our holiday roots. Rain will always be an event that would forever be etched in my mind as solitude in its purest form…*my delight in living!*

As we arrived at *Misthaven*, I was overcome with joy to be in my favorite place in the world, during a season I didn't much remember being there before. It was a welcome opportunity for making new memories and new traditions. I knew at that moment I would reflect upon this for decades to come.

Since our tree was only in the light rain for a few moments in transit, we were able to bring it inside the house to embellish, right away. Tree decorations were simple for our newly-found, conifer friend. We strung cranberry and popcorn garlands, and found a box of handmade, origami crane and frog ornaments, as well as walnuts, topped with glued-on ribbon hangers. They made for a homespun, holiday look. We topped the tree with the one, ornamental extravagance I smuggled in my suitcase from Boston: our beloved, cut, crystal star. With intermittent moonlight between waves of rain shining in from the windows upon the showpiece, it made for a very brilliant effect.

After some traditional toasting of hot chocolate, Father adjourned to his study, for what I thought was quiet contemplation. A few moments later he called to me with his usual, *"Eliz-aaaah?"*

As I peered through the doorway, his reflection in the mirror over the hand-hewn fireplace mantel surprised me, as he was opening the antique sea captain's safe and rummaging through its contents hurriedly. He turned around with something in his right hand. He showed me a document of some sort. It was his will and he had recently had it amended to state that *Misthaven* would be mine upon his death. Despite the previous stipulation in the deed regarding firstborn sons having it willed to them by default, somehow that clause was circumvented. "It doesn't hurt to know a good lawyer," I just mumbled to myself under my breath.

Father's sudden showing of this will instantly made me leery of the timing. We were celebrating our return to *Misthaven*, and here was Father discussing his death without words. We agreed to table it for the night and I was off to my room to embark on the preparations for a restful slumber and bigger plans for the next day.

With the rain still gliding downward upon the window panes of my bedroom, I began to become hypnotized to a small degree—not truly, mind you, but mesmerized at the grace and beauty that surrounded the characteristic droplets. I was in deep meditation—peaceful beyond belief. I was imagining all sorts of things to accompany my aqua orchestration of sounds. Just as I was about to truly lose myself in the experience, I heard a louder, "*clink*" upon my window. As I gazed out toward the dark night, there below, standing in all his rain-swept glory, was Caleb. He looked up and motioned for me to come outside. I gave him a quick shrug of disbelief, then I went downstairs and grabbed my coat and wellies, as if on autopilot. Forgetting that I was already in my long, flannel nightgown, I proceeded to throw on my coat anyway. This moment was surely a rarity, and I wasn't going to miss it.

I casually mentioned to Father I would just be right outside talking to Caleb, as I grabbed my umbrella and headed out the door. There in the rain, drenched from head to toe was my long-lost friend of island fame. He stood there with this expression of solemnity across his face with a small box in the palm of his outstretched hand.
"What is that you have in your hand?" I inquired with sincere interest, but wondering if it was some kind of joke, given the time of evening and the weather.
"Here—I have something I wanted to give you that couldn't wait for New Year's Eve," he sputtered, in between his teeth chattering. The joke idea quickly evaporated and I suddenly couldn't contain my

excitement, as this was spontaneous and rather strange, even for him. I gave him a quick hug, "Hello," then shyly accepted the box and lifted its lid to reveal the magical contents.

Inside, what appeared to be a handmade box of driftwood with a simple, antique clasp of pewter, was a stunning bracelet, amidst a dusky purple, velvet shroud. This gift was most unusual, as Caleb was always a practical person of modest means. The bracelet was obviously an antique; the well-made, box chain link and settings were at least 18 carat gold, with six or seven, vibrant green, oval tourmaline cabochons, about one quarter of an inch in size, spaced vertically, every inch. It was the most beautiful bracelet I had ever seen; it was meticulously crafted and very old. *How unusual to have the colors green and purple paired together,* I observed.

Stunned beyond belief, I managed to utter some recognizable words of gratitude, although I still was quite astonished this gift was for me, and not kept in his family.
"This is absolutely beautiful, Caleb," was my pitiful acknowledgement of such a generous work of art. Trying to recoup the misfortunate utterance of thanks, I augmented, "What did I ever do to deserve such a striking treasure?"
"Eliza, my Nana gave this to me a year ago and I've been holding onto it ever since, waiting for the right moment. Your out of habit return to *Misthaven* during this holiday season was cause for me to celebrate! It was given to my great-Great Grandmother Settle when she was growing up down in York, and Nana wanted me to have it," he went on, to clarify its past ownership.
"Caleb, why do you want me to have something of such great worth to your family?" I inquired, as I realized that we were both fully soaked to the bone from standing in the rain for so long. I had completely forgotten to open up my umbrella.
"Eliza, you and I have been best friends for years; we've sailed together, grown up together, been there for each other and I can't

imagine anyone else I'd rather give this to than you, nor find a reason to delay giving it to you."

Still in shock, despite the numbing chill from the rain-soaked clothes I was wearing, I threw my arms around his neck with a smile so wide, the rain was splattering against my teeth. Just as I thought I would be able to compose myself, Caleb began to give some conditions that accompanied his conveyance: "By accepting this gift, I need you to promise me Eliza that we will always be friends; that growing older and becoming adults will not change us; and that we will always be able to pick up where we left off." His requirements were starting to sound very serious.

"Are you *dying* or something, Caleb?" I half-joked rather loudly, to compete with the rain drops that were growing larger and more deafening by the minute. These momentous acts by Father—and now Caleb—seemed ominous; they were causing me to grow more anxious by the moment.

"Don't be ridiculous!" he laughed, ensuring this was to be a moment of joy, not deathbed urgency. "No questions, please! Just accept it and be done with it already!" He verbally reprimanded with the greatest sarcasm and widest smile.

Just then, Father stuck his head out the door and called me in, so I wouldn't, "catch my death of cold," as he always said.

"I better run," I said, as Caleb started jogging across the yard already.

"I'll see you right after I get back from visiting my uncle!" he shouted happily, as he dashed out of sight into the night.

In a trance still, I sloshed my way back into the house on a quest for a giant towel. After I changed my clothes and dried off, I went into the study to say goodnight to Father and then sought the seclusion of my room, to surround myself in replaying this moment over and over in my head. *I thought I knew Caleb completely, but even still, he surprises me.*

Chapter 9

I rose to a beautiful day; the sky was a vibrant blue with white, cumulus clouds, beckoning me outside. *What an atypical Christmas Eve morning,* I thought, recalling all the holidays-past, spent in Boston.

Father and I decided to eat out for breakfast and took a leisurely stroll up the dirt road in the center of the island to Dottie Look's Place—a rustic diner on the waterfront, replete with lobster buoys and traps scattered around. It was located in what used to be the old post office. The local hotspot overflowed with Downeast hospitality, as Dottie, like Caleb's uncle, was from Little Falls in Washington County—the epicenter of coastal, Downeast, Maine.

We began the meal with scones and butter, and Dottie herself ushered in a few crab cakes and eggs for each of us. Several of our island neighbors were there, so we got caught up on all the local happenings, while savoring the delectable cuisine.

Caleb was the talk of the island; everyone was so proud of our Harvard Man from home, making his way in life on the mainland. Just as everyone was finished with their renditions of all of Caleb's mischief, out from behind the counter came a question poised for embarrassment: "So when are you planning to marry Caleb, before, or *after* graduation?" was Will Look's inquiry, clearly forgetting I was only sixteen. Will was Dottie's husband and the island Moderator for all the open town meetings, as well as the Postmaster and local paramedic. He also was a lobsterman in his negligible spare time, and had island ancestry that dated from the 1700s. He was a descendant of generations who never left the island.

Sensing a feeding frenzy on the horizon no matter what my response was, I decided to show no embarrassment, only indifference, as I didn't want anyone to think anything that wasn't so. So, without any delay, I quipped, "Haven't you got your Christmas shopping done yet? I think you'd better get busy, as there is only one more shopping day left before Christmas." All diners present were bellowing with laughter at my response, and once again, all was right with the world on Hales Island—at least at Dottie Look's.

The rest of the day was spent enjoying nature, despite the chill, as the sun was out, the sky was sapphire and it was Christmas Eve! After spending the day touring the island, Father and I stopped to watch a bright, red cardinal soaring back and forth across our front lawn for several flights. We both agreed it was a good omen.

Christmas Eve was spent watching holiday movies, drinking peppermint hot chocolate and eating hors d' oeuvres beside the roaring fire. The evening continued in casual fare, until at eight o'clock, a large contingent of carolers came calling. I was surprised that they would come on Christmas Eve, but as it turned out, there were entire families singing together as a happy tradition; this was how they chose to spend their time together on the holiday. Since we hadn't spent Christmastime on the island for many years, we were not aware of this lovely tradition that these singing families would participate in. After we shared hot chocolate with our friends in the parlor, the carolers left. We then resumed our agenda and finished watching movies. When the films were over, we discussed what we were truly grateful for in life and made plans for the next day— Christmas Day. Other than the beautiful serenade, it was a very quiet, family evening, without fanfare or pageantry. I enjoyed the peaceful time together with Father and the change in tradition. I was soon off to bed dreaming about the magical morn' that would greet us in a few hours.

I jumped out of bed on Christmas morning to the sounds of a blender whirring, utensils clanging, and the aroma of fresh pastries, straight from the oven. I put on my robe and slippers and let my nose lead me downstairs. It always amazed me how wonderful foods could float throughout such a large house and reach me so many square feet away from the source.

I was old enough now to have patience to skip the immediate gift opening and postpone it until after breakfast, a sure sign I was growing up. Christmas music was playing and we enjoyed our festive meal to the tunes of holiday, Celtic harp melodies.

The phone rang shortly after I finished the last crumb of my pastry. When I answered, I could barely discern the voice with all the static on the other end. It was Uncle Seth, calling from jolly old England, wishing us a, "Happy Christmas!" He wanted to let us know that a package should be arriving any day. It was so nice to hear his voice and catch up on all his adventures.

After the phone call ended, it was obviously time to open gifts. We gathered around our fragrant fir tree and exchanged a few presents. I got to open mine first. A beautiful, handmade, wheat-colored sweater from proud, Maine-grown wool and two leather-bound books for me were hiding in gift wrap. I couldn't believe my eyes when I discovered who the authors were. There, laying in tissue paper in the box was a leather-bound copy of *Walden*, by Henry David Thoreau, as well as, *The House of Seven Gables*, by Nathaniel Hawthorne. I was in heaven! The ties to home and to Mother were not unnoticed, nor underappreciated by me. "Thank you Father!" was all I could muster up, feeling a tug of emotion.

My gifts to my father weren't as magnificent as his to me, but nonetheless appropriate. One thing we each gave in common was a sweater. I bought Father a handmade, Nordic-style sweater with engraved, pewter buttons in a deep, ocean blue with cream pattern. I bought it from an island neighbor who spun her own wool. When he got to opening the next gift box, I instructed, "Close your eyes as you open it, please."

"Eliza, what have we here?" was his question, as he felt something wooden.

"Open your eyes now!" was my cue for him to end the suspense.

There in front of him was a hand-carved decoy of a loon by a local artist. The realism was exceptional and the detail of the feathers was meticulous. I could tell that he was enamored with it. My plan to buy him a great present seemed a winning success!

The remainder of the day was spent playing social card games by the fire and just conversing. It was a joy just to listen to Father laugh and recall happy pastimes during my life, as well as his when he was growing up. I thought to myself that any girl would love to have such a wonderful relationship with their own parent. I knew that I was truly blessed.

Chapter 10

It had been quite a while since I anticipated an event quite like this New Year's Eve. Since receiving the bracelet from Caleb, it was all I could do to *not* dwell on that rain-soaked moment that eclipsed all others in my immediate lifetime. I was proud to wear it often, when I wasn't doing active things. I was very careful to protect it. I gazed upon it repeatedly throughout the hours, even on Christmas day, when thoughts should be turned toward family and tradition. I would angle my wrist toward the sun, watching the rays cascade through the stones, leaving green shadows.

I began to wonder why I was so preoccupied with this particular New Year's Eve party, and especially how I would look that night. It had never mattered on the island before—not here, not where appearances were secondary; it was a person's substance—their essence—that mattered most. I realized that I was definitely bordering on obsessing about the event.

The week passed and caterers appeared at *Misthaven* in throngs, setting up their warming trays and ironed linens, while they shivered from having been just outside in the frozen air. The unusually rainy weather prior to Christmas had quickly plunged to more mainstream freezing temperatures, in time for the grand event. Beeswax tapers and black and silver candlesticks were strategically placed throughout the house. This was a black tie affair. Every detail was not to be overlooked. Musicians arrived and the lead vocalist demanded a tall glass of water, threatening laryngitis as a result of their daunting boat ride from the mainland.

I took that as my cue to go upstairs and primp and pause for reflection for the coming evening. As I surveyed my closet, it didn't take long to locate the dress I had already chosen, after meticulous perusal of dress shops in Boston. Besides the crystal star, I also brought along this little fabric number. For someone of age sixteen, when you aren't quite an adult but want to look like one, couture is everything. I chose a deep, forest green, satin dress with capped sleeves, a scoop neckline and draped, empire bodice, hemmed at the knee. Strategically placed at the bodice was an opal-encrusted, 18 carat gold, broche-like piece of jewelry that was beautiful, and yet, still drew your eyes up toward my face. It didn't overpower the dress; it positively accentuated the slimming lines. As additional accessories, I chose an emerald and opal pendant and earring set, crafted by the same jeweler from India who designed my broche. I would wear my hair in an updo, reminiscent of Princess Grace. I was striving for sophistication, timeless elegance and heart-stopping impact. It was only two hours away that I would see if my intentions would be successful.

Wait a minute! I shouted to myself loudly in my head. *Caleb is my friend, my best friend of so very, many years. Why now am I so caught up in trying to impress him?* Logic prevailed, and suddenly I was analyzing the recent events, scouring my vast pool of memories that revolved around my dearest friend. I was becoming obviously too concerned with such things, such as how I looked, and if he would notice. The more I thought about it, the more I began to find my behavior quite premature. As I began to overanalyze the situation further still, Father gently knocked on my door, saving me from my internal debate.

"Eliza, your mother would have been so overcome with emotion upon seeing you looking so beautiful," Father said, almost choked with tears. "You are absolutely breathtaking and will most definitely be the prettiest girl at the party," he added, most sincerely.
"Thank you Father, but I am wondering if I am dressing for the wrong reasons," I replied, as I gingerly accepted his compliment.
"What do you mean by that, honey?"
"Caleb gave me a green, tourmaline bracelet the other night out in the rain; it was a gift of friendship, but it's a family heirloom. I find that I

am becoming very much caught up in how I feel about our relationship now."

"Eliza, you and Caleb have been friends for years. You both have your whole lives ahead of you. If he gave you this gift out of friendship, then that is the reason it was given, with no pretenses," Father responded in his voice of reason. "If you choose to dress up for this party and have his reaction foremost in your mind, then perhaps Caleb is becoming a different kind of friend now."

"Thank you. I appreciate your opinion," I added and continued to finish my hair.

"By the way Eliza, green tourmalines are found in Maine. I can't imagine a more perfect gem choice coming from Caleb." With that parting remark he was off to tend to the guests.

I was alone in my thoughts, pondering the meaning behind my motivation for the reaction I was trying to achieve for the evening. I halted the analysis in its tracks and opted for resuming the festivities.

By the time I was ready to make my way downstairs, it was already nine o'clock and the party was well underway. I made a deliberate pause in front of the mirror, assessing the ensemble I chose and surveying what could possibly be added to complete the effect, but also not wishing to overdo accessory-wise, as was a tendency of mine in times of nervousness. Embarrassed, I realized that I had neglected to put on the bracelet that Caleb had given me so very recently. As I slid it on, it occurred to me that it matched my gown *perfectly*. Gazing at my wrist, the green tourmaline and the deep green of my dress were an inseparable pair of blended, harmonious notes.

Not to be overshadowed by the real thing, but music was drifting throughout the house to the tunes of some magical, swing composers. The band that was hired played a myriad of musical genres, but it appeared that "big band" was the flavor of the moment. As I descended the staircase, a sea of partygoers flooded the foyer and central hall. Dancing above their heads were stars all a-glitter, hanging from every sconce and chandelier. As I gained entrance to the expansive parlor that doubled as our ballroom through the throngs of attendees, Father was standing there to greet me and introduce me to his most honored guests. I did my best to pay as close attention as I possibly could to each face and name, but Father's voice was becoming more and more distant in my mind, as my thoughts were elsewhere. At first moment to sneak away from my obligatory introductions, I did not hesitate to make a quick departure, in quest for company of someone closer in age.

As soon as I found a more comfortable spot to linger and watch the crowd, my ears were treated to a most entrancing and melodic voice. Mesmerizing all, to a familiar, 1940s sentimental ballad, I attempted to gain access through the wall of people before me to see who this vocalist was. It wasn't the pompous and arrogant lead singer who demanded his thirst be quenched upon arrival; it was a different, more earthy and captivating voice. I thought that I had found a perfect place to sneak a peek, when an attorney friend of Father's found me and proceeded to "enlighten me" about the benefits of Eastern Time versus Pacific Time, and how much she thought that those in Maine were blessed to see the stroke of midnight first in the U.S. I soon escaped to the other side of the room and found out that the guest vocalist was none other than Caleb.

I never knew he could sing! I chastised myself mentally, for neglecting that very important detail of his many gifts. I continued to argue the reasons why I was so misguided in the talents of my friend to myself, when Caleb's gaze was directed solely toward me, with a smile that not just entranced, but had my stilettoed feet frozen to the floor. I suddenly became acutely aware of how painfully handsome he was. His cream with black lapelled Rolex jacket; neat, black bowtie; and perfectly pleated white shirt with French cuffs and onyx cufflinks were unfamiliar attire for him, and yet, they suited him very well. In fact, he looked so suave I couldn't take my eyes off of him. *Wherever did he get that ensemble?* I wondered. *Never mind—Father.*

Everyone in the room abruptly turned toward us. All eyes were intent on watching the display: of me looking at Caleb utterly astonished, and his singing pure, timeless prose with such melodious force that it captured my heart. Everybody knew it. As I allowed myself to let the shock of his hidden graces subside, I actually began to enjoy this interlude—so much so, that my heart figuratively—and literally—skipped a beat.

Caleb was a person of intensity and adventurous qualities that mystify, and yet he could be so very charming, gallant and expressive—*and dashing!* Loyal to the end, his ability to befriend all was what endeared him to everyone who knew him well. Even those in the audience who knew him as a young boy, running about Hales Isle knew he was most definitely the greatest surprise of the evening's festivities.

Returning my focus to this monumental display of talent, I listened with a pure intent for this melody to envelop me with a sure knowledge of who Caleb really was. I thought I knew everything about him, but my understanding obviously came up short. At the conclusion of his performance, he took a bow to thundering applause and lithely leapt off the stage, to quickly make his way toward me, his eyes intently focused on mine.

"Eliza, you take my breath away," Caleb announced in his confirming voice of breathlessness, after his impactful solo.
"Thank you Caleb. Thank you for never ceasing to surprise me," I replied, still stunned. Before I could think of another witty response to divert the attention from my obvious enchantment with his public, vocal display, he grabbed my hand and insisted we dance.

Before I could catch my breath, we glided across the ballroom floor. Caleb made a deliberate glance toward the bracelet on my wrist and said with controlled enthusiasm, "I see you are wearing the jewelry I gave you. That makes me *very happy,*" he offered with a deliberate, slow blink to solidify his words.

Trying to concentrate on not stepping on his toes and focus intently on his words, I attempted to bring myself to speak what was on my mind, but couldn't.

"Just dance with me, my lady," he said with a grin that beamed clear across the room.

I could just hear all the old biddies in the room sighing and "oohing" and "aahing," trying to comment with authority on our little moment. I quickly tuned out the static noise from their low murmurs and enjoyed this semiprivate milestone. As we glided around the room, it was obvious that Caleb had had dancing lessons. Another untapped attribute I was in the dark about came to light.

"When did you learn how to dance like this?" I gestured, trying not to lose my breath.

"Well, I wanted to get an elective out of the way early in my career at Harvard, and opted for 'Ballroom Dancing, 101,'" Caleb admitted. "In fact, my instructor thought I had so much promise, she asked me if I wanted to join the dance team."

"I had no idea you could be so graceful," I muttered, almost to myself.

We continued to marvel the onlookers, mostly with Caleb's fancy footwork, which appeared effortless. He wasn't focusing on his feet one bit, but instead, directed his attention to me with, "Eliza, you really do look beautiful tonight; you are beautiful beyond words, really." This compliment meant so much, coming from him.

As we continued to dance to this slow waltz, I was no longer enthralled with the glitter and lights of the ballroom, but became increasingly aware of everyone in the room becoming a rather large blur—everything and everyone, except Caleb. He became so acutely in focus, that I was amazed at the clarity from my perspective. It was an odd reality. Here I was dancing with my oldest and best friend, and I was gaining insight into the depth of our friendship with each, choreographed dance step. I was in awe of the perfection of our relationship. There was such a deep trust between us that had endured over the years. *Such a surprising time of our lives,* I thought to myself, as I glanced at the token of beauty gracing my wrist from my best friend. We continued to dance the night away, amidst the mob of spectators in our own, little world. It was truly an unforgettable evening.

As midnight neared, I started to panic. I politely excused myself after the song ended and went upstairs to my bathroom, anxiety building with every, upward step. *What would I do when the clock chimed twelve? Would I kiss my best friend, or hug him?* We were both dressed up in unforgettable attire and I was wearing *his* gift—an unabashed token of affection. He had serenaded me and I felt like the "Belle of the Ball." *What better way to cap off the festivities, than a customary, Happy New Year's kiss?* The tug-of-war of thoughts went back and forth in my mind, as I debated internally. *It will certainly change things!* I lectured myself, repeatedly.

I decided I was tired and was being atypically irrational, so I discreetly walked back downstairs to the kitchen to get a glass of water. After a few gulps, I felt amazingly revived. The music had stopped and my father, the self-appointed MC announced that the countdown to midnight was about to begin in fifteen minutes. I finished the last of my glass and tried my best to make a refined return to the ballroom. Sadly, Caleb was nowhere to be found.

I took a quick look around the room and started to briskly weave my way in and out around the guests, but couldn't find any trace of him. I flashed a look out the windows and saw a silhouette outside, standing on the dock, moonlight casting its dreamy spell. Instinct made me turn to immediately rush out the door, but I hesitated, for what felt like a split-second, to switch my shoes for snow boots and grab my parka—after all, it *was* winter in Maine! Despite the plowed path to the shore, I did my best to not get anything soaked in the fresh snow. As I took a few steps along the dock, Caleb turned and smiled.

"You disappeared. Nobody knew where you were," I chastised.
"I needed to revive myself a bit. Sorry I worried you," he voiced in contrition.
"Why did you come outside?" I inquired, trying to not sound possessive.
"I had to see up close this 45-foot wooden ketch that was sailing by. It was covered—and I mean *covered*—in twinkle lights. They must have wanted to ring in the New Year just off the eastern shore, so they could claim at midnight they were the farthest east where the New Year hits the U.S. first. I bet they didn't know that they needed to be Downeast, near Lubec, for them to have made that claim legitimate."
"They were the farthest east for here, anyway," I offered in support of the sailors I missed. "They should have steered for the candy cane stripes of Quoddy Head Lighthouse as their mark," Caleb noted.
"Too bad they couldn't have had *you* as their guide," I stated in mock sincerity, knowing that I wasn't about to let anyone have Caleb at this prime moment.

The moon was reflecting an endless shimmer upon the waves, a perfect accompaniment to the mesmerizing sounds of the sea. The timid swells were rhythmically lapping up against the dock. Caleb's face was also in reflection. Just as the water sparkled, he couldn't have looked more *dazzling*. Perhaps it was the sudden surge of cold air circling about, but my breath was momentarily taken away.

Just then, we heard the shouts of the countdown begin: "TEN! NINE! EIGHT!—" from the party guests inside, many of whom were peering out the picture windows of the ballroom at us. I felt my cheeks blush from both the frigid temperature and my embarrassment. I looked up and discovered Caleb had closed the three feet of distance between us, to only one.

"SEVEN! SIX! FIVE!—" I glanced back down, as both of my cold hands where instantly clasped; my fingers were suddenly entwined with his. His hands were surprisingly warm, for not wearing gloves.

"FOUR, THREE, TWO—" the crowd shouted. I looked up again at Caleb. In that split second, I knew that we were about to embark into unchartered waters.

"ONE! HAPPY *NEW YEAR!*" echoed from the house, the celebrants actively cheering.

Instantly, Caleb bent down his head closely, brushed his lips to my ear and whispered, "Happy New Year, Eliza." As I was about to share the same sentiment, in one, fluid movement that seemed to stop time, his hands softly cradled my face and he offered the most gentle, *perfect* kiss. He didn't offer multiple kisses, or a drawn-out, lingering kiss— no, *this* kiss was too complete to trivialize it with repetition. My lips began to tingle—and not from the snow that had started to fall.

"Happy New Year to you too, Caleb," I managed to vocalize, as I closed my eyes, and smiled as wide as the ocean was before us.

Chapter 11

Five months later

"Eliza? Earth to *El-i-zahhhhhhh?*" was Ashleigh's unsubtle attempt to reel me back to the task at hand in my dorm room, albeit momentarily without me, evidently. My best friend at Hawthorne was clearly demonstrating her intolerance of daydreaming during "study time," which really didn't amount to much actual study today. Her elongation of the syllables of my name immediately caught my attention, as Caleb and Father said my name the same way to me, many times.

"What?" I asked, sheepishly. "Can't a girl think about the Best New Year's Eve, *EV-ER?*" was my reply, validating my departure from the mind-numbing process.

"Eliza, it's now the first of June and we're supposed to be studying for finals. You're off in 'La-La Land' obsessing about something from five months ago!" she scolded. "Besides, it's not like that was the last time you saw Caleb," Ashleigh reminded.

"It might as well have been," I mildly argued with a sigh. "Caleb has been so busy since we all returned to school that I really haven't spent much time with him at all, other than the rushed dinner with Father at the townhouse on April Fool's Day and a few phone calls, texts and emails," I pulled from my brief, mental catalog of our sparse communications.

"What do you expect 'Liza? May I remind you that he's at *Harvard—HARVARD?*" was all Ash' needed to say to bring clarity to Caleb's chronic unavailability.

"Okay, let's get back to work," I reluctantly conceded.

"You know, we should take a break; after all, it's Friday night!" she offered as a truce. "We can pick up where we left off on Monday after class. There's a party at Noah Olmstead's house tonight. Want to go?"

"That braggart's house? The last time I had to endure his blathering-on about himself at Father's firm's office anniversary party, I wanted to jump off a cliff! I had to listen attentively because his father is my father's business partner. I'd rather have my fingernails ripped out!" I grandstanded, as Ashleigh's mouth dropped open in amazement at my uncharacteristic protest to party attendance.

"Okay, I can see the party is a no-go," Ashleigh sputtered, clearly stymied on ideas of what to suggest to do next, since she planned on an immediate, resounding, "Yes!" from me.

"Hey, why don't we head over to the MFA?" I suggested. "Because of my mother, I have a lifetime membership, and you know how long it has been and how much we—I—enjoy seeing Boston's showcase of fine art. Father had just emailed me today, in fact, about the new Impressionist Exhibit. I wondered if you and I would be going this weekend."

"Let's go first thing tomorrow, okay? We can take the 'T' and save us the hassle of driving ourselves," Ashleigh compromised.

"Sounds like a plan! I have something to do until nine in the morning, so I'll meet you by the big maple tree outside, around a quarter after nine. I'll be the one wearing the Monet t-shirt!" I cheered.

First thing the next morning, in one, brisk movement, I jumped out of bed, took a quick shower, then got dressed. What I didn't share with Ashleigh the night before, was that I had an early morning agenda to go and have a surprise visit to Caleb on campus. Wearing my specified white, Monet t-shirt with the *Water Lilies* image on the front, favorite jeans and the perfect, gray tweed, newsboy cap with cute wisps of my hair hanging out, I hopped in my new, sun yellow Volkswagen convertible. I then cranked up the music and drove over to Harvard for my quest to establish contact again with Caleb. The vehicle was a recent gift from Father for passing the driver's test. He wanted me to get something with more horsepower, but I opted for the car that made me smile.

I arrived at Caleb's dormitory and rang the buzzer. His roommate, Dan answered and gave me bad news: Caleb had just rushed home to Maine. His father had passed away from a heart attack. Stunned, I managed to thank him for the information. As I walked back to my car, I pushed aside my grief and contemplated how I could best help ease Caleb's pain. I knew this was going to change his life immensely.

I took my cell phone out of my pocket before I eased into the driver's seat and locked the car door. I called Father immediately to break the bad news and ask for help: "Father, I just found out that Caleb's father died of a heart attack. He's on his way home to Maine already. Would you please call his family and find out if there is anything we can do?" I anguished, as the tears started to flow. My heart was breaking, as I knew how close Caleb was to his father.

"I'll call his mother right away. I'd like for you to please pack some clothes for a few days and come home to the townhouse tonight, as we'll need to head up to Hales Island tomorrow, to lend our support and to attend the funeral that will most likely be taking place in the next few days," Father calmly itemized. "Don't worry about finals; I'll call the school for you to let them know there's been a death in the family—not to worry," he added protectively, knowing I would stress over missing my Trig final. *A death in the family*, I thought. *They were indeed practically like family, that's for sure.*

"I'll see you in a few hours, Father. Thank you," I replied, then ended the call with, "I love you."

My cell phone was now ringing; it was Ashleigh, wondering where I was, since she was at the maple tree impatiently waiting and I was nowhere to be found. Her ringtone on my phone was uniquely hers; it was a song about the finer things in life she can't live without. It was part fact and part jest. She would never put things before friendship, but she sure did have insanely expensive taste. I told her the sad news and we agreed to talk more in the dorm room while I packed. The MFA would have to wait.

"How awful for Caleb and his family," Ashleigh offered in a solemn tone, as she supervised my suitcase organization—or rather, disarray—on top of my bed. "Be sure to bring the black sheath dress I brought you from Paris," she urged in typical, Ashleigh-like form, despite the sad circumstances.

Always the fashionista no matter what, I thought to myself, as I managed a wan smile.

Jacob and Mary Longfellow were hardworking parents. Caleb's father's shipbuilding kept him away from home for long periods of time. Mary's three local jobs kept her on the island, but worn-out at the end of the day. Mary helped out at Dottie Look's diner three days per week, banded lobsters for a few local lobstermen as catch came in, and worked the volunteer, emergency radio dispatch from home on Saturdays. All of that would come to a halt for the time being. *Poor Caleb and his family*, I anguished inside. His three, much older brothers would be coming from the mainland to stay, prior to the funeral. They co-owned a Maine recreational adventure business together in Danforth and rarely returned to Hales Island. Hopefully, one of his brothers would stay behind with their mother for a while, so Caleb could return to Harvard soon. It would be just like Caleb to feel responsible for his mother, since he'd been home with her the longest. He knew better than anyone the loss she must now be feeling.

After several hours of Ashleigh's dictatorial—and at times, annoying—fashion direction, coupled with truly sincere compassion and understanding, I was ready to escape the dichotomy playing out in my dorm room and go home to see Father. After we loaded my small car trunk with the excess placed on the back seat, I hugged Ashleigh goodbye and drove off.

Father had just picked up another celebrity client from one of the Boston sports teams. He was neck-deep in contracts, so this was not a convenient time for him to leave. Father always stood by his friends, so, despite his busy schedule, we wasted no time and transferred my luggage into his Bentley, loaded his suitcase, and were ready to leave first thing in the morning.

The day dawned and we headed north on I-93 toward I-95 in the soundproof comfort of Father's luxury sedan. Wanting to ease the tension, Father broke the silence. "How's your car working out for you?" he inquired. "Are you sure you don't want to upgrade to a different one?" His wish to replace my car was totally transparent.

"While I do appreciate the superior accoutrements of other vehicles, mine just makes me grin. It's such *a happy car!* Besides, I ordered some daisy accessories for it, to promote maximum cheer!" I defended.

"Well, I guess you're right," Father conceded. "Maybe after graduation you'll change your mind," he offered, as one last attempt to win me over to his vehicular preference.

"Smiley-car, Father, happy car," I stated matter-of-factly and ended the discussion.

I must have snoozed for quite a while en route, because next thing I knew we were on the ferry to Hales Island and almost there. I didn't even remember boarding.

"Wake up, sleepyhead," Father chimed, as he handed me a cup of decadent hot chocolate. For a ferry galley, the beverage was supreme. The mornings on Casco Bay were still chilly in May, especially on the water, so I appreciated the cocoa as it warmed my hands and my stomach. With all my practice on the water sailing, I was used to comfortably eating and drinking on a boat. I could see others on the ferry were getting a bit nauseous, even with the waves as smooth as they were today. Father and I sat in silence for a bit, then landed and grabbed the taxi to *Misthaven* to clean up, before we went over to offer our condolences in person at the Longfellow's.

Father already had a bouquet of flowers delivered to Caleb's family. We also ordered a casserole and several side dishes from Dottie Look's restaurant. We arrived at the same time as Dottie at the Longfellow's federal blue with white trim, circa 1910 New England farmhouse; we helped her carry our delivery inside, giving her the lead along the brick, Flemish bond path toward the entrance. Caleb's home offered a welcoming front porch and a big picture window out the back, overlooking Longfellow Cove.

While Dottie entered their house assertively and made herself at home in the kitchen to set up the food, we stood at the front door to talk to Rick and Mike, two of Caleb's brothers. After our wishes of care and concern, we were invited in and were ushered to the living room, where Mary sat in a red, bustle-back wing chair facing the sunshine, cascading from the big window. She was staring blankly out at the cove, where a couple of blue and white lobster boats were mooring. Her plaid, fringed blanket was neatly tucked around her; clearly one of her sons had done his best to make his mother comfortable.

"Hello Mary," Father made our presence known. "We were so deeply sorry to hear about Jacob's passing," he compassionately added. "Since we were traveling from Boston, we asked if Dottie could deliver some dinner for your family; she's setting it up in the kitchen right now," Father offered, knowing Mary was probably not feeling much like eating, if she had even heard what he said. She was clearly in deep thought and dealing with the sudden shock of everything.
"Is there anything we can do for you?" I sincerely inquired.
"Oh, hello Eliza, *Benjamin*..." her voice trailed off as she still faced the window. It was evident she wasn't up for visitors yet, so we paid our condolences once more, then took to the kitchen, where we found Dottie straightening things up. Dottie and Mary were lifelong friends, as well as cousins, so we consulted her on what we could do for the family. I left Father behind to chat with Dottie, as I went for a walk looking for Caleb, as he wasn't at the house.

It didn't take me long to find him, as Caleb was down the hill in view of the house, sitting cross-legged on the deck of their red-roofed, storm gray boathouse, robotically throwing stones into the ocean. I caught myself staring off in the distance toward *Misthaven,* magically shrouded in the afternoon sun along the point. I recalled how our home and Caleb's were the only two, deepwater frontage properties on the island. Not catching him off-guard on my approach, he quickly stood up, walked toward me, gave me a hug and offered appreciation for arriving so quickly.

"How did you find out so fast?" he asked in disbelief.

"I stopped by your dorm yesterday to re-establish contact with the 'elusive Caleb Longfellow' and your roommate gave me the sad news. Father and I made immediate plans to come up."

"I'm so sorry Caleb about your father. I'm so, so very sorry," was the best I could offer, the sad circumstances limiting me on how to respond.

"I'm glad you're here," he replied, as he walked back to his boathouse roost overlooking the sea and sat back down. I followed and parked myself beside him on the weathered decking, attracted by the distinct color combos of the lobster buoys hanging on the post nearby. The windowpanes of his boathouse allowed you to peer deep into its windswept soul. *What a fitting structure for a boat-building family*, I thought.

Caleb brought me back to the conversation, announcing, "Mr. Hampton just left. He came by to offer his support. As I'm sure you remember, he understands what it's like to lose a spouse. My mom appreciated him sharing his direct experience, but I think his visit upset her. When she sat in the chair and stared out the window, I knew I needed to leave and to give her some space," he shared.

"So, you think I'm *elusive,* huh?" was Caleb's attempt to be witty and cut the silence. It was too painful to see him feign trying to lighten the mood.

"We can talk about that later," I redirected the dialog. "Let's just continue to sit together for a while, okay?" I gently pleaded, as I tenderly brushed the side of his cheek with the back of my index finger. I noticed that he needed a shave, but didn't say a thing. His normally bright blue eyes were a bit stormy in color, matching his boathouse more closely than usual.

"Sure, let's just sit," he conceded, as the wind blew his hair awry. He unconsciously put his locks back into place.

The warm breeze was relaxing. I adjusted myself to a more comfortable position, listening to the lobstermen off in the distance making plans for their next acquisition. I had no idea what Caleb was thinking, but just offered my support in solidarity, my place beside him a humble offering.

Next thing I knew, Father was nudging my foot with his own to wake me up, as Caleb and I had both fallen asleep, sitting side by side with our backs against the clapboards of the boathouse, my head resting on his shoulder. It was almost dark outside; the afternoon had slipped away. I was glad that Caleb had taken his mind off of his Dad, at least for a little while. I felt so helpless, as Caleb was always such an easygoing person. He obviously had the wind knocked out of him with this tragic news.

"Time to head home," Father urged. Hearing a voice, Caleb woke up and wiped the imaginary sleep from his eyes, as he spoke with a yawn. "Thank you—*yawn*—Eliza, for coming today—*yawn*. I appreciated the company," he confessed, while stretching. "It was exactly what *I needed*," he said, as his eyes pierced mine with an unusual intensity, the sunset reflecting off of his pupils. I raised my hand in a "goodbye" with a timid smile, as I was reluctant to leave him.

"We'll see you and your family tomorrow. Goodnight, Caleb," Father offered in quiet consolation, as he gently led me by the elbow toward the front of the yard to walk back home.

"Goodnight!" I echoed to Caleb, craning my neck back to see him get up. In a few, quick strides he was back inside his house.

In silent, comfortable solitude, Father and I didn't say a word to each other walking back home. We were each deep in our own thoughts. I wondered what Caleb's mom had said to Father. I wondered if Father was able to cheer her up after Mr. Hampton had unintentionally stirred up such fresh and raw emotions. If anyone could calm an otherwise bad situation, it was Benjamin P. Hales; the "P" should have been for "persuasive," not "Paul." Besides, he knew exactly what she was going through; he knew what it was like to lose the love of your life, too.

When we got back to *Misthaven*, neither of us had a real appetite, so Father and I each grabbed a snack—he a pear and I a peach yogurt—as we both said our "goodnights" and I retired to my room. Father went to read in the library. I changed into pajamas and sat up in bed for a while, trying to think of ways to bring a smile to Caleb tomorrow. Goofing-off didn't seem appropriate, nor did playing any jokes, as would be our usual. I decided that having gregarious fun tomorrow to take his mind off of things was out of the question, under the circumstances. I slid farther down in my bed, to quickly drift off to sleep. I'd come up with something to do in the morning.

Chapter 12

Something in the end of a dream startled me; I abruptly woke up and couldn't get back to sleep. I leaned on my elbow and looked over at the clock; it was two thirty in the morning, the glowing, turquoise numbers read. I knew I wouldn't be dreaming again anytime soon, so I put my slippers on to avoid the chilled floor and walked to the window seat to catch a glimpse of *Eliza's Wake*. As I shuffled over, I realized that this visit to the isle would not welcome a well-deserved sail, as that was too much fun to have in a time of mourning. My beautiful boat from those whom I loved most would have to wait, despite it being "open season" for sailing.

Amid the myriad of pillows along the window, I kicked off my slippers and clasped my knees up to my chin to get comfortable. I stared out at the moonlit water, the outline of my sailboat perfectly in silhouette, down below. Just then, I did a double-take, as I thought I saw a shadow of someone busily moving aboard my boat, which was a clear indicator of someone preparing to set sail. I looked again more closely through my antique telescope; sure enough, there was someone aboard. I knew it was locked up, *but that never stopped a determined thief.*

My heart pounded as I dressed in a flash. I was livid that someone had the nerve to steal *my beauty, RIGHT UNDERNEATH MY NOSE!* All I could think about were the people I loved who had worked so hard on building her—*nurturing* her—including Caleb and his father with crafting the hull. That brought my blood to a boil, knowing that I would not have the words to explain to Caleb how *yet another* part of his father was missing. The anger seethed within me almost to a guttural roar!

Furious, I shoved my arms and feet into each sleeve and pant leg, fighting to free them, as my anger made this task difficult. Without even thinking of my safety, I forgot to wake up Father. I grabbed a flashlight from the mud room and a croquet mallet from off the back porch, then I stomped off to the dock to make someone really pay for their audacity. *The nerve of some people!* I shouted at the top of my lungs in my mind, as my agitation grew in leaps and bounds with every step toward rescuing my vessel.

"GET OFF MY BOAT, YOU TOTAL, SCUMBAG-*LOSER!* DON'T YOU KNOW THAT STEALING *IS A CRIME?*" I screeched angrily, almost out of breath. I started to swing the croquet mallet back and forth with total, bodily force, with a fierce and menacing facial expression. I wanted to demonstrate that I meant business, and connecting with any part of this offender's body was my goal. It was going to hurt—*really HURT!*

At this short distance, I had figured out that it was indeed a man aboard; the realization of me against a strange man had my resolve waver a bit, for a moment. Father must not have heard my yelling, as the nights were still cool, so the windows were shut. Luckily, I remembered that I had left my cell phone in my jeans pocket, so with my free hand I pulled it out in one, flowing motion to wake up Father, as 911 would only call Portland on the mainland. Father was my only hope for prompt backup. He would no doubt bring a gun—*fully loaded.*

"Eliza, what in the world are you doing?" a calm, familiar voice in the night inquired, easing my quest for justice. It stopped my postured, mallet-swinging and phone call in their tracks. "Eliza, hon', it's just me, Caleb," the confirmation came, so I put away my phone and let the mallet drop on the dock. I wanted to be fuming-mad at him for scaring me, but I couldn't, as the realization of the death of his father sunk back in. As quickly as my anger rose, it fell just as swiftly.

With no further discussion, Caleb reached out his hand to help me aboard. The emotion of his pleading eyes in the moonlight made my knees momentarily weak, causing my boarding of the boat more of a hoisting effort on his part than it should be. He sat down in the cockpit and patted the spot next to him for me. As he could see I had rushed out of the house without a coat and was cold, he climbed down the companionway and grabbed a blanket from the salon, as he had a key—and rightly entitled to it—as my master shipbuilder. He wrapped the heavy, wool, point blanket with dragonfly detail around my shoulders and sat by my side, draping his arm casually behind me, but unmistakably, *around* me. I leaned closer toward him and rested my head on his shoulder, as I had fallen asleep doing so earlier in the evening. I closed my eyes for a moment to take in this indelible impression: the salty night air circulating around us, the sound of the boat's bumpers gently tapping against the dock, the polished, moonlit gleam of the boat's varnish and Caleb's own fragrance—a woodsy, fresh essence that didn't come from a bottle of cologne. I let it all envelop me in the moment. "I'm in Heaven," I murmured under my breath, inaudible to Caleb, even in such close proximity.

"I couldn't wait until tomorrow; I needed to be near you 'Liza. You are the only person who I don't feel so hopeless around," was Caleb's sincere justification for commandeering my boat in the middle of the night. "Since I wasn't about to disturb you and your family at such an unreasonable hour, *Eliza's Wake* was the best place to be to pass the time," he added.

Remembering where I was, who I was with and the late hour, I excused myself briefly and ran back inside the house to leave Father a note, to let him know when he woke up where I was, in case this impromptu visit lingered to the dawn of a new day. Even though I knew he'd understand that I needed to help Caleb during this difficult time, I didn't want him to worry when he got up at his usual, early hour and found that I was alarmingly absent. We didn't need another heart attack to deal with. When I returned to the boat, I resumed my spot next to Caleb.

We sat together talking until first light. It had been a long time since I had a captive audience for an extended period of time with my favorite native of Maine.

I did my best to keep his mind off of his Dad and help him focus on happier times. When I thought I had conquered the opportunity to ease his pain by chatting all night, Caleb looked out at the sunrise and expressed, "This reminds me of the time my father and I were finishing up building the hull of your boat; it was sunrise and the start of the last day we were working on it together. Looking back, it was a bittersweet moment; it was the last boat we built together *and* the last bit of quality time we spent together. I'm sure you can understand why I like being aboard *Eliza's Wake* so much."

I smiled up at him, then put my head back on his shoulder and gave him a one-armed squeeze around his waist. The blanket fell off my shoulders and Caleb instantly returned it to its proper place. *Caleb must have been the one to tuck his mother in with the plaid blanket yesterday,* I surmised.

We both knew a sail was not appropriate today, as the funeral was taking place late afternoon on the mainland in Portland and extended family members were arriving soon. Mary Longfellow didn't want to waste any time with the funeral plans, as everyone coming was within easy driving distance, so no need to wait another day. She wanted to move forward quickly, so she didn't have to keep putting on a brave face, hiding her sorrow from all of the guests in town. "The sooner they all left, the better, so she could finally grieve," Caleb professed of his mother's emotional condition.

Caleb excused himself down to the galley briefly and came back up to the cockpit with a couple of mugs of hot cocoa. It was just like Caleb to find the food aboard. I had forgotten Uncle Seth had put in a small microwave and stuffed some fun things for me to eat down below. It was also nice to have the convenience of electricity, dockside.

"Thanks. Here's to happier times," I said, as I clanked my mug against Caleb's.

"Cheers," was Caleb's reply, then he downed the mug's contents in three, huge gulps.

"Well, I better head back home, as I need to help Mom get ready for company," Caleb announced, as he set the empty mug on the cockpit table. "I'll see you at the funeral then?" he asked, his eyes hiding something.

"Sure, we'll be there, but we're planning to leave Portland for home right after the funeral," I cautiously mentioned. I wanted us to stay put longer so I could help him more, but realized he needed to get home. He would deal with his grief in his own way, on his own time. I just wished I could stick around for a few more days and spend some more time with him.

"I'll have to see you again when I'm back at Harvard, in a week. My brother is staying with Mom, so I can get back in school right away."

I was relieved to know that he would get back to campus soon, and resume his life away from home. Being away from Maine would hopefully take his mind off his Dad and help him heal more quickly.

Just as I thought Caleb was going to leave the boat, he took a step out of the cockpit and hesitated, leaned his head back turning his face toward me and whispered, "Can you stay another day or so?"

I saw his eyes glistening, confirming that my suspicions were correct; his previous composure was a facade, so I offered instant support: "Of course I can stay another day. What would you like to do tomorrow?"

"Let's sail. I need to," he said with total conviction.

"She'll be ready at dawn, or whenever you want to go," I assured him.

"See you at the funeral then," were Caleb's last words, as he leapt out of the boat and walked toward the sunlight, its beams fully breaking through the trees.

The funeral was somber, but not overly so. Caleb and his family sat off to the side of the front of the room. The partition separating them from the audience was wide open. Attendees could view them at various stages of discomfort from being in the public eye: Caleb's mother was stoic, but her eyes and nose were red; his brothers were fairly composed, the eldest handing Mary a tissue from time to time. At first glance, Caleb appeared to be in deep thought, but not excessively distraught-looking. I noticed him wearing an extra-wide, earth-toned tie that was clearly from the 1970s; it must have been his father's.

The Westwood Funeral Home service room was decorated with two, ornamental trees flanking the closed casket and several, potted plants in the front. Always the practical family, they felt that flowers would die; plants had at least a chance to survive. There had been a viewing prior to the service. Now the casket was closed.

After some scripture and poetic prose were read and personal remarks given by family—with the exception of Mary—the service concluded. The organ hummed a reverent melody in the background, signaling that guests were free to pay their respects one more time to the Longfellow's.

As each guest filed by the family, words of clichéd condolence were not spoken; only heartfelt dialog was taking place. Yankee funerals were not overly-emotional, yet never lacked in sincerity. This was especially evident today. The Longfellow family was working through their grief, just not in the "made for reality TV," sort of way. As I approached them, I followed Father and paid my respects. As I reached Caleb, his arms encircled me with a gentle embrace and a quiet, "Thank you for being here," for me. His parting words were, "I'm still going to meet you to sail tomorrow at dawn, okay?" I mouthed, *O-KAY* and smiled warmly at him, as Father put out his arm for me, to lead the way out of the room.

Father gave me permission to take the ferry back to Hales Island, as so many other Longfellow friends were traveling with me. He gave me a hug and said he'd see me back at the townhouse next weekend, as he had to return to the firm, as anxious, celebrity clients were losing their patience. Arrangements had been made for me to take a commuter bus from Portland to the Boston terminal, then take a cab home in two days. Father knew I would sail and with our housekeeper/chef, Mrs. Eddleston manning *Misthaven*, I was in good hands.

The next morning I was up at dawn, making way to set sail. I let Mrs. Eddleston know of our destination plans and estimated return the night before, so we were free to go. The weather was cooperative; bright, blue sky and calm waves awaited our departure. As I drifted into a momentary daydream, mesmerized by the watercolor palette of nature's expanse before me, Caleb hopped aboard, redirecting my thoughts to him.

"Let's get this show on the road, okay?" Caleb urged. I wasn't one to delay, so I followed his lead as he instinctively took over captain's duties.

We worked together quietly, intuitively, and in perfect tandem. As we sat back to enjoy the wind in our faces, we both looked at each other briefly and knew that this was an existence worth living. Life was good, despite loved ones leaving us prematurely. We continued to enjoy each other's company with small conversations, interspersed with the ongoing busywork of sailing, while taking in the breathtaking majesty of the bay. No serious discussions were engaged; we just enjoyed being together, at sail. There was a great therapy in this peaceful journey. By the time we returned home at dusk, the sun was setting on the memories of the past couple of days, blurring out the pain and ushering in healing in abundance.

Chapter 13

"Father? I'm back!" I blurted out, as I came in through the front door on Beacon Hill. I had already loaded my luggage back in the trunk of my sunshine-on-wheels, as I wasn't staying long. I needed to get settled back at Hawthorne for my morning makeup final in my Trigonometry class, after missing a couple of days of exams. I wondered how Caleb's workload was waiting for him too, upon his return to campus.

"I'm in here," Father's voice directed. As I followed it to the library, I found him sitting by the fireplace, clearly engrossed in a presidential memoir. "Eugenie has dinner waiting for you in the kitchen," he added, not looking up from the pages. By the time I finished my last bite of Chicken Cordon Bleu, washing it down with an uncustomary glass of milk, Father was done reading and came into the kitchen to finish the conversation.

"How is Caleb? How is his family?" he inquired with a tone of concern, as he pulled up a chair next to me.

"Caleb and I had a nice sail two days ago. I walked around the island yesterday before I stopped by his house to pay my respects again to the rest of his family," I answered. "I think Caleb's mother is glad to be rid of all the fuss and company. I think they are all on their way to some normalcy—as normal as can be, under the circumstances."

Father must have been reading my mind about the exams waiting for Caleb back at school, as he exclaimed, "I spoke to the powers-that-be at Harvard, to make sure they gave some leniency for Caleb to finish his delayed finals in peace."

"That will be a huge burden lifted from his shoulders, I'm sure," I said in appreciation.

"You are a good friend to him, Eliza. Your level of compassion and support is beyond your years," Father boasted.

Sensing my shifting anxiously in my chair, he deduced, "Don't tell me—you need to get back to Hawthorne, right?"

I gave him a big hug and a kiss goodnight, thanked him for everything and headed for my happy, yellow, German chariot to carry me to my dorm.

As I let my bags fall to the floor in a thudding, *SLUMP*, I noticed a note had been shoved under my dorm door. One, quick glance of the small envelope on the floor and I knew it was from Ashleigh. In the age of texting and other high tech media, my best friend still loved the fine art of written correspondence—particularly, "girlie" note cards, often scented. I had rebuked her for not being more eco-conscious, but to no avail. I would never fault her for sentiment, so I opened it with a smile. "WELCOME BACK!" was all that the note said. I knew I'd wake early to a call in the morning from her wanting details, so I promptly donned my pj's and climbed into bed, falling fast asleep.

A trilled, *"RING!—RING!—RING!"* went my cell phone abruptly at 6:00 a.m. *What, no trademark, "Ashleigh" ringtone today?* I thought in a foggy haze, as I answered the phone, knowing instinctively it was Ashleigh calling for her early report on my trip for the funeral.

"Whose phone are you calling from, Ash'?" I mumbled, half asleep.

"I switched phones for a day with a new friend who was thinking of buying one like mine," she replied sheepishly, knowing my default ringtone for unknown callers was the generic, old-school telephone ring that jolts you awake from even the deepest REM sleep. I had been meaning to switch it to something less annoying, and forgot. *Note to self: change ringtone for unknown callers and turn off phone at bedtime.*

After a few minutes of expected interrogation, I told Ashleigh I'd meet her in between finals in the lounge to catch-up, in person.

Reluctantly, she hung up, then I closed my eyes for a few more minutes before I had to start the day.

I sent a quick text message to Caleb, welcoming him back to Harvard, letting him know I'd be around if he wanted to talk, or get together after finals. I knew he'd be swamped with getting back into the routine at school, so I didn't expect to hear from him until later in the week. What I didn't expect, was for the week to go by and then another week, and then the semester was already letting out for summer, with still no word from him. After the closeness I thought we'd felt during the time we were both there for the funeral, as well as New Year's, I thought he'd be more in contact. I became very concerned.

I called Caleb's cell right after school got out as I was packing up my dorm room to head back to the townhouse the next day. I left him a voicemail—still no response, even after three days. I decided too much time had passed, so the next day I texted his roommate at Harvard before I left campus, in hope of some information. I got quite a shock: his roommate advised me that Caleb had taken an impromptu internship for the summer at a law firm in New York City. I was told not to expect to hear from him anytime soon, as they were, "working him to death."

I couldn't believe Caleb would take off without saying a word, and not even call me to let me know he was okay. My intuition told me that Caleb was dealing with his grief still. Being in entirely new surroundings, with little time to think, this was probably a deliberate grasp for survival.

I immediately called Father at work to find out if his firm—who sponsored the Harvard scholarship—might have some information on Caleb's NYC stint. I always thought internships came later in college.

"All I know is that he was offered and took an early internship this summer, but I thought you knew," was Father's reply, clearly surprised at my being kept out of the loop.

I did my best to be un-phased at the surprise information and found a quick excuse to hang up, so that I could sulk in private dejection. After a few minutes of dealing with the noise of everyone escaping the building, I slung my duffle bag over my shoulder, grabbed my other suitcase, flipped off the light switch and headed to Boston Common, before going home. I ignored Ashleigh's frantic texts and just sat, staring at the swans and boats on the lake, trying to concentrate on the birds singing and breeze tickling my face—a futile attempt to tune out the thought most prominent in my mind: Caleb left without saying goodbye. *Sure, he was dealing with grief, but wasn't I supposed to know about something like this?*

I pulled into our townhouse driveway and couldn't help but notice the Porsche already there, with Ashleigh leaning up against her flashy car, clearly agitated.
Ooops…I probably should have answered her texts, I realized.
Expecting a shrill lecture, I was amazed at being offered only a hand with my luggage, quietly following me alongside, into the foyer.

"I know why you didn't answer my texts," Ashleigh offered, as she helped me finish carrying my bags upstairs. "I heard all about Caleb's sudden departure from about three other people today." Her news was a total strike to my pride, in that I figured *everyone* was in the dark. *No, not everyone—just me*, it seemed.
Continuing, she went on, "The internship was too good to be true; evidently it came at a convenient time to escape. He's staying with a cousin—a starving artist—and takes the subway to his new firm."
I couldn't believe that I was the *last* person to know about *my* best friend.

Ashleigh, ever the problem solver had her own agenda: "Let's go visit my Aunt Linda in Kahala, on Oahu for a few weeks!" she cheered. "Sun, fun, surf and relaxation are just what you need—right now!" completed her pitch for summertime bliss.

"Okay," I conceded, with no fuss, whatsoever. My inability to counter her vacation plans with something else took Ashleigh visibly aback, but I paid no attention, and she moved on to the next topic of importance: what to pack.

"I think I better go ask my father about this first, before we get ahead of ourselves," was my voice of reason.

"He'll say 'yes,'" she countered in a snap.

He did. In a week I was to bid, "Aloha" and was off to Hawaii to bask in the sun, enjoying a tropical summer, the dream of just about every teenage girl. *The drastic change in climate and scenery will do me good*, I repeated to myself, like a mantra.

Chapter 14

"Is that a 42-foot ketch I see, way out there?" I lazily asked, sunspots in the way of my vision. Ashleigh was not paying much attention to my question, trying to get sunscreen on, as we lounged in her aunt's backyard for the third day in a row.

"It looks like a sailboat to me," was her inattentive reply.

I shrugged off her disengagement and flipped over to my other side, avoiding sunburn.

The amazing, lapis waters, swaying banana trees and warm, salt spray in our front-row view were mesmerizing—therapeutic, actually. We had been at Ashleigh's aunt's house in Hawaii enjoying the gifts of the tropical isle in abundance for a week already: mahi mahi, spam musubis, ramen, multiple, fruity concoctions—*sans alcohol of course*, Korean barbeque and shave ice, just to name a few, were dietary staples. We had eaten our last bite of chocolate macadamia nut confectionery, when Aunt Linda yelled out the sliding glass door, asking if we wanted to head over to Hanauma Bay to snorkel.

"Grab the frozen peas!" Ashleigh shouted jubilantly, as she snatched up both of our towels and headed to the car. I picked up the snorkels and fins on the deck and loaded them into the trunk. As I circled around the car to climb in, I noticed a bit of rust on the bumper of the nearly new, large model BMW. *Even nice cars don't escape the hazards of nature*, I thought.

Hanauma Bay is a popular tourist destination, but worth enduring the crowds. Ashleigh and I were thoroughly enjoying ourselves, standing in waist-deep water feeding peas to the fish by the dozens. They tickled as they swished around my knees, swarming for their spherical bites of wrinkled, green veggies. The vibrant, yellow fish reminded me of their miniature counterparts I'd seen in the fish tank at my pediatrician's office in Boston. Even with all the people, it was strangely peaceful—almost hypnotic—just standing there quietly feeding our little friends, tracing the surface of the warm water with our fingertips.

After we finished snorkeling and seeing some interesting fish up close that chewed on coral, we made plans for our next excursion to the North Shore. The Polynesian Cultural Center in Laie was our trip for the next day. I couldn't wait to see all the different cultures exhibited—especially the Master Woodcarver in the Maori village, as they had a hand-hewn canoe that would marvel any sailor or boat builder. The intricacies of Maori carving were a true art form; their designs were totally unique. Thinking about boat-building caught me in a moment of surprise—I realized that I hadn't thought about Caleb, all week.

Breakfast the next morning was truly gourmet. Our pancakes with coconut syrup and fresh mango, pineapple and papaya in footed, glass dishes with fresh guava juice, capped-off a scrumptious cuisine. We would need all the energy we could generate, as we'd be walking a lot today at the PCC.

We took the Kamehameha Highway—known as "Kam Highway" by the locals—from Kaneohe, stopping at a deserted beach in Kaaawa to stretch our legs and get our feet wet. Then we visited a roadside, Korean barbeque stand in Hauula for a quick—but, oh-so-worth-it—bite to eat. We took our time getting there, learning patience and more fully acclimating to "island time" along the way.

We needed to stop for a bit and regroup, as we were still living like stereotypical, "Type A" Bostonians, prone to rushing things. I was reminded how there was nothing more indicative of being from the home of the Red Sox, than the hurriedness of passengers riding the commuter trains. The inability to wait for anyone trying to board was oft-seen. Fellow commuters walking ahead of you that weren't walking fast enough were cause for exasperation. In fact, my mother told me once, when I was little, that when I was a baby and she had me in a stroller, she tried to make her way through Quincy Market and found it so difficult to gain entry with all the people moving, that she had to bulldoze her way through. Then, after that, she tried to sit down outside on a bench to rest with me and two businessmen rudely took her spot, right in front of her, with no apologies, whatsoever. That was her one, single complaint about the city that she adored.

I had yet another realization. I hadn't thought about my mother in quite some time. Perhaps it was because I had a strange comfort in knowing she was in a good place, smiling down upon me. Father and I spoke of her so openly, it was if she was still walking the earth, painting all that was glorious to see. She would have loved the flora and fauna I witnessed already today. I laughed to myself as I remembered the time I spoiled her helicopter ride, viewing similar plant life from above.

Arriving at the PCC, we found several tour busses unloading hoards of people. Ashleigh's aunt reminded us that we should try to exit the park as soon as the night show was over, or we'd be stuck behind all the tour busses for most of the trip back to Kahala. We said our goodbyes and headed to the ticket counter, with plans to be picked up promptly after the show.

We had the VIP package, so upon arrival, we received our shell lei greeting by some local college students with perpetual smiles who worked there. We were still full from our roadside treats, so we bypassed the snacks near the entrance and hurried on our way to see the sights.

"Hey 'Liza, let's get our photo taken with that statue, over there—you know, the tiki guy," Ashleigh urged. We took turns posing with the wooden warrior amidst the lush, tropical plants, then a passerby offered to take our photo together.

"That's one for the scrapbook," I offered, with a grin.

"Don't be so, 'old-school' Eliza; there are so many other, cutting edge technologies. That's the way to go to promote our vacation," Ashleigh commanded. I had forgotten Ashleigh was everywhere, using every social media method, accounting for her life 24/7, it seemed. With the exception of her unusual proclivity for formal, paper stationery, I was a dinosaur compared to her. It was an odd contrast to her commitment to the dying art of handwritten correspondence. Ashleigh was a communicator, plain and simple—whether in person, online, phone, or via note cards, it made no difference.

After touring the Tahiti, Hawaii, Tonga, Samoa, Fiji and Marquesas villages, as well as the quilting hut, we felt quite knowledgeable about many of these countries and arts of the Pacific. We finished off our tour in the New Zealand area. I found a marquise-shaped, Maori warrior pendant, hand-carved in steak bone, made by a local artist; this necklace was truly remarkable. It reminded me of a double-ended dory in shape. On the surface was a face with his tongue sticking out; his image was a testament of fearlessness and independence I wanted to emulate. I tried it on, smiled at myself in the mirror and knew my souvenir shopping was complete.

"Don't mess with you, eh Eliza?" was Ashleigh's sign of approval of my purchase.

"I'm going to wear this symbol of empowerment every time I sail; with it, I'm going to be protected from all threats—foreign and domestic, too," I added with my most presidential voice. I turned on the heels of my flip-flops to head to the luau and night show dinner area of the park. Ashleigh slowly followed behind, unable to take her eyes off the coconut tree climber scaling the branches above us, chucking the fruit to the ground in a neatly stacked pile, nearby.

"Wake up girls," Aunt Linda announced. So full from our luau dinner and exhausted from the day-long tours and night show, we slept the whole way back to the house. Ash', still in a coma, climbed out of the car and went straight to bed. I managed to wake up enough to catch a glance of the moon over the ocean off the back deck, so I sat for a moment to enjoy the scene. Shimmering wavelets continued to hypnotize, so I went in the house and fell on my bed, not bothering to change clothes. I was tired; clothes could wait until morning.

Chapter 15

I woke up on my back, staring at the ceiling. The morning rays were cascading through the louvered windows, as my eyes partially focused on what appeared to be something rather large—*crawling*. The foreign creature jarred me wide awake in an instant. I covered my mouth and stifled a shriek. As the cloud of brain fog dissipated, I could see my luck had just changed for the better: *a gecko crossed my path.* I had heard about them, seen photos of them, knew having them inside the house was considered good luck, but never had seen one in person before. *He was really, quite cute!* I watched him scurry around the ceiling for a minute or so, then he came down the wall near my bed for a closer look at me. I held my position and kept my breathing shallow, so as not to shake the bed, scaring him off. After a brief pause, he turned the opposite direction and disappeared.

It didn't seem possible that a month had already passed by in Hawaii; it was time to head back to Boston. School was only a few weeks away. The change of scenery and nonstop adventures were unparalleled for a girl who knew wool better than tropical-weight linen, boots better than flip-flops. For as busy as this summer vacation had been, I felt completely rested; my head was as crystal clear as the vast pool of aquamarine before me. *Must be the mauka showers,* I acknowledged.

Packing my duffle bags—including a new, pink one with tropical print I picked up just to house all my souvenirs, I felt a renewed appreciation for family. As much as I enjoyed "hanging ten" with Ashleigh, I really missed my father—not in a clingy, homesickness-y kind of way, but just feeling an acknowledgement of the importance of family, being forever.

Not seeing Father for over a month was a definite first for me. I realized that it wouldn't be long before I'd be off to college and on my own, fulltime, which made me feel a bit melancholy. It was appropriate to miss being, "Daddy's little girl." After all, I really did like spending time together, as strange and unusual as that was for a teenager to think. I'd even be so bold as to say it out loud—in front of other people, *other teens*—even.

Barreling into the room, Ashleigh stated the obvious, "Well, it's time to get back to reality and blow this shave ice stand!"
"I've finished packing, Ash'. Here, please help me out and take my new duffle bag to the car." I could see a look bordering on coveting cross over my BFF, so I cautioned her: "Don't look at me like that Ashleigh. You should have bought one for yourself! You *know* you wanted one!"
"I don't need Aloha accessories where I'm going," was her snide remark. I had forgotten that as soon as I landed in Boston, Ashleigh would be off to New York City until school started, to shop till she drops with some of her "silver spoon" cousins on Park Avenue.

Before we got in the car to head to the airport, I took one, last check of my texts and email on my cell phone, in case—*by some miracle*—Caleb reached out for the first time all summer. No such luck—*hermit is, as hermit does*. There was no response from him. I quickly emptied my thoughts of him, determined to maintain my Zen-like, "state of being" for as long as I could. *I'll miss the warm, early morning swims, right outside the door.*

Chapter 16

"El-i-za!" came the familiar-sounding call of my name, from one who helped bring me into the world. My mother had progressed so quickly in labor that she had given birth to me in the bathroom. Father helped deliver me, until the EMTs arrived.

"I've missed you so much!" was all I could say out loud, before Father swept me up in his arms and squeezed me with a huge bear hug, next to the baggage carousel. Ashleigh knew it was time to let me have my reunion, so she nodded in my general direction and headed to the next terminal for her flight to New York. I knew that I'd talk to her soon, so I offered her a brief wave farewell.

"I didn't think you could get any blonder," Father assessed, "—or tanner," referring to my richer skin color. Even sailing in the sunshine in Maine never offered this drastic a change.

"One of the things people forget about tropical locations, is the close proximity to the sun and ocean; it generally lightens hair and darkens complexion," was my facetious reply.

Our banter continued all the way back home to the townhouse. Ash' and I had taken the red-eye from San Francisco, so I was starved, having slept through the middle-of-the-night snack offering on the plane.

"How does a hearty breakfast of blueberry pancakes sound?" Father inquired, as we walked inside the townhouse from the garage, having heard my stomach growling in surround-sound.

"Like heaven!" I enthusiastically replied. "It's *sooooo good* to be home!"

"Great! See you in the kitchen in half an hour," he added.

I schlepped my baggage to my room, took a quick trip to the bathroom to wash my face, then headed back to the kitchen ready to plow breakfast—I was ravenous! In between mouthfuls of pancake perfection, I did my best to hold a conversation with Father, without choking. I gave him the rundown of our Hawaii itinerary, told him all the crazy things Ashleigh and I did (leaving out the part where I got a bit homesick, even if I didn't fully acknowledge it, to preserve the jovial mood), then thanked him again for my summer fun.

As breakfast was nearing its end, I was getting ready to leave the table and take my dishes to the sink, when Father's facial expression became serious. *Uh oh. That expression doesn't look good.*

"Eliza, I'm just going to come right out and say it: Caleb got a new scholarship offer from the firm he was interning at in New York and he's going to Columbia University this fall. He clearly wanted to distance himself from my firm, evidently. I'm sorry, but I've been advised that he's not coming back before school starts."
"Wh— *what? Who* transfers *from Harvard?*" I asked sternly, clearly in shock at the news, *and at the stupidity*. "Well, I guess that changes my plans for Thanksgiving this year for sure," I continued, half-dazed. "He didn't even call, email or text me, *all summer long!* What a COWARD!" I screamed, throwing my hands up into the air in frustration.

Seeing how I had all but lost my "Aloha Spirit" in my unveiled anger at Caleb and my blatant prejudice between schools—as Columbia is a fine institution as well, despite family allegiances—Father steered me to the stairs. He knew that I was tired, devastated and needed time alone. It wasn't like me to become so emotional and he fully understood that. I ran straight up to my room, threw myself on the bed and cried myself to sleep.

One hour later, I woke up to my cell phone buzzing with repeated texts from Ashleigh. *She must have landed and immediately texted me*, I thought, as the fog was lifting from sleep.

I looked at my phone and it read: *911—Guess who I saw?*

Oh, I don't know Ash', your favorite designer purse on the clearance rack? I texted hazily, not quite fully awake.

No, not what—*WHO! Don't be stupid! Besides, you know I don't shop*—in bins. *I loathe them. I saw Caleb, Eliza. He was having brunch with the family at my cousin's house, when I arrived.*

I texted I'd call her right back. I needed a moment to compose myself.

A million thoughts rattled around my brain as to how to handle this. Knowing he was there was just too big of a coincidence. I had forgotten Ashleigh's uncle was a lawyer, so his firm probably was the sponsoring organization for his Columbia scholarship. They were likely just getting to know their scholarship recipient and thought a fine, family meal with the founding partner was the way to go.

Ashleigh had two, beautiful cousins who would happily make it their "pet project" to show Caleb all that NYC had to offer. Since I obviously didn't know Caleb anymore, who was I to guess whether he'd have anything to do with these cousins, or not? They were sailors themselves, as they had a "summer cottage" on Long Island—actually, a gargantuan estate that, "made *Misthaven* look like a shack," from what Ashleigh told me. Caleb would overlook their privilege if they were down-to-earth enough, and I believe they were, as Ashleigh used to complain they'd choose a sail over shopping, any day. They were going to shop with Ashleigh right away, just to get it over with. I guess I better get this phone call over with, too.

"Ashleigh?"

"What…took…you…so…*long?* I've been *holding it* since San Francisco! I need to go to the bathroom and I've been waiting and waiting for you to call me!" she shouted.

"Ash', that was way, Too Much Information. Calm down. I won't take long. What is the mailing address for your uncle in Manhattan?"

"Why? You aren't planning on *coming* here, are you? Should I warn my cousins to disappear, just in case?"

"Ashleigh, call off the dogs. I'm just mailing you a package, overnight. You'll know what to do with it."

Before she could forget she *had to go* and interrogate me some more, I said goodbye and hung up. I had made up my mind, and that was that.

Needing the best therapy that I could get on short notice, I took off to the Museum of Fine Arts on a quest for solace, amid the beauty. Seeing the artwork would be just the remedy I needed for an aching heart. I decided not to bring along my watercolors or sketch materials for action on inspiration from the galleries, as I was not in a participatory frame of mind, but instead, strictly an observer.

The next morning, a small package arrived in Manhattan via overnight, secure shipping, addressed to Ashleigh, with a brief note included inside:

> *To Caleb Longfellow:*
> *Return to Sender.*

That was all it said. Enclosed was the wooden box and green tourmaline bracelet he had given me, with his verbalized, accompanying requirement:

> *By accepting this gift, I need you to promise me Eliza,*
> *that we will always be friends,*
> *that growing older and becoming adults will not change us,*
> *and that we will always be able to pick up where we left off.*

Clearly, the "contract" of his bracelet gift was null and void after his behavior all summer. *Guess he's getting, "Legal 101," in how to break a contract—and a heart!* I fumed internally. Regardless of his father's death, friends don't disappear on each other. It's completely disloyal. There was no "picking up where we left off," as Caleb left with no word and with no intention of returning. I didn't need this "gesture" constantly reminding me of his abandonment of our friendship—of our growing relationship, nipped in the bud before it ever fully blossomed. I knew Ashleigh would deliver it to Caleb right away, so I could close this chapter of my life, nice and tight.

Chapter 17

The last few weeks of summer I was on autopilot, just biding my time until school started. At school my usual routine would emerge, allowing me camouflage and distance from my father's almost-daily inquiries into how I was feeling. He surely meant well, as he assumed the news of Caleb would devastate me; strangely enough, I felt *powerful*. I ushered in my senior year with a fervent drive to succeed in all of my classes, which included my fourth year of French and Art, along with a full spectrum of AP/college prep courses in English, Calculus, Physics and Economics/Government. Running for Class President again was not insurmountable, even with a heavier than usual class load with plenty of after-school activities. Surprisingly, I won the election for the second year in a row, which provided more escape from idleness, a state of mind I wanted to avoid, to keep my thoughts off of Caleb.

My senior year was supposed to be a meaningful rite of passage, a period of immense hope for the future. In between studies, gatherings of friends, student government, additional, extracurricular activities and the numerous college applications to complete, I was fulfilled with busywork. After a few weeks, the "work" in busywork wasn't really evident anymore. I was at ease—contented, really. I even enjoyed a few dinners and picnics with Stewart Grey, IV, the son of one of Father's best friends from college, Dr. Stewart Grey, III, a high-profile cardiologist in Boston from very old, New England money.

Stewart IV was every bit of New England aristocracy that Caleb wasn't. Despite the wealth of his family, he was well-rounded; he was engaged in things of purpose, other than the expected, expensive, fast cars and ridiculous keg parties that many at Hawthorne regularly participated in. He was well-read; his interests included equestrian, daily writing and several, philanthropic pursuits, in addition to being Editor of the school paper, the *Hawthorne Herald*. He worked tirelessly on his family's charitable foundations; he was slated to be a board member for two of them, once he finished college. He was already accepted to Harvard, presumably Pre-Med, thanks to his long line of alma mater history in his family. It didn't hurt that the Grey Family funded the revamped medical technology wing on campus.

Stewart was classically handsome and cultured. He wore timeless, designer clothes and handmade shoes from Italy. On him, houndstooth and English horse riding attire were especially dashing. He was six feet tall, had smooth, dark brown hair that was almost black, and mesmerizing, pale green eyes that when he smiled, lit up and reeled-in every girl's attention at school.

His regal good looks were initially sought out as a distraction for my mental musings, but he turned out to be a great partner for my own desire to help others. His arts foundation regularly donated to the MFA, so naturally, my interest was piqued when the annual gala was announced, seeking volunteers. *A résumé boost and something I really wanted to be a part of!* We had a great time working side by side, ensuring that the gala offered something other than stodgy fare, to broaden the attendance age to include young adults. It was a huge success, evidenced by so many of our own age, as it resembled a sort of "mini prom." Stewart and I toasted our triumph with his grandmother's recipe of autumn fruit punch at the event. He whirled me gracefully around the marble floor of the MFA. During our first dance, I briefly caught myself thinking of Caleb and last New Year's, but quickly put him out of my thoughts. This exercise in mental control worked, as it would be the last time that I thought of Caleb for quite a while. Eyes sparkling—perhaps a tiny bit from a captured tear of a memory now shelved, I smiled up at Stewart, happy for our friendship and mutual service to the community.

Three weeks before Thanksgiving, I happened to arrive at the townhouse just after the mail did. An engraved invitation, addressed by hand in graceful calligraphy to, *Miss Eliza Hales* was waiting for me on the foyer table. It was too early for any friend's graduation announcement; a wedding invitation would have been addressed to Father, not me. I promptly opened its oversize, cream-pressed, linen envelope, revealing a red paisley, foil inner flap. The interior envelope shrouded one of the most impressive invitations I had ever seen. *What? I'm invited to the Grey's Annual Family Thanksgiving Dinner!* I was speechless.

The Grey's had a yearly tradition at their country estate in Dover, but had never invited Father, despite their old school ties. Only family and their closest inner circle—a select, few friends—were ever invited. Horse riding was expected over the weekend, as they had magnificent stables, a covered arena and acres of groomed trails for their myriad of warmbloods, including a Hanoverian dressage champion imported from Germany, nicknamed, "Liebchen." Thankfully, as animal advocates, they always passed on fox hunting.

I had no idea that my friendship with Stewart warranted this gesture, but I was definitely going. Now I just had to convince Father I needed to buck our own tradition and be elsewhere. This wasn't going to be easy—or so I thought. I showed him the invite, explained the magnitude of my inclusion and surprisingly, he was fine with it, as he knew them well, of course. He was happy I could finally meet these fine people. He too had been invited elsewhere for Thanksgiving this year, to New York City CEO, Dana Hyde-Randolph's penthouse in Manhattan. They had been introduced by one of Father's clients a few months prior. Although I hadn't met her in person, I knew from the tabloids that Ms. Hyde-Randolph always surrounded herself with many celebrity friends, made through both of her ex-spouses' connections; both former husbands were film producers. One would expect a few of the celebs popping in during dinner on Park Avenue, chased by the paparazzi, which was sure to liven the atmosphere. I congratulated him on his adventure, feeling rather amused as I was leaving, reminding him to bring home some autographs from her colorful dinner guests as mementos, as well as buying me one of the luxury, signature bath sets from the hotel he'd be staying at.

I gave Ashleigh the news the next day at school that I was inducted into the elite sphere of the Grey's, as well as Father's uncustomary holiday fete, *sans moi*. My best friend filled in the blanks that Father overlooked, by giving me a comprehensive overview of the Grey family and of the entire Dover event, including everyone expected to be there at dinner. She also offered some valuable counsel on who to avoid. Evidently, one of Stewart's great uncles was fond of certain foods that didn't agree with him; he would forcefully belch, always to his right, while unsuccessfully covering his mouth. Hopefully I would not be seated near him. By her account, the rest of the weekend was sure to be stellar.

What truly intrigued Ashleigh, however, was Father's "certain demise" at the hands of the expected NYC celebrities on hand during Thanksgiving. Evidently, one paparazzi magnet in particular hated lawyers with a vengeance, due to his ex-wife taking him to the cleaners for a mammoth settlement. We both agreed, however, the experience would be good for Father, especially since this was the first time he'd outwardly shown an interest in any woman for quite some time. I certainly didn't expect anything to come of their budding relationship, but regardless, he needed to dive back into the dating pool!

After a two week cold snap, the weather warmed up to ideal for outdoors in autumn, just in time for my "Dover Debut." Thoroughly prepped by Ash', I felt as if I knew the extended Grey Clan already.

Stewart offered to drive me, so he picked me up Thanksgiving morning at a comfortable, ten o'clock. Confined to the snug cocoon of his environmentally-conscious, electric roadster, his understated, yet memorable cologne was captivating, transporting me into a wistful, dreamlike state. I thought ahead of how I hoped the day would evolve, picturing a duet horse ride, amidst the fallen leaves of gold and auburn, scattered.

"I'm looking forward to you meeting my family," Stewart interrupted my visualization. "My sister is in her car right behind us, by the way. Since my car only allows for two, she opted to follow."
"Me too," I bounced back into reality, referring to his original comment that just registered. "At least she won't have to smell exhaust," I interjected, trying to catch up in the conversation, with a wink in his direction. "Oh, I hope your mother likes this bouquet," I added. "The sunflowers and blue-violet irises just spoke to me."
"Your taste is always so artistic, Eliza; she'll love them," he assured in confidence, taking his focus off the road momentarily to seal his comment with a penetrating gaze. I nonchalantly tried to regain my composure, caught off-guard by his sudden intensity and the formality of the imminent occasion.

Despite my well-to-do upbringing, I was somewhat casual by comparison to Stewart. I suspect he never wore flip-flops in his entire life, or had a funnel cake at Lake Winnipesaukee. He did, however, spend the bulk of the past summer abroad volunteering in Chile, helping rebuild houses from earthquake damage—a character reference of immense proportions, in my estimation. He felt impassioned to help them, since he felt they didn't get the PR that the hazardous aftermath of another region did. Not to forget his own, American backyard, he spent the previous summer helping with ongoing reconstruction efforts in the Midwest. I admired his commitments. His heart was in the right place, with an internal compass on track, to match.

The rest of the short drive Stewart talked about their stables, which reminded me of my early riding school days I had all but forgotten. The few ribbons I had won were still neatly pinned to my bulletin board in my bedroom at our townhouse. With a sense of awe for the equus kingdom, Stewart shared specific handling instructions for his prized, dapple gray gelding, set for my enjoyment. I thought the color of his horse was appropriate. Stewart was clearly looking forward to our ride together after the meal.

Arriving at the estate, marked by a pillared, wrought iron gate, with an intricate, "G" flourish and imposing urns, my heart fluttered, seemingly nervous about the impending introductions. We swung into the circular drive and parked near the existing vehicles. His sister proceeded further down, her Porsche out of sight. Money and style were all represented. The last-ditch effort to bring out the flash before the frost—an imposing Lamborghini and Bugatti, as well as an Aston Martin, suitable for a world-class super spy—were neatly lined up like piano keys, ready to play. These were in subtle contrast to the more stately, but equally prestigious Rolls Royce nearby. Their images evoked an effortless panache, but Stewart's choice of vehicle spoke of eco-warrior decisiveness that impressed me much, much more. *Beauty* and *brains,* I thought.

Before I could manage to lean in the direction of the passenger door, Stewart was already at my side, gesturing to help me out of the car. As my hand glided into his, I caught a glimpse of an exquisite, family crest ring with ornate leaves. It was clearly quite old, yet the patina still shone as it would for its original owner, I suspected. I wondered how many generations of Grey men had worn this remarkable token. He noticed my visual pause with his ring and offered a quick explanation with, "My father gave it to me for my birthday this year; five generations of Grey sons have worn it."

As we walked to the entry, I marveled at the state of perfection of his early, twentieth century, English style manor. The grounds were manicured. Deep, forest green boxwood adorned the path. The muted, multi-hued stonework facade was precise. The slate-colored roof was pitched and gabled, drawing the eye to the detailed chimney brickwork with herringbone pattern. As fall had descended, only the evergreens were still present as the perennials slept, but the variegated cream and soft jade leaves of the ornamentals were a showy display against the hedge and milk-white planters, with tapered arborvitae flanking the entry, as well as the arbor off in the distance.

I expected his mother to be inside with the other guests, but she surprised me and greeted us at the front door, wearing a crisp, white, linen and lace half-apron over her muted, pink Chanel wool suit. *Classic, "American First Lady,"* came to mind. *All that was missing was a pillbox hat.* Stewart looked over at me as if he was reading my mind, and smiled. After a gracious welcome, Caroline Grey ushered us into the drawing room for hors d'oeuvres, while we waited for the main event. She politely excused herself to attend to the kitchen, which included waitstaff for the crowd of thirty-plus family and guests. I wondered where his sister had disappeared to.

We weren't abandoned long, when Stewart Grey, III entered the room in more regal fashion. His "surgeon ego" did not disappoint, as he carried himself with a bravado, resolutely sure. Despite his longstanding friendship with Father, I felt visually probed by Dr. Stewart's discerning eye, summing up my substance to associate with his only son. Philanthropic tendencies aside, the senior Stewart presented an entirely different demeanor than his more congenial son, who, I reminded myself, *was just a friend,* despite my growing wish for something more.
"Well son, aren't you going to introduce me to this pretty, young lady?"
"Dad, this is Eliza Hales," the introduction in full-swing. "And Eliza, this is your father's long-lost friend from Harvard, Dr. Grey."
"Call me Stewart, young lady. You don't look a thing like your Dad, thank goodness," 'III joked with a thinly-pressed, Cheshire grin. I

appreciated the humor, as it offset his unconcealed swagger nicely, putting me more at ease. *Perhaps the Spanish Inquisition won't happen after all?* I mused in thought.

The commotion in the dining room brought Stewart and me to our feet. He gently placed his hand on the small of my back, guiding me toward the rest of the guests. Entering the room was a grand experience, an expansive, yet intimate space, with extensive mouldings and millwork on the stained, coved ceiling, leaving a large, square, depression effect. Adorned with multi-tiered, eye-catching crystal chandeliers, affixed to ornate ceiling medallions, the refined room offered a Georgian mahogany dining table, reminding me somewhat of a banquet in regal fashion. The table was long and narrow with carved, claw pedestals underneath, providing substantial seating for our merry company. The six sets of painted, white, double French doors—three on each side of the room—let in filtered, autumn light that graced the woodland scene of the red, toile wallpaper; it accentuated the highlights of each, perfectly coiffed attendees' hair with a subdued radiance. The china, crystal and silver were placed at the proper locations; the linens and other culinary appointments were equally dazzling against the backdrop of flames from the oversized fireplace, with hand-carved rosettes on the oak mantel.

We were the last to be seated, so all eyes were riveted on me: the fascinating new fodder for dinner conversation, perhaps carrying over to the country club circuit as well. I wondered what was on their minds, as I walked past almost each and every guest. Their eyes trailed my every move. In grand propriety, Stewart was seated across from me and did not assist me with my chair, as it was the job of the waitstaff instead. *Another nod to the regal effect.* I rearranged my napkin that had been placed in my lap and felt the richness of the heirloom fabric leisurely roll back and forth between my fingers. I attempted not to appear nervous, so I kept my strategically-placed hands folded on my lap under the table, out of sight.

Stewart quickly stood, catching everyone's attention, to make a brief, but charming introduction, before his father was to take over as MC. "Everyone, this is Eliza Hales. Our fathers were college mates at Harvard. She is Senior Class President at Hawthorne and the finest example of a person I have ever met." It was decorous, but let on in no uncertain terms that I was not an ordinary dinner guest. The fact that I was even present sealed that status. I was certain that I blushed a vibrant pink. As I looked up, I found 'III tilting his head to one side in a forthright, questioning look. I could feel my face turn a deeper shade in response. I swiftly glanced in the other direction to our hostess, to regain my composure. Caroline beamed at her son with such a gentle fondness, clearly proud of him. *What I wouldn't give to have my mother still here to gaze at me that way.* My mother didn't wear pearls or delicate, ecru half-aprons more suited for petit fours; she wore a utilitarian, white, butcher-style apron to actively paint and get messy in. Mother's elegance shone through the broad strokes of her work; its magnificence permeated the souls of all who gazed upon its beauty.

Seated to my left was not the great uncle I had been warned about, but Stewart's only sibling—his older sister and our traveling companion— instead. *So I finally get to meet our motorcade escort.* Gillian Harcourt Grey was a former Hawthorne grad two years prior, who happened to share her brother's love of horses and an evident predisposition for pearls. She was currently attending Wellesley, majoring in Classical Studies. Her hair was the color of walnut with auburn highlights; its sleek, gentle waves undulated past her shoulders. Her locks nicely contrasted the lovely, cream cashmere sweater set she paired with an earth-toned, wool pencil skirt with camel-colored, leather buckles and matching, opaque hose. Glancing from brother to sister, I concluded they could easily grace the runways of the most esteemed, Fall Collection together.

"Eliza, tell me something juicy about my baby brother," came the icebreaker that brought me back to the event at hand.

Just as I was about to do injustice to her request—as there really was nothing alarming to share—their father launched his annual ode to family and Thanksgiving. As 'III droned-on, waxing nostalgic with his abundant puffery, my thoughts wandered to the view outside, focusing on a rather vibrant cardinal sitting on the branch of a nearby birch tree. He hopped twice more within view, before taking flight, out of sight. I felt a twinge of disappointment that surprised me over something so momentary.

The Thanksgiving feast did not disappoint. The conversation was kept mostly between Stewart, his sister and me. I met those in my immediate vicinity during the meal, namely Stewart's paternal grandparents, as we were close enough to 'III and his wife. After dinner, I met the rest of those fortunate enough to be included. I was most impressed with Caroline's two great aunts who were twins, that even at age eighty-seven, still dressed alike and finished each other's sentences. These ladies had been seated at the other end of the table from us. They were the life of the party; every nuance of their shared life together was not missed by anyone.

Upon the conclusion of dinner and dessert, Stewart's eyes grew wide as he segued to what mattered to him most: riding. Both he and Gillian got up at once, thanked their mother, nodded *adieu* to all those present and broke open the door nearest the stables, like giddy kids seeking out their gifts beneath the tree on Christmas morning. I tried to keep up, until Stewart realized his stride far exceeded mine and he curbed his excitement momentarily. Gillian validated the change of pace and fell in step with us.

As we approached the stables, the full-bodied scent of the hay and tack offered a dramatic, sensory transcendence; it was almost as transporting as these examples of robust horse perfection themselves. I read the nameplate, before my eyes rose to face my champion partner in this adventure: *Carpe Diem*. This fine example of a horse was to be my trusted companion for the rest of the day. His magnificent coat did not disappoint, nor did his musculature or conformation. His shadowed color matched my hosts' surname expertly.

After donning the riding gear I stashed in Stewart's car that was magically waiting near Carpe's stall, Stewart helped my foot in the stirrup with courtly care. With the grace of a Victorian lady riding sidesaddle, I was comfortable, demonstrating confident respectability as an equestrienne. I quickly acclimated to Carpe's tendency to nip at unknown riders with a brisk, "Walk on" command, which he followed promptly, forgetting his aversion to strangers. I gathered speed, but quickly found myself lagging behind both of the Grey siblings. Always the gentleman, Stewart backed-off and let his sister ride on ahead of us.

I enjoyed the solitude and having a more private moment, as there had always been a crowd surrounding us. Stewart had a look of planned strategy appear on his face, as he clearly took advantage of the fleeting secrecy with a surprising and bold proclamation: "Eliza, we've worked side by side on many events and activities. I've watched your graceful leadership, your selfless service, your kind example and admired your beauty for many years, even before we really knew each other. I love everything about you…" his voice trailed off, as Gillian interrupted by rejoining our ranks. All three horses resumed formation, in equal pace with one another.

"Did I interrupt something?" she coyly interjected. Not to appear flustered, Stewart offered me a gallant wink, snapped up his reins and challenged his elder sister to a race. I stayed behind, enraptured by the surroundings of the trail. The chickadees were chick-a-dee-dee-dee-ing, as if in celebration of the thrill of the chill in the air. The fence rails lumbered along, defining a path and confining it at the same time. *If I had a run at it, I could jump that rail.* Better judgment got the best of me, mainly due to not knowing if Carpe would take a run at it with me still astride, or not.

I did exhort my steed to pick up his pace a bit, to rejoin my party. As we ascended the next ridge, I stopped, so that I could see the pair in the distance; they were still at a full-on run, with no visible sign of ceasing anytime soon. I slowly circled Carpe back around, and took a leisurely stroll back to the barn.

Greeted by the head stableman, Mr. Rutgers, I dismounted, leaving the cool-down and grooming for someone more familiar with Carpe's preferences. I sought out a sunny spot in the garden adjacent to the outdoor arena, to wait within view for Stewart's return. It seemed a contradiction to have a place of fragrance and floral beauty in such close proximity to a manure production plant. No matter, as it was fall; the most fragrant of blossoms were slumbering. A brisk wisp of a wind shadowed by, followed by subdued laughter traveling on the breeze, emanating from the Grey household. Captured by my thoughts, an unknown span of time drifted away. Soon after, a distant call grew in magnitude, until the bearer was standing right in front of me.

"Eliza, I was trying to get your attention, to see if you wanted to go for a walk—just the two of us. I need to beg your forgiveness for abandoning you, of course," Stewart offered in sincere apology.

As I was sizing up the remorse, I gave a head-to-toe assessment, visually. I surmised a perfect specimen of refined handsomeness. Like stepping out of the pages of an elite horseman's pictorial, Stewart was a tweed-clad Adonis. He didn't look like the other boys at school. Here was a genuine person with class and maturity. His moving smile was in heated competition with his sinewed physique. I was marveling, and he was trying to talk to me, as he demonstrated his intentions to get my attention by way of the back of his fingers gently brushing along my jawline. It worked. I wasn't used to him touching me. He had never done that before. I was back to reality.
"Sure. A walk sounds divine!" I answered, almost breathless.

As we sat down together on a rough-hewn bench in the stables, I watched Stewart methodically take off his black and russet-topped, leather riding boots, leaning them neatly against the wall, all the while he was carefree in his sharing of his plans for his future. I listened attentively, admiring his wistful, reflective countenance that was far beyond his seventeen years. I found myself dreaming and wondering what it would be like to be in this future with him—this wide-open, expansive future. For the first time in I don't know how long, I surprised myself with a flash of memory of Caleb. A record player needle screeching to an abrupt stop brought my thoughts of Stewart to a halt in my mind. A strange, almost guilty feeling of disloyalty started to come over me. I countered back and forth to myself with outrage from within, for thinking about someone who abandoned me, angry that my psyche was trying to deny myself happiness with someone else. *Caleb is not here! Forget Caleb!*

"Eliza, what was that you said?" Stewart prodded. I took a deep gasp of breath through pursed lips, petrified my thoughts might have been spoken aloud.
"Nothing important," I answered guardedly, assessing any potential damage.

Satisfied he didn't hear my thoughts, I stood up and reached out my hand in gallant gesture to pull him up. He obliged. His hand lingered in mine. It was warm, steady and strong—a *deliberate strength* was my immediate thought; there was nothing spongy or clammy about his hand—no trust fund-languidness of any kind.

Experiencing this closeness of contact brought warmth to my face which gave me away, as Stewart's eyes twinkled with a knowing look. He caught me in my embarrassment, which caused me to feel even more unsettled. Without hesitation, he scooped up my arm through his, to properly escort me on our sojourn, to considerately take my mind off the awkward moment.

My fingers gently perused the articulated folds of his jacket sleeve, as I appreciated the conversation while walking the grounds on the perimeter of his beautiful home. We circled around the north wing of the house and found an enchanting pavilion in the near distance, outside of earshot of some of the guests who were now outside on the patio. Upon closer proximity, the architectural magnificence was revealed in brilliant light. The chalk-white, Corinthian columns were standing circular, as sentinels to the central focus: the transporting, Greek statue of a goddess, reaching out, as if longing for someone. Her gown was effortlessly wraith-like, the swells of the marble "fabric" almost translucent. As my eyes reached skyward, it was evidenced boldly that the dome above was massive. Its concave design incorporated acanthus, working their way along the edge, freeing the classic lines to launch the eye to the very center overhead, where a woven cluster of varying leaves and scrollwork chose to reside. *A major feat must have been in order to position it atop its supports.*

We sat side by side on one of the five, marble, arced benches surrounding her serene, alabaster beauty. The dew on the nearby grass glistened in the sunlight, but could not compete with this breathtaking story in statuary. There was no sound in the air, except for the branches overhead dancing a lighthearted waltz to the voluminous breeze, beginning to build up a following.
What a perfect setting. What must have been on the goddess' mind? My thoughts wandered off. *She's clearly longing for—*

Suddenly, Stewart leaned his face in close to my own, his heathered breath anticipating. His purposeful gaze locked with mine as he paused for approval, then offered his full-bodied lips with a lingering kiss, as his fingers gently folded into the strands of my hair, cradling the nape of my neck. Like cashmere and chocolate, this belonging— this intertwined, emotional decadence—enveloped me. Like the outstretched fingertips of the stone lady before us, my heart had been seeking, and now was found.

Heavenly. A piercing energy captures my soul. These thoughts opened my eyes to find myself basking in Stewart's radiant smile. "Perfect," he quietly triumphed, as his eyes closed in deliberate pause. The warmth from his closed-mouth smile transferred. I too, was beaming.

"Absolute bliss," I added. My words were such a small offering in response to a truly significant moment.

Before Gillian could gallop her way into destroying the magic still permeating the air, we stood simultaneously and walked back arm-in-arm in a calm serenity to the house, to say our goodbyes to his parents—my gracious hosts.

Not being immediately excused to leave, and after several hours of visiting with Stewart's relatives and parents, we found Gillian revving her engine, blatantly urging a prompt departure to follow us in our two-car caravan. With a stern look over his shoulder to keep his sister's impatience curbed, Stewart opened his car door for me for our return drive, to take me back to Hawthorne, since Father was not home. As I stepped into the car, Stewart added a footnote of remembrance with a gentle brush of his lips across mine. My heart stopped simultaneously, as did the engine noise. I suspect the fleeting silence from Gillian's car wasn't coincidental, but instead, reactionary, to our momentary display of affection.

Upon returning to Hawthorne I found my dorm room undisturbed—evidence that Ashleigh hadn't pilfered something that she really didn't need. I fell into the armchair and cozied-up with a book, intent on some recreational reading to pass the time. After reading the first line about ten times in a row, I let the book fall in my lap and my mind wander, recalling this wonderful day. The only negative was having to say goodbye to Stewart when he dropped me off at my residence hall.

The perfect gentleman, he sweetly offered a goodbye, with a kiss of my hand.

This is it; it's time to move on and really mean goodbye to Caleb, then.

Chapter 18

The following weekend I got a call from Father, sounding out of breath.

"Where *are* you?" I anxiously inquired, frustrated that he hadn't come home right after Thanksgiving, or called me to mention his delay. I heard a feminine giggle in the background; curiosity was now fully engaged.

"I got *married*, Eliza," was his sly explanation. He sounded like someone who might be in trouble for sneaking in past curfew and got caught. "Dana and I decided that life was too short not to have fun, and that we should have fun together as man and wife," he added.

My voice must have let out an audible gasp, as I heard a lighthearted chuckle from over the phone.

"What happened to just getting a few, celebrity autographs?" my voice instantly tapered off, knowing full well that a man in love—and a man like my father, who makes strategic moves in daily living, and who doesn't make important decisions until he definitively knows what he wants—is not to be trifled with.

"What, are you—*disappointed*—to not have needed to endlessly shop for the perfect bridesmaid's dress? *What*—are you like *Ashleigh* now?" he joked, excitement like a giddy child in his still-winded voice. He was really laying on the sarcasm.

My father got remarried. Wow.

It was good to hear him so happy, and I told him so. I had never met Dana before, but could feel her warmth over the phone, when I offered her best wishes on her marriage to the most wonderful man on earth—a designation of which she wholeheartedly agreed. I instantly liked her and couldn't wait to meet this new, female role model, as I knew Father's good taste would not have his new wife be anything less than the perfect complement to our little family.

"Oh, and guess what my wedding gift was from Dana?" he hinted, with a tease in his voice.
"I can't imagine," I answered in sincerity.
"She bought me a Harley, Eliza—a motorcycle—with *all the bells and whistles!* We're going on a road trip next spring to Niagara Falls and Mount Rushmore, but for now, we're off to Bermuda. If you need me, call of course, but you should be fine at Hawthorne with class and your studies."
"Wow!" was all that I could offer in response. For someone who didn't joke at all, and mostly traveled to Maine, it was good to see him branching out.

"When we get back, we'll celebrate Christmas in New York—all three of us—together. What do you think, Eliza?"
I didn't dare spoil his moment, complaining of a change of tradition. I had a feeling several traditions might be challenged in the future, with another person in the decision-making. I concurred with the holiday plans, happily congratulated him again, then said a cheerful goodbye, measuring the full weight of the reality of my changed, family dynamic.

"Ash', guess *what?*" I abruptly began the conversation, knowing that my phone call woke her up from her beauty sleep. "I have—a *stepmother.*"
"What?" she yawned, not offering the level of shock that I expected from her.
"Get dressed. We're going to the MFA. I need art therapy." It was my way of dealing with the aftershock of a marriage I wasn't quite prepared for. It was finally sinking in, and I needed time to adjust to

the change, to relax about it and give it a chance.   Perusing the museum was the ideal method of facilitating a seamless transition.

"Okay," was all Ashleigh could sleepily respond.

Comatose—great.

"Ash', don't fall back asleep, 'cause I'm coming right over.   I need you."

With winter now nipping at my window, I grabbed my banker's gray, wool pea coat, along with my blue, gray and teal, loosely knitted scarf—the blended hues of wool and mohair reminded me of a Downeast blueberry harvest.   Despite the emotional turmoil, for a brief moment, I stood in front of my mirror, noticing the knee tear in my jeans and the supple patina of my boots, finally broken-in to perfection.   I placed an earth-hued, knit beret on my head, letting my loose braid cascade over the front of my left shoulder.   *Casual chic that will keep me warm.*

I spent ample time listening to Ashleigh's tale of woe about her Thanksgiving, en route.   I purposefully drove us, so that I had a brief excuse to concentrate on the road and not have to comment as frequently.   She shared the play-by-play of her parents' huge argument, over such an insignificant thing: it was over their disagreement in choosing the brand of turkey.   I yawned unintentionally, and Ashleigh assumed it was meant for her annoyance, so she got very quiet, very quickly.

Uncustomary to the usual time spent with my best friend, I had to reintroduce the conversation.   I was still trying to get Ashleigh to start talking again, when we arrived at a series of stoplights.   Changing from stop to start allowed Ashleigh the opportunity to change her mood. She talked continually from that point all the way to the museum.   I was glad she got it out of her system, as the MFA docents always frowned upon Ashleigh's voluminous depictions of her life, echoing in whichever gallery we were in.   I wished to let the art offer a visceral connection, without having to tune her out to be able to maximize the experience.

I wanted to sit and ponder, so we found one of my favorite paintings to gaze upon: *A Boy with a Flying Squirrel*, by John Singleton Copley. There was something about this work that always spoke to me, no matter what was going on in my life at the time. Perhaps it was the luminosity of the rich colors, or the sheen of the table, as well as the boy's hair and collar. The highlights made the canvas come to life, even centuries later. I'd like to think it was the squirrel that did all of the talking. Its eye was a window to its—and perhaps the boy's— soul, as well.

Ashleigh knew to be silent during these abbreviated vigils in front of each masterpiece. When I rose to move on to the next work on our journey, she stood, made a visual sweep of our resting spot to make sure we removed all of our personal belongings, and without a word, followed my lead. Next, we paid homage to Monet's, 1907 *Water Lilies*. Out of his vast collection on this subject, this was a particular favorite of mine. The depth of the water and its reflection from the sky, along with the dewy, pink flowers evoked a serenity that always came in handy.

"Are you still considering studying art in Paris?" Ashleigh broke my concentration.
"Yes, I think at some point I will definitely need to cross that off my to-do list. I don't think life will be as rich and full if I don't. I'm looking forward to it. Perhaps after my first year of college, I'll study abroad," I shared.
"Good. Because if you weren't going to do that, I'd have to find another excuse to spend a lengthy stay in the 'City of Light.'"

In pursuit of turning the spotlight on the urgent matter of my familial shock, Ashleigh got to the point: "Eliza, enough small talk. I know you need to talk about your Dad's uncharacteristic behavior. I'm sorry to have rambled-on so much about my own family issues, but I was nervous. You've never said you've needed me before." She grabbed both of my hands with absolute intention and pierced my eyes with her own, as she commanded, "Talk to me."

Despite the appearance of shallowness at times, Ashleigh was truly a caring person. I was grateful for her listening ear. Words poured, a few tears were shed and fears were promptly alleviated. Surprisingly, it was not such a traumatic change after all. *I was seventeen, after all, not seven.* Unlike other kids my age, whose parents were getting divorced and changing partners as often as kitchen trash can liners, my father was a widower who was not reckless; after so many years of being alone, he deserved to be happy. I wasn't going to stand in his way of spontaneous marriage, or throw a tantrum, pity party, or anything else that would diminish his joy—*their* joy.

I thanked Ashleigh for being there for me. She offered a candid relief that my neediness was ever so brief, and we moved on to other exhibits. We toured the entire collection of Winslow Homer next—a favorite, due to his residence in Maine, and his ability to capture the soul of the sea that I loved so much. The crescendo of our tour ended with Renoir and Rembrandt—blatant contrasts in mood. Renoir's works always radiated exuberance; the vibrancy of the palette, as well as the people always seemed engaged in *joie de vivre*. Rembrandt's works, in all their value of dark, perfectly married with light, brought a weighted seriousness that always lifted my spirits, while grounding me at the same time. Perhaps the black dominance of the compositions reflected the stark distinctions in my own life.

We both selected some note cards from the gift shop, and grabbed a bite to eat in the café before we headed home. The serenity of the gallery environment from whence we came seemed to remain with us both. We both hardly said a word on the ride back to Hawthorne. Ashleigh offered me a hug, leaving behind a little gift of perfume she had been saving to surprise me with.

"No need to thank me. It's my own fragrance line! I wanted you to have it before it goes to market next week. It will be at every fine department store, licensed under the 'ASH' brand."

She blew a kiss as she waved goodbye and ran off to her own hall. I parked my car in my assigned parking spot and spritzed a whiff of the scent in the chilly air. It had a woodsy base, with citrus and Asian top notes; something about it reminded me of a familiar moment, although I couldn't quite put my finger on it. The more I tried to remember what it reminded me of, the more agitated I became, so I decided I should study a bit, so I could fall asleep quickly. I made it inside my dorm just in time to watch the first snowfall of the season, from my window overlooking the famous, Hawthorne maple tree.

Chapter 19

A few days later, Father called me, contrite that he had, "sprung too much, all at once" on me about his marriage and changed plans for Christmas. He wanted to make it very clear that he was just thinking out loud and did not want to mandate any alterations for such an important, family celebration. I was relieved that he left it up to me, and that Dana was in complete agreement: Maine, or the Beacon Hill Townhouse were equally brilliant to her. There was clearly no need to appease the new wife or witness the petty demonstration of expected, marital allegiances, like so many of my friends had to encounter.

Twice-divorced, this MBA grad from the Wharton School of Business was a diminutive native of Door County, Wisconsin; she was from hearty farmer's stock and had no children of her own, so she was quite adaptable to whatever transpired. A serial entrepreneur with considerable, self-made wealth, in addition to that from her former husbands, I appreciated her trust in my ideas, as well as the sanctity of tradition; however, I was open to change as well. I had always wanted to see the beautiful tree in Rockefeller Center, and if all went well, staying for New Year's Eve in New York—in magical, Times Square—would be a dream come-true! Father set the Manhattan plans in motion and Dana offered her private jet from Logan to La Guardia, with her limo driver to bring me to her penthouse there.

Before we hung up, Father assured me that Dana's former spouses were flagrant cretins, and that he had no fear whatsoever about the success of their marriage. Dana's exes treated her badly, he said, so she kicked them to the curb. With Father, Dana had found abiding love and someone to trust for the first time.

I had only seen Stewart across the quad between classes a few times, with only a few, sporadic phone calls since Thanksgiving. I was beginning to think that our time in Dover was a figment of my imagination, when he surprised me from behind, cupping his gloved hands over my eyes, then whirling me enthusiastically to face him. The leather aroma lingering from his gloves reminded me of the tack stored neatly in his stables. *Was that all a dream?* I asked myself. I fought to return to the present.

"Are you a new student at Hawthorne? I don't believe I've seen you around before," I teased, gauging his unusually effervescent mood.
"I suppose I deserve that," he countered, eyes apologetic, his overworked breath a perceptible mist in the chilly air. His demeanor noticeably changed; where there was once a hint of groveling remaining, there was now an unconcealed excitement in his voice, building up as if he was about to burst if he didn't shout from the rooftops. For such a composed individual, this building animation was intriguing to watch unfold.

Amused, I encouraged, "What is it Stewart? What has you so excited? I'm dying to find out—*Spill!*" I took a deliberate step back out of range, waiting for him to explode from joy. In most relational dynamics, I was always the even-tempered one, as was he, so for him to be so atypically herald-like and for me to rally him on like a hyper cheerleader, just to hear his news flash was a bit nonsensical for me, but I indulged him anyway.

"I got accepted to Harvard for next fall, AND I'm starting a unique nonprofit that's going to CHANGE THE FACE OF ALTRUISM!" he gleamed, triumphant. Normally, this kind of news—especially from a genuine philanthropist as him—would intrigue me wholeheartedly within the thrill of the moment, but my enthusiasm was somewhat detained; in fact, it was tangibly *absent*—coma-like, even. *Was I simply preoccupied with finals?* Perhaps I was, but there was something significantly missing from my congratulations to this handsome and sincere do-gooder. It didn't feel like a lack of support or interest, but my mind was definitely *somewhere else.* I was rapidly becoming quite adept at second-guessing myself. *Was I wrong to think I was falling for Stewart Grey so quickly?*

As compassionate and confident as he was, and more important—as self-assured a person as I was in my path in life at all times—was I just attracted to him in a silly, shallow kind of way? I always thought of myself as a person who stayed true to herself and held right on course—always. To miss the mark in falling for the wrong guy would be just so—*misdirected*; it would be so *not* like me. If I kept pursuing this almost post mortem analysis, I would soon be hatching an escape plan, talking myself right out of Stewart, so I stopped, immediately.

I smiled at him, gave him a quick peck on the cheek and ran off to class, before the magic of *the* kiss and promise of a future at Thanksgiving was shot right out of the air, like the pheasant trophy on display in the headmaster's office at Hawthorne. I didn't want my meandering mind to culminate into a death of a relationship as instantaneously as it began. Right there behind my eyes, in the frosty winds of the campus my ancestor founded, my imagination wavered and my heart challenged. Whether it was from the cold, or burgeoning love, I did not know. I *always* knew what I wanted. I offered my best attempt to shake the uncertain thoughts out of my head for good, before they took root.

As I made a graceful exit and made my way to class, alone in my head, I resurrected my pointed conversation with myself against my own counsel, for a blatant epiphany: *why have I never bothered to share with Ashleigh about his kiss on Thanksgiving? If Ashleigh doesn't know about it, it isn't real.* These were wise words—wise words indeed.

Chapter 20

With Father and Dana back from Bermuda and staying in New York until New Year's Eve on their extended honeymoon, I stopped by the townhouse to see if I too had good news in any thick envelopes on prestigious, collegiate letterhead. Waiting in a neatly stacked pile on the inlaid, mahogany table in the foyer were not one, not two, *but six* envelopes, each addressed to yours truly. Brown, Harvard—Father's clear favorite—Stanford, The School of the Museum of Fine Arts-Boston—Mother's alma mater—Wellesley and Yale—each in their corresponding stationery—all jockeyed for my attention. I decided to open them alphabetically, my smile increasing in width with every, unfastened piece of correspondence. *Wow! I was accepted to all of them!*

I had choices, more than most seniors had. I wasn't naive; I knew that the long hours of studying and extracurricular measures would be hard, but it would be well worth it. So far the efforts had paid off. The big decision I had to make was whether to choose Ivy League, California prestige—with a more temperate climate—or Art School. I knew that many would consider Art School seriously limiting myself and passing up "real school," but in my mind, I could always expand my horizons and attend more than one school and obtain more than one degree. My options were not limited; on the contrary, they had considerable range.

I called Father's cell to give him the good news. Like any parent living on planet Earth, he beamed with pride. Dana had also voiced a biased preference for anything I accomplished, wanting to tell all within her sphere. I had to beg her not to ask for a mention on the society page in the New York Times, as she knew the Editor. I was amazed at how quickly and easily I felt close to her, this woman who championed me just as enthusiastically as Father had, even though I had never even met her in person. That would quickly be a thing of the past, as we were soon to be celebrating the holidays together. Without wasting any time and without any fanfare, I sent in my acceptance to the MFA, for their freshman level, Art Study Abroad Programme in Paris, but decided not to tell anyone yet.

The jet taxied down the runway in Boston and we ascended lazily into the air, our climb as smooth as silk. I must have dozed-off for a moment, as the cabin steward woke me to offer a bottle of water to take along, as we were already going to land; I missed my chance for a mid-air mineral water. Dana's limo driver, who was waiting on the tarmac did not disappoint; he looked more like a bodyguard than a person normally behind the wheel.

As I arrived at Dana's swanky address, the doorman greeted me at the curb, ushering me into a building that didn't hint, but *shouted* its architectural pedigree. The elevator opened, revealing Father with a wide smile, waiting for me. Ever so happy, he almost crushed me with his paternal hug. I could not have been more pleased for him for his matrimonial blessings. As I stepped away to look at him, I could see that here was a man who was completely in love.

As if on cue, Dana walked into the foyer and kissed my cheek, embracing me at the same time. Her hair was pale blonde—almost platinum—in a sleek bob to her chin, hinting to her Midwestern Norwegian ancestry and accentuating her cheekbones, along with her graceful, long neck. Of petite stature, her deep, blue eyes were almost violet, validating every word she uttered of unabashed zeal and uncompromised eloquence. Clearly a fashion plate, I assumed she would be a trophy wife; on the contrary, she was a pleasant mix of loveliness, intelligence and substance—and not just financial. Like a shooting star, my father caught on and was along for a captivating ride. He was in heaven—they both were—and it emanated decisively.

Dana's generosity was demonstrated immediately. She wanted to show me her city in style, so we soon left her penthouse for a tour. While we were out on the town, she frequently asked if I wanted or needed anything, as the three of us window-shopped together. I was just happy to be done with finals and enjoying this new excursion; shopping was more social for me than productive.

Figuring out I was not one to ask for anything, my not-evil-at-all stepmother bought me a diamond key necklace from a prominent jeweler, a telling symbol and extremely gracious gesture, all-in-one. At dinner, at one of the hot spots in the city, she explained the meaning behind this key: "Your father is the key to my happiness; he unlocked my heart. As his child, you too will unlock many exciting, wonderful experiences and doorways to pass through on your journey through life. One day, you will find true love and together, you both will be the key to unlocking each other's hearts, as well."

I found her tribute offered a flair for the dramatic, but the sincere words resonated something within me, an abiding understanding. I knew that I would never need a man to "complete" me—and it was clear that she too was of that belief—but together, someday, the love of my life and I would be an ideal complement to one another, doing great things in this world. Dana would never replace my mother, but from the moment we met, she was an empowering, feminine example to have as an instantly endearing and genuinely caring, family member.

On the way home from dinner, we stopped by Rockefeller Center to see the brilliance of this year's Christmas tree. As I stood at its base and gazed skyward, the lights shimmered, showering multifaceted sparkles on all those who stood in awe beneath its lofty splendor. The crystal star at its peak was its crowning glory. It was everything I always imagined it would be, and more.

I felt compelled to make a wish. As my closed eyes opened with a twinkle and smile to match, for just a split second that felt more like a double-take, for the first time in months, despite its very short stint in my possession, a perceptible absence was felt on my right wrist—the place where Caleb's heirloom bracelet once rested. At that moment, I was reminded that Caleb was living in this very city. I pondered what he was doing, if he was happy and what the future held for him. I entertained his memory for another brief moment, then shut it up and locked it away in my heart—for safekeeping, or self-preservation, I was not completely certain. All I knew was that I was not the pining type, nor one to pursue futile endeavors.

Father and Dana chanted in unison that they wanted to keep moving, as their toes were starting to show signs of frostbite, so we returned to the car and drove back to the penthouse. Along the way, I watched the people busily living their lives, the hustle and bustle of the Big Apple. I unconsciously craved its sweetness. I knew in just a few days I'd be hearing the famous, seasonal melody of the city blasting in Times Square, feeling like a New Yorker for a few hours, and not just a transient visitor.

I began to daydream in the car but was speared by a question about what I wanted from Santa. Dana couldn't help having this discussion; she was beside herself in yet another opportunity to find out what things I liked and wanted. She already bought me a necklace that probably cost one thousand dollars. It was a very lavish gift—much too generous. It was obviously pocket change for her, but I didn't want to start any precedent of, "a gift equals a healthy relationship." Besides, I couldn't be too candid, as some of the things that I wanted were impossible; they weren't tangible, or buyable. Dana seemed determined though, and it surely seemed to make her happy to play Santa, so I just told her my interests and let her come up with whatever made her feel good. I didn't like spelling-out gifts to people. My belief is that part of gift giving is to allow the giver some sort of influence in the choice, not just the recipient. I know people who get embarrassing gifts, year after year, clear into adulthood who would disagree with me, vehemently, however.

Chapter 21

Christmas Eve morning I received a phone call from Ashleigh. She was now in New York City also and wanted to get together. I wasn't sure if it was okay for me to take off from my *parents*—it sounded weird to say that word, but good at the same time—so I told her I'd consult with them and get back to her.

At breakfast, Father, Dana and I dined on fresh strawberries and crepes prepared by some celebrity chef Dana kept on hand in her beautiful breakfast room. The presentation was superb. The food was marvelous! As I savored the delectable fruit, I noticed the gargoyles across the street on another building competing for the sun. There was something about viewing this city during a meal that made it very difficult not to ingest air while I was eating; it was a breathtaking vista of architectural masterpieces. Both art and architecture were equally important to me.

I swallowed a mouthful of whipped cream and asked, "I'm sorry to spring this on you on such short notice, but I just heard that Ashleigh is in town. She invited me to meet her today. Is that okay?"
Father looked at Dana to answer, and she graciously approved: "Sure, we'll see you in the morning. Be prepared to open a really, *big* present!"
"Now the pressure is really on. I hope you like my gift to you both. It's sort of a combination Christmas and wedding present," I prefaced.
Father smiled an unusually wide grin, so I knew something was up. There would be no stopping them, this lovesick duo trying to outdo every parent in the tristate area. It wasn't Father's typical behavior, but I didn't care. He knew that I wasn't swayed by money and I was happy that he was happy. Having Dana was the best Christmas present he could have received.

I hoped that this, "big present" was not in addition to this Santa stash that she had been hinting at. I didn't want to be spoiled. I had a feeling that "spoiled" would be an understatement, however. Ashleigh will probably be jealous. She'd probably spend all day trying to guess what their gift would be, so I figured I would only mention it in an emergency situation.

"Wow! Right on time," Dana enthused, regarding Ashleigh's punctuality. I ran to the foyer to meet Ash' and brought her in to greet the honeymooners, and meet Dana in particular. I was certain that the two of these females with exquisite tastes were both fluent in "posh-speak." Ashleigh brought the fluency right out of my new stepmother, while Father gave me a side smirk—more of a half grin, actually, glowing with pride at his new bride.

I took my cue and Ashleigh and I left the building to find a stretch limo waiting for us. I wasn't thrilled with the waste of fossil fuel this super monstrosity consumed, but I stepped inside, with Ashleigh patting the seat next to her.

"It *is* a pig of a vehicle, isn't it?" Ash' assessed, the driver's smile in the rearview mirror directed plainly at her. "My parents forgot to book something more eco-friendly, well in advance. Who knew that so many would need transportation during the holidays?"
"I thought people only *walked* in 'The Big Apple,'" I dryly quipped.

"So tell me about your wicked stepmother. Is she really as great as she seems?"
"Ash', I can't even begin to tell you; she's unbelievable—truly. I feel like I'm in some surreal, alternate reality. Every piece of media always portrays the new stepmom as some conniving, evil witch. She's not like that at all. She's gracious, kind, witty, smart and very

generous, in a thoughtful, sincere way. Father didn't know what hit him when Dana set her eyes on him."

"Wow. I guess you and your Dad are equally smitten."

"Amazingly so," I concurred.

"Let's do lunch somewhere fun," Ashleigh urged.

"What do you have in mind, lunch counter at the nearest diner?" came my dead-in-the-water zinger.

"Don't be droll. You know I've been drooling to go to that new, five-star place! The Chef is a friend of my mom's dog breeder," Ashleigh offered with pleading eyes.

"That's practically *family*, Ash'!" Continuing while laughing, I suggested, "I don't care where we eat; just help me buy a present for my *parents*," emphasizing the plural. It sounded just as weird to Ashleigh as it did to me, indicated by her wide-eyed response. I haven't talked about parents together, in the present tense, *ever*. This was a real first for me.

After a superb dining experience—even getting to meet the Head Chef, who normally wasn't on duty during the day, nor greeted anyone, unless they were world-famous—we thankfully found the perfect Christmas/Wedding gift quickly: matching motorcycle jackets. I happened to find a custom leather tailor who would wrap them and deliver them by courier by ten o'clock, tonight.

After several hours of shopping, we toured the town in our massive, black chariot. Our driver kept to himself, but occasionally was overheard whistling Christmas carols. We enjoyed the background music.

"Eliza, you really outdid yourself on this one! They are going to LOVE those jackets!" Ashleigh offered in full support.

"Yeah, I did well, didn't I? It's the perfect gift—*inspired* really."

"Inspired... the perfect segue into Christmas Eve, wouldn't you say?" Ashleigh exclaimed.

I smiled in response, knowing that tomorrow morning would be the first time I'd had a mother to share Christmas with since I was a little girl. I felt a pang of excitement, anticipating the festive morning to come.

Ash' and I finished the evening with the best slice of New York City pizza I could have ever imagined. Every mouthwatering bite was to die for. Thank goodness, "diet" wasn't in my vocabulary. This was too good to pass up.

We attempted to chat some more while we ate, but instead waited until we were finished, to avoid awkward pauses while we chewed. As chatty as Ashleigh was, we were good enough friends that silence was not a negative. Of course, the waiter came to ask us how our meal was when our mouths were full of cheese, so we just nodded and smiled. I always wondered why they did that—strategic really, as if they knew you couldn't complain, unless you were an outright heathen. We must have looked polite enough for him to risk asking. At the end of our meal, our tip reemphasized our nonverbal, generous praise.

We drove a few blocks, taking in all of the splendor and magic of this most special of nights, when an ice skating rink emerged, beckoning us to go for a glide. The little girl in me was joyful as I donned my skates. Even Ashleigh was overcome with childhood nostalgia. This wasn't the Frog Pond, but there was still a lightness from within that soared.

As we were both bent over lacing up, I looked over at Ashleigh, and she at me. I realized that next year at this time we would both be in different spots on the planet, making our own, separate ways in the world. I felt my nose burning—not from the cold, but from stifling back the tears that I knew were about to spill.

"'Liza, are you *crying?*" Ashleigh asked, her voice beginning to choke now too.

"What a couple of sentimental fools we are, eh Ash'?" I managed to spurt out, in between fumbling in my pocket for a tissue, to head off what was only momentarily away from reaching my nostrils; it was betraying my emotions in tandem with my eyes.

"You really are my truest friend, Ashleigh; you're my sister, you know," I pledged. "Knowing that a year from now we'll both be apart, doing our own things has me feeling a bit, you know—*weepy.*"

"Yeah, I feel it too. We still have six months left of school, and I'm already feeling the weight of adulthood being thrust upon me. If my parents ask me what I want to do with my life one more time, *I'm going to explode!"* she blurted out. "I told them once that whatever it is, it will have to do with fashion and beauty. I thought that would suffice, but I guess not. They're intent on me presenting them with a life plan before I even graduate high school, it seems!"

"Let's skate!" I urged, putting my best friend's arm though mine as we pushed off from the edge, steadying ourselves along the way. Bound by an allegiance that transcends all the miles that will soon be between us, we skimmed the surface of the frozen ellipse, feeling the icy breeze touch our cheeks, fueling each breath in solidarity. We toured the perimeter, the surface like glass, our blades leaving behind an etched memory of our lives.

As I stepped out of the limo at the curb after our enchanted evening, I gave Ashleigh a sustained hug and wished her a Merry Christmas and a Happy New Year. As she blew me a kiss goodbye, I thought I saw a glint of a tear as she quickly ducked her head back inside the vehicle, speeding away instantaneously.

"Well, that was a special evening," I mumbled aloud to myself, causing the doorman to wonder if I was speaking to him. He quickly figured out that I was in my own, little world. I'm sure he'd seen much more lively entertainment this evening than to bother paying attention very long to "almost-normal" me.

After the jackets were discreetly delivered, I hid away in Dana's guest bedroom and crawled into bed to read. I still felt excitement on Christmas Eve, always hopeful, especially in regard to Dana's new presence in our family. Tonight I also felt a tad somber for the imminent change about to take place in my life in a matter of just a few months. Who would be there to catch me in this wide world of adult living?

I overheard Father and Dana rustling wrapping paper, laughing and what sounded like tickling each other in the next room. I rested my head upon my pillow and smiled at the thought of having not just one, but two parents to back me up. I had forgotten for just a moment that I was not alone. I wouldn't let that happen again. With that happy thought, I slid off into a dream of fruit-flavored candy canes and stockings stuffed with gingersnaps and spritz cookies.

Chapter 22

Christmas morning in New York was a brisk one, as I could see steam rising from every rooftop in the vicinity out my window; the vapors were competing with the first snowfall of the season in Manhattan, affording a frosty display. The smell of pastries fresh from the oven was wafting under my bedroom door. Cinnamon, cloves, nutmeg— perhaps a hint of apple—the symphony of these familiar, holiday scents was resplendent. I grabbed the plush, spa-like bathrobe that Dana had left for me and beelined directly to the kitchen. Everyone but the chef was still sleeping, so I took advantage of the momentary silence to have a cup of hot cocoa with a cinnamon stick, enjoying the uncustomary stillness of the streets below, before I headed to the shower.

After breakfast as we sat around the living room, I pleaded excitedly, "Father and Dana, I want you two to open your present first," hoping they wouldn't guess what it was.

Father gave Dana the honors; she daintily separated the red, green and gold wrapping from the large box. After the lid was removed, the punch of leather scent doused the room with its signature bouquet, before the tissue paper overlay was even considered.

"Wow! What do we have here?" Father asked, anticipation curling up his mouth on each side.

"It's perfect, Eliza! No, *they're* perfect!" Dana gushed, while slipping her arms in each sleeve, deliberately breathing in the weathered fragrance and parading her jacket around the room. You could just see her imagining herself revving the motorcycle throttle.

"Try yours on too, honey," she lovingly advised her new partner in life.

After a few more, smaller gifts were given from my parents to each other, Father arose from his chair in a commanding motion and asked me to meet them by the expansive picture window. I knew something was up, because there was no finesse in Father's attempt at concealing there was a surprise for me, not to mention Dana's rather blatant, "big" hint already given.

"Ok, I'm ready for whatever it is you're doing a lousy job at hiding from me," I announced to our family gathering. As we all looked out the window, I confessed my state of feeling clueless, to which Dana encouraged me to look in all directions. After staring across and beyond, I steered my eyes down below. There on the curb was a shiny, jet-black, horse-drawn carriage with not one, but four pristine, white, draft horses. Even at this great distance above, I could see that they were meticulously groomed, their manes combed in tiny wavelets, contrasting the massive power of their frames. The front horse on the left—perhaps the lead of the foursome—was demonstrating his spirit—perhaps annoyance—pounding the pavement with his front left hoof, over and over. This gift was "classic Father," and a most welcome surprise!

"Let's take the elevator down and get a closer look, okay?" Dana eagerly suggested. As we left together to greet my fairytale gift, I sensed that this may not be the end of the bestowals. I glanced over at Dana; she nonchalantly composed her face with no evidence whatsoever of the games that were afoot. Dana expedited her pace a bit, emerging an anticipatory grin from ear to ear as she waltzed along, arm in arm, with Father.

We soon arrived at the garage level. As the doors parted, a polished automobile with a giant, red bow affixed to the windshield was waiting only a few feet away. Without need for closer inspection, I could see that this was not just any car, but a Lamborghini, with deep, metallic, charcoal gray paint. The machine projected a Le Mans racing sound in my mind, with gears briskly shifting as it sat there poised to pounce in all of its shiny splendor. Father was speechless, but ran to the car like the proverbial kid on Christmas morning.

Father, for the "man's man" that he was, didn't get excited much about cars, with very few exceptions; however, this was one of them! In a priceless, exaggerated wonder, he opened the compartment and found the engine that people only dream of. *Beauty and power for the future,* I'm sure he imagined. Not usually impressed by modes of transportation, I too was envisioning myself behind the wheel with my hair suspended in the tempered breeze, wearing large sunglasses to complete my adventurous persona in transit. *Perhaps I might ask for the keys and borrow it sometime.*

"Well, what do you think, dear?" Dana's words brought us all back to the present, while I was hopping from one foot to the other to keep warm.
"I'm speechless! I can't believe it! Thank you so much!" he shouted, picking up Dana and spinning her, his glee not even remotely subdued.

"It's not like I talk much about cars, so how did you know this was 'the one?'" Father's inquisitive gestures painted an almost childlike countenance on his face, the shadows of the parking garage not hiding the shock.
"Your brother-in-law, Seth told me," Dana answered, matter-of-factly. "Evidently, Seth had seen a car magazine that you had at *Misthaven*; he said that you had tore out its Lamborghini photo and posted it casually in the barn," she continued. Obviously, Father didn't think anyone was paying attention, or that it even mattered.
"The magazine clipping was entirely a whim," Father admitted. Evidently he had a deep appreciation for the car's mystique—as would just about anybody. "I didn't even remember what happened to that car image, come to think of it," Father added. "I think it must have fallen to the ground at some point, buried under some gear."
"So when do we take her for a spin?" Dana interrupted Father's—as well as my own—musings.

"No time like the present to show off your *present*," I punned, with shameless corniness.

"We've got an appointment with a coachman, if I do recall," Father reminded about my carriage, waiting in the light snowfall, just yards from where we stood.
"I need to go pay those horses a visit, right now, as I'm sure they want to let off some steam," I solidly stated. "However, if you two want to go drive your new car, Father, I wouldn't blame you one bit. I wouldn't mind my grand city tour by carriage on my own," I assured them. They both seemed to want to part ways for a few hours this morning and go test out their own brand of horsepower.

Before I left the garage, I hugged them both—one at a time, then initiated a group hug. I surprised myself at my outburst of elation. "I really am deeply touched by this thoughtful gift; it's amazing, really!" I professed, as I practically bounced my way out the garage door. On the way to my ride, I sent a text message to Ashleigh, confirming the magic of their gift was so creative. She instantly responded, "U2COOL," an inside joke, as we both had absolute disdain for abbreviations in text or email messages.

As I introduced myself to the coachman, I stepped up to sit on the comfortable seat inside its covered protection and smiled to myself, as I buried the side of my head into the backrest, about to launch on my jaunt in style. Their mission to catch me off guard was thoroughly accomplished.

Two hours later I returned to Dana's apartment and found the two lovebirds sitting by the fireplace, roasting marshmallows.
"We've been thinking, Eliza, that we should take some time and head up to *Misthaven*. What do you think? We could all go and take the

Bentley on the ferry, no problem," Father offered with a wink, in between bites of his gooey treat.

"I've wanted to see this special place of yours, Eliza, for a long time," Dana interjected. "Besides, I've been feeling you need to spend time with some tradition for the holiday, at least for a little while. Then we can come back here for the ball drop on New Year's. How does that sound?" she added.

"It sounds absolutely *perfect!* I've been having dreams about *Misthaven* at least once a week for the last month I think, so it has definitely been on my mind," I agreed.

"Done, then!" Father's voice surged from behind the swinging door between the butler's pantry to the kitchen, where he had ventured for a piece of apple pie for each of us.

Inhaling the fragrance of the freshly baked slice, I asked the important question: "When do we leave?"

We decided to depart first thing in the morning, stopping by the townhouse to pick up a few items, including my heavy, cold weather gear. From there, we continued north on I-95 from the New Hampshire border, making our way to take the exit to Portland. Dana was clearly enjoying every moment of this joyride with her newfound love, and even with me, the hostage daughter in the backseat. I didn't mind too much though, as we were getting closer by the minute to my island refuge. It had been far, far too long since I'd been back.

While Father stored the vehicle in the barn at *Misthaven*, I sprinted down to the water's edge on this atypical, late December day with no snow on the ground. A warm front had passed through on Christmas Eve, with evidence it might stick around for a while; this was no problem for me, as I had hoped to sightsee in relatively "warm comfort" around the island for a bit. With no precipitation, I was tempted to ride my motor scooter all around; however, this was Maine, not New York. Despite the "warmer temps," it was too cold with the brisk wind in my face for even me to be so bold in the winter as to become the island, "babe on wheels." If I had, it was sure to start some interesting conversations, like my trying to get attention or prove something. It was best to be discreet, so I opted to be a pedestrian for only short distances during our stay.

I wanted to be present for the grand tour inside the house for Dana, so I'd wait to go terrorize the neighborhood. She "ooh'd" and "aah'd" in all the right places, Father overflowing with pride as he showed her all of our family treasures. His show and tell included my spyglass; I had brought it with me from the townhouse the last time that I was here, forgetting to take it back after Caleb's father's funeral. *That's right; that was the last time I had been back.* It had indeed been far too long since my last visit. I pushed aside the memory and sprang out the back door to the boathouse, to take inventory of the rigging and sails stored for winter. Father and Dana were engrossed in their own conversation, so they didn't even notice I had left.

I found everything to be stored in its right place and in shipshape. Gear was hung from the rafters, like ghosting vapors of summers past. I walked the perimeter of a new dinghy sheltered there, alive with white and blue paint by window-lit rays of sunshine streaming, its oars stored opposite, braced along the planked wall. Just outside the window under the weathered eaves, were four, untouched icicles, reaching toward the earth, steadily shedding their volume from the slight rise in temperature. They marked the time of winter thus far, their mass accumulating under the overhang.

Turning the corner outside the boathouse, the crescent seashore came into view. Clouds were nowhere in sight—the permeated sky of muted lapis complemented its mirror image in hue below, an ocean of nostalgia, its tide riding in and out, in and out, taking memories along with it. Tossing a few pebbles into the ocean, I walked parallel to the shore for several hundred yards, looking for sea glass. Winter was the ideal time to find unusual samples, as the tumult of the currents brought forth many gifts in unlikely colors—if the shore was not buried by snow, that is. I found tiny, cobalt and pale turquoise glass pieces spread in the pebbles near a large shard of driftwood, calling out my name to take a break and enjoy the sights, sounds and smells of my favorite domain. I decided to keep moving, but swiped the glass jewels on my way by, for my never-ending collection.

The solitude wasn't deafening; on the contrary, for the first time in many a moon, I felt grounded. Pure. Unshaken. No more fears of adulthood were looming. I glanced ahead of me to ensure footing, distracted momentarily by the steeped-in-crimson cardinal, perched on a low-hung branch, echoing softly the flutter of my own heart with its wings. *Cardinals have definitely been most-present throughout my life, a vibrant, vital symbol.* Suddenly, *vital* could not be more appealing—a stripped-down, raw version of my essential self was within reach, as long as I stood in this very spot. I let out a deep sigh, then cast aside the deal-breaker and meandered further, hoping for an additional epiphany.

Circling back toward the house, I stopped to walk along the dock and listened more intently to the clapping waves upon the shore, its blithe mist hissing in relaxed tempo. Too cold to sit upon, its creaky slats heaved with each step, despite my mere, 110 pounds. I slowly paced to and from the shore, drafting an invisible path on the wooden boards. This sudden distraction came from nowhere, or rather, *perhaps it came from within*, I concluded.

I deliberately strolled toward the front of the house and looked across the coastline of the island. Jutting out above the craggy rocks was a structure I had seen a hundred times before: Caleb's boathouse—an iconic tribute to Maine with its red roof and storm gray clapboards. Like the buoys gently sounding in the harbor, it was sounding out for me. The echo of Caleb was calling out to my heart.

A creature of habit, Caleb was always home for Christmas and New Year's. I was bound to see him on Hales Island; it was just a matter of time. With an island so small, there was no way to hide politely. I determined to get it over with and appease my curiosity. I wanted to see if perhaps I might receive an explanation for his disappearance act.

I decided to bundle up better before I made my way over to the Longfellow's, so I went back inside to grab another layer and a warmer hat and scarf. I switched my stone-colored, wool-lined field coat for my heavier gauge, red one. Both were from the iconic purveyor of all things Maine, in terms of clothing and gear. The articulated sleeves were a marvel for any outdoor activity, an ease for even swinging an axe or chopping wood, which I had made use of many times. My Boston Red Socks beanie was cast aside for a khaki bomber hat that covered my ears more fully, lined in lustrous, Leicester wool from local farms. I topped it off with a scarf my mother had knitted right before she died; it too was red—a rich scarlet, with woven hues of amber and sienna—the colors of the blueberry barrens in the cooler months. It had an open chain— ethereal-like, yet generously wrapped around my face and neck; it sequestered the warmth and staved-off even the most brazen winds. It was one of my most cherished possessions. *Despite the "tomboy" appearance, Caleb had always loved this ensemble on me*, I mused, but I didn't wear them for that reason. I was being practical now. I had an agenda, and I wanted to be protected against the elements as I traipsed my way over to the moment of truth.

The wind had surely picked up, but that didn't stop me from my journey on foot. I stayed close to the side of the road, taking my time to enjoy my surroundings along the way. I could hear wood chopping and a couple of chainsaws shredding off in the distance, overshadowed almost by the wind building up a small tantrum of its own, along the edge of the forest. I finally arrived at Caleb's house, plodded right up to the front door, and knocked. I wasn't sure what to expect. I tried not to let my mind second-guess my previous lather of mustered

144

courage. Just as I was about to give up, the door opened brusquely. It was Caleb's mother.

"Eliza, how good it is to see you! Merry Christmas and Happy New Year," she proclaimed, inviting me in with the wave of her hand, anxious to close the door on the elements. I walked over by the fire. Like a sheep about to be shorn, my outerwear came off hesitantly.

"And you too," I countered, as I put the last of my evidence it was winter off on a nearby chair. I tried to make small talk with her, assessing her place in the grieving process, when Mrs. Longfellow doused my hopes.

"I thought you should know that Caleb isn't here. He left about an hour ago," her embarrassment, clearly unveiled. She knew Caleb had seen or heard of my arrival and then left abruptly; that was certain. He must have taken the last ferry out for the day, as we were still on a holiday schedule.

"I'm sorry that I missed him," my robotic response held together quite well.

After about an hour of hearing all about Caleb at Columbia, his interning at his firm in New York and all of his accomplishments—which was only right for a mother to brag about—I bid my leave and headed back toward home, wishing I hadn't paid the visit. Along the way, I saw a curious bird—perhaps an oddly-hued heron—off in the distance, perched upon a rock. Heading down toward a stretch of beach I rarely traversed, the bird quickly became a symbol of sought after achievement—a light at the end of the emotional tunnel. I wanted to hang on to my composure just long enough until I reached it. I had no such luck. I fell to my knees in the sand, broke down and cried into my gloves. I didn't care that there was a serious windchill brewing. My tears felt steaming hot against my face.

I went to bed that night listening to Father and Dana cooing incessantly downstairs, feeling angry for the first time at their newfound love for one another. It wasn't like me to feel so put off—to feel envious or jealous. The anger and resentment of Caleb—the memory of abandonment—not once, but now twice with his total avoidance today—hit me with a ferocity I wasn't prepared to receive. I opened up that lock I had hidden away for just a moment in reconciliatory hope, only for it to be dashed upon the rocks, as in a wicked storm. I poured out my soul in anguished sobs. It was a nor'easter of the worst kind.

Chapter 23

Two days of slovenly haze passed me by, when I received a welcome phone call from Stewart. He knew it was last-minute, but he wanted to know if I would celebrate New Year's Eve with him, as his family's plans for a trip to Paris had been cancelled, due to a medical emergency of his father's patient that had since been resolved. He was no longer leaving the country, so he was hoping by some miracle I might be available. I told him about going to New York to see the ball drop in Times Square. Sensing he was willing to travel, I invited him to meet me at Dana's in Manhattan so we could all go together in her limo.

The date was all set. Now I could get on with the rest of my holiday respite on the isle. I was really looking forward to the New Year. I felt an electric charge run through me suddenly, like an exciting kind of change was tangible in the air. I was definitely up for it. I welcomed it, in fact.

The next day I only ate dinner with Father and Dana. I spent the rest of the time walking the island, enjoying the brisk sea breeze and grabbing things to eat here and there, at the house, or at the diner, periodically spending time indoors to keep from incurring frostbite. I also began work on a new watercolor painting, keeping me busy. Oddly, the subject was Caleb's boathouse. In the back of my mind, I anticipated that this piece may never reach a completed state—or at least not right away.

I needed to continue to give my parents some private time, as well as visit with my island friends, so I took a break from painting and went for a walk. On foot, the unhurried pace of my stride allowed my thoughts to churn. I realized that the last time I was here was the funeral, which wasn't a happy occasion, fitting for catching up, so I meandered over to Dottie's Place for some welcome cheer with my extended, island community. If this winter was like any other, everyone had been staying busy making balsam wreaths and the traditional, decorative New England kissing balls, while keeping up with plowing snow and splitting wood.

I plopped down on a stool, front and center, still deep in thought. As my thoughts circled back to the present, Dottie came over to the counter to see what I'd been up to. Everyone else became engaged onlookers, clearly eavesdropping on our every word. I kept my remarks to all about the newlyweds in our family, so they would keep me out of the topics of discussion. Dottie hinted that everyone was so excited to meet Dana, but I knew it was equally in part because my stepmother knew so many celebrities. I gave in to my better judgment and offered a partial, verbal list of some of the A-listers Dana knew. I had a captive audience. For me, this list was bordering on meaningless, as all of the famous people who mattered to me, who I would want to rub shoulders with were all dead, some of them centuries ago. After a slice of warm apple pie I began to feel tired, so I wished everyone a cordial, "Happy New Year" and jogged back home for a nap before dinner.

The brisk air on the way back to *Misthaven* gave me a resurgence of energy. I was no longer sleepy. My alert, but reflective state offered the perfect mood for starting another watercolor painting, one that allowed me to focus my emotions elsewhere. I decided to paint from my bedroom window, my art supplies at the ready. The view of the rocks, beach and balsams was a fitting subject matter. All my tools of expression were neatly placed on my art table, which was easily accessible to capture the essence of the coast in its last moments of muted light, before sunset.

I placed the paper on the table, affixing it with painter's tape along its edge. Mother always preferred cold press paper, as I did also. The tooth of the white fibers eagerly welcomed the thinly washed measures of pigment. Other than my intensity of mood, nothing was quite so absorbed and ready for transformation as this particular work of art in progress.

My art teachers at Hawthorne and private instructors always encouraged me to paint in broader strokes—to paint a greater area with larger brushes first, so as to open up myself to expression more easily and expand my technique. Not only did this speed up the execution with improvement—not sacrifice—in quality, but this direction helped me considerably; it made all the difference in me considering becoming a professional painter. With this exercise in grander scope, these gestures of artistic method became more implied, instead of blatantly spelled out in unnecessary details. These subtleties provided more substantial impact. This manner was vital to creating a worthy watercolor. It was a marvelous moment the day I understood this secret.

I got lost for the next few days in the immersion of art, only coming up for air for the bare necessities. Father and Dana didn't seem to mind. Soon it was time to leave for New York and prepare for the eve of a new year.

All the way back to Manhattan I made mental notes for the remainder of my senior year, as well as life after graduation. I knew plans were made to be broken, but I also wanted a semblance of focus. For the first time in my life, I wasn't entirely certain of what came next, despite the inscription on my spyglass, blessing my life with direction.

Even though I had already submitted my acceptance to the School of the MFA, I wasn't sure if I should attend one of the other choices—these institutions of higher learning—I had already been accepted to, instead. I decided to talk to Father and Dana about it right after the New Year, before the next semester began, as there was gravity in making such an important decision. Having Dana's perspective added to the mix would surely offer me a broader range of ideas to consider.

The afternoon of New Year's Eve I became increasingly nervous. The last two months since Thanksgiving with Stewart had been mostly superficial conversations, frequently in passing; they were quite a contrast to what took place in Dover. I stopped obsessing on our fleeting exchanges and tried on a few different outfits, smoothing the fabric as I simultaneously tried to calm my nerves.

Dana's guest suite offered a sumptuous bathtub, so I opted for a therapeutic bubble bath to maximize my quest for relaxation. After my bath, I gave myself a pedicure of metallic, cerulean blue, with dainty, white, opaque snowflakes on each toe. Even though my toes would be hidden, knowing of their frivolous existence was excuse for inner celebration! I finished admiring my artistry and fully styled my hair. I spent more time than usual on my makeup, then got dressed for the festivities.

Stewart arrived early, greeted by Dana. I found them chatting casually in the living room and went to give him a hug. Before I got within close enough range, Dana made a graceful exit and Stewart's beaming smile gave great hope that the night would indeed be memorable. As he met me halfway across the room, there was something in his eyes that truly danced—a joyful consideration in his expression. Charmed, I matched his smile with equal zeal. Still within earshot, we exchanged hellos and "Happy New Year" to each other.

I noticed his charcoal wool topcoat still glistened from melted snowflakes, as did his hair; the moisture turned the deep, sable color to nearly black. Each raven-hued strand was tousled ever so gently, yet still his appearance was in perfect order. I wanted to make him more comfortable before I embraced him, so I offered to take his coat. We were still waiting for Father to finish an urgent business call before we left for dinner and the midnight festivities. Stewart followed me to the closet. Contrary to the last several weeks of almost nonexistent interest in anything more than passing pleasantries in the halls at school, he proved his distractions were far behind him.

"Eliza, while we have a minute to ourselves, I wanted to tell you how sorry I am for being 'not present' for the last five weeks. You must have been wondering how I could go from intensely interested at Thanksgiving, to what I'm sure must have appeared as indifference. I don't have an excuse that would justify my distance. I had been working on the nonprofit idea I had mentioned to you and it became all-consuming. I wanted to show my father what propels me in life, so he'd back off a little and let me drive my own future. He's been relentless in trying to make his agenda mine, and I needed to show him what I want to do with my life. I've decided it isn't medical school, and needed to show him I can lead a meaningful life and let him down easily, as his heart was set on me following in his footsteps. As it turns out, the business plan impressed him so much, that I think he's now considering my ideas." I smiled at him, happy for his success in overcoming this barrier between him and his father.

"While my focus was from the good of my heart on behalf of other people," Stewart continued, "I missed the mark on not dedicating myself just as fully with building things with you. To be candid, I wasn't sure if you'd even want to spend New Year's with me after my 'checking out' for the last month, so thank you for that. I hope you can forgive me."
"Of course I forgive you, Stewart," I responded, while pausing at the closet, a feeling of warmth pervading. There was nothing to forgive.

"I admire your dedication to a cause you believe in; besides, I've been pushing myself this past semester as well, so it's likely you wouldn't have seen much of me anyway."

I closed the closet door and turned back toward Stewart. He was now standing right in front of me, his expression, tender. His arms circled around me as his voice caressed my ear, "Eliza, you're so easy to love." Gently lifting my chin ever so slightly with his finger, he sealed a kiss, rich in promise of a more committed future. Marveling, he took a step back, admiring his handiwork at rendering me momentarily speechless. The effect of his look of warm admiration certainly made an equally profound impression; the depth of his pale, gray-green eyes—the color of lichen in filigreed sunlight—penetrated any facade of composure I tried to will within myself.

It was useless to force a verbal response, as it wouldn't do justice to what just transpired. As trite as it may sound, I felt a bit dizzy. To steady myself, I simply put my hand in his and walked him over to the window to admire the sweeping view of this masterful, grand city in lights. We stood there in solitude for a few moments, until Father and Dana came out.

"Ready for celebrating?" Father asked the obvious, with Dana smiling broadly behind him, a sparkle in her eye. She knew exactly what had been going on, and she continued to smile approvingly. She clearly liked Stewart.

Father shook hands with Stewart and we were off to dine at one of the fanciest establishments in town. It was still lightly snowing, adding more magic to the evening. It could have taken longer than usual to get to the restaurant, but our driver was quite adept at maneuvering around the myriad of slush, taxis and traffic, so we still made our reservation. Once inside, Stewart took the opportunity to smooth the snowflakes off my shoulders as he removed my coat for me, which the waiter whisked away immediately. He then held the chair for me, catching my attention once again with a gentle stroke of my arm, before he stepped aside to sit next to me. This time, Father was paying attention. He gave me a look of, "What have we *here?*" as he raised his eyebrow in silent inquiry.

"So Stewart, I understand that you are launching an exciting, nonprofit organization. How wonderful for you and those whom you will serve. I'm sure your father is very proud of you," Father spoke, listening intently for Stewart's elaboration. Father was in full, "fatherly assessment mode" now. Somehow, my previous Thanksgiving dinner invitation or follow-up conversations didn't register for some reason—perhaps he was too busy being in love himself to notice who might be important, who might be vying for my affections. Father wouldn't be caught off guard again.

"Yes, I'm happy to say that my dad is quite pleased, which is pretty remarkable for someone who was dead set on me following him into the medical field as a surgeon," Stewart replied. "I guess I must have monumentally swayed him."

Sensing the need to interject, I qualified further, "Father, Stewart can't share the details yet, as it's not to that point, but I'm certain it will be a huge success, and even more importantly, a way to help a lot of people." I didn't even know what it was yet—not a clue—but I didn't need to. Stewart was a strategic thinker with a business mind even his own father couldn't match. He'd succeed at whatever he put his sights on.

"What I *can* say," Stewart concluded, "is that the business model incorporates methods to produce a high volume of assistance without a lot of manpower, saving the funding more for programs, and not personnel." I could see that both Father and Dana were impressed with such an effective, yet often overlooked approach to philanthropy. I couldn't help but feel proud, knowing that such a kindhearted and determined person loved me. He *did* say I was "easy to love." *I assume that he meant it. I...believe... I–I love him too*, I silently realized, as I felt my smile beaming from ear to ear, undetected by anyone but me. In that moment I was set free from any emotional contrivances of the past; it was liberating.

As dinner progressed through the courses of exquisite cuisine, Father and Dana—myself included—were no match for Stewart's charm. We laughed out loud repeatedly, a jovial atmosphere surrounded us as we became better acquainted—even Stewart and I—since not much time had passed between us. Stewart blended us all together effortlessly. We were all besotted with him. He had an air of nobility—a valiant confidence and sincerity about him that drew you in, without arrogance or tiring self proclivity. He exuded a strength of character far beyond what I had previously witnessed—perhaps understood. It was like removing the many petals—revealing the essential layers—of a rose in his essence, and finding the center even more sweet-smelling than before, having experienced the full weight of his fortitude as a human being. Mixed with this handsome rose was a cedar aroma of sage-like wisdom and presence that towered, providing a heady canopy of protection. It was a treat for all the senses. *A rose not like any other...*

After dinner it was onward to the Party of the Year in Times Square. I was grateful I chose my attire wisely, as it segued nicely from the elegant meal to the messy magnitude of the masses and inclement weather. Once outside the fortification of our limo, hand in hand, Stewart and I braved the mob of partygoers and made our way over closer to the countdown platform of performers and announcers. Dana had VIP access for each of us, courtesy of one of her celebri-friends. Stewart and I danced on and off to the beat of the performances, mixed with all the visuals of the marquees of the Square—each, equally powerful. The lights and sounds, the frivolity and anticipation for something new on the horizon provided a backdrop for a winsome surprise.

Father and Dana were nowhere to be found, so I assumed they escaped somewhere less frantic. I seized the moment of intimacy in the middle of the swaying populace and reached both my hands around Stewart's neck, drawing his face closer to mine. Despite the escalating noise of nearby celebrants, I wanted him to hear me the first time I said it. I looked into his eyes, tears starting to well up within mine as I offered my heart: "I love you Stewart." That was the life-changing statement, right there. I said it. *I meant it.* I really, truly, ardently *felt it.* As if the crescendo of the music playing was conducted just for our own purpose, the notes were timed perfectly, as Stewart lifted me and spun me around, the radius of my heels thankfully making no contact with anyone around us. Contrary to our expectations, the music, however, was building up to begin the countdown to the New Year, not our own, private moment. Along with all the others in the crowd—a city within a city—we each cheered loudly, shouting the descending numerals signifying the world was about to embark on a new journey of another 365 days of opportunity.

For those brief moments, however, the world stopped for Stewart and me. Like the elusive flickers of light and sound between a hummingbird's rapid wings, we seized the moment for a New Year's kiss like no other. Hundreds of thousands of people surrounded us, yet we were entirely alone. We held onto each other, my ear next to his chest, hearing the palpable beats of his heart through all the layers of winter clothing. It was a spirit-speaking-to-spirit experience, a feeling of understanding permeating every fiber of our togetherness.

As if on cue, the snowfall ramped-up in both speed and quantity, quickly putting a damper on the celebratory crowd. As the huge gathering began to disperse, I looked across the Square and did a double-take. Like a direct view from my spyglass, my eye zeroed-in between the scattered snowflakes to what felt like a mirage; I could have sworn I saw Caleb, glaring at me for a split second, before instantly turning to disappear into the mob of revelers. I felt it was clearly my imagination and dismissed it, as nothing was going to upset such a perfect evening.

Stewart wrapped his arm around me, shielding me from the mass exodus, as we made our way back to where the car was to wait for us. Father and Dana were already inside sharing chocolates with our driver, as we hopped in and shut the door behind us. I kissed both Father and Dana on the cheek before we set off, singing a quick rendition of "Auld Lang Syne," before we dropped off Stewart at his hotel. Dana was asleep before we arrived back at her apartment. After a few moments of silence, Father offered a welcome vote of acceptance of, "You picked a good one, 'Liza." *I couldn't agree more.*

Chapter 24

Six months later

"Eliza, please hand me those red, peekaboo pumps over there," Ashleigh gestured with a sweep of her nose, her hands too busy, coiffing her hair for her Salutorian Graduation speech of the evening. I was already dressed and ready, my Valedictorian address prepared and practiced, ad nauseam. Always two peas in a pod, we were now bookends for this most important of events—a milestone that seemed to sneak up on us, as the second semester of our senior year left no moment for pause. The only thing in my blur-of-a-schedule I made time for was Stewart. Ashleigh didn't mind my absence, as she had been booking nonstop modeling shoots. Had she not been so busy, our speech roles would most assuredly have been reversed.

"Eliza? PLEASE HAND ME THOSE SHOES!" shattered the peaceable moment. I sought out to obediently fetch, but had to laugh out loud when I saw that there were several pair of "red, peekaboo pumps" in her closet. *Someone has way, way too many shoes...I shudder to think how many more she has at home, since this is only her dorm closet.*
"Uh, which ones, Ash'?"

Frustrated, Ashleigh marched in exaggerated steps over to her closet and flipped them over her shoulder by the straps. "See, these are what I meant," she scolded. With an easy flick of her finger, both of the velvety, rouge beauties adorned her feet, surely to complement the black of our gown and cap and Hawthorne crimson nicely, although Ashleigh was murmuring repeatedly how badly the cap fit on her head, surely to undo her dramatic 'do.

"Beauty *and* brains, that's my Ash'," I congratulated, trying my best to nudge her out into the hallway, to show up on time. "You know how Professor Stevens hates tardiness; if we're both late, we're going to give her a heart attack," I added, pushing her again for emphasis.

We were able to make it to the stand on time and found our seats among the esteemed guests and presenters, including our Key Note Speaker, Sir Reginald Haversham, an Elizabethan actor of the stage and copious period movies, most notably an alumni of Hawthorne—in addition to being knighted, of course.

From Norfolk, England of strong, societal ties, Sir Reg' was part of the 1960s influx of Brits who sought out a "change of pace" in U.S. prep schools. Tiring of our foreign land, he went on to finish his education at Oxford, but toward the end of his stint there, acting snatched him away from the lofty pursuits of incessant academia. Now mostly retired from acting, his travels brought him back to the land of Yanks, for what I suspect was a bit of a "comeback tour" in some off-Broadway play. Regardless of his reasons for setting foot on American soil, we were surely in for an entertaining address. His booming voice was truly majestic, his timing, perfection.

Even at the late hour, daylight was still shining profusely, blinding the podium. Ashleigh had a permanent crease in between her eyes from squinting. As she sat back down, she let out a "Phew!" under her breath, marking the end of her agony. I whispered to her that I thought her remarks were witty, noting that she had managed to incite all-out laughter and guffaws from most of the audience, multiple times.

The pressure was on now for me to do well, as Ashleigh would never let me forget it if I slipped up, got tongue-tied or forgot my words. I was prepared—more than prepared, really—so I stood up and looked out over the multitude of people. The sun had just set behind the trees, giving me a lesser advantage of being forced to make eye contact with all those in attendance, eagerly anticipating what profound utterances I came to share. I did have a message of significance; it culminated the last four years of living and thriving with a vision for the future. If only my parents would be impressed, I would have done my job.

My eyes searched for a moment, row by row, until I found Father and Dana, with Stewart's parents, Caroline and 'III sitting beside them, with 'III's genteel, half-pivoting wrist-wave causing me to stifle a chuckle. *He's Father's good friend from college, but could they be in-laws someday?* I was getting way ahead of myself.

Since New Year's Eve, I had been spending a lot of time with Stewart's family, and he with mine. Clearly, things had progressed, as I had all but forgotten, "C." His name had been reduced to an initial only. *But I digress...* To regain focus, I pulled my perspective in closer, to the front row before me for a momentary look at Stewart's radiant smile amongst my fellow classmates before I spoke. I drew in a deep breath and took a quick glimpse at my notes, before I forgot what I was going to say, as Stewart had a look about him that almost melted away my concentration. He was important to me, so I wanted to lock eyes one, last time before I dove into the formal responsibility of Valedictorian-ness. We had spent what little free time we had over the past six months understanding each other's deepest secrets, championing each other's greatest hopes and dreams, all the while, falling in head over heels, unabashed love, so no wonder severing my gaze wasn't easy.

It seemed as if time stood still, then Professor Stevens coughed a not-so-subtle, "A-hem," so I got down to business with what I hoped would be my most poignant effort of remarkable eloquence, *ever*.

"Eliza honey, that was the most magnificent Valedictorian address I have ever heard—and I've heard quite a few, being on the Board of Regents for Hawthorne," Father gushed.

"I echo that sentiment," Dana added, while Father lovingly adjusted her pashmina on her left shoulder, putting it back into place. "If only I could have summed up such optimism when I gave my own speeches, even in the boardroom, she added.

"You have the makings of a fine orator, which will come in handy for just about anything you end up pursuing," Father exclaimed.

My future, at the moment, was focused solely on one thing: attending the Regent's Ball, a graduation tradition, with my beau, in period dress. My Hales ancestors would have appreciated this event, as it began in 1850. Retaining that period as inspiration, waltzing was to be expected.

In existence for over one hundred and fifty years, the Ball was an opportunity to promenade in style, and celebrate this segue into adulthood at a level of class not found in the usual, "Grad Night" party fare of most of the area schools. The Ball had always been an elegant affair. Its annual setting was at the regal Bridgeton Estate, adjacent to the campus. I was looking forward to focusing on fun, friends and an epic time in history, instead of thinking about my future. There was plenty of time to be a grown-up. I had my whole life ahead of me to concentrate on that; for this evening, it was all about fanciful frivolity of a more decorous time.

Stewart had already secured his dashing attire for the evening; his parents had it custom made in England. It was hinted by his mother that despite tradition for formal black and white, there were also subtle, green elements in his waistcoat to complement his eyes and black, velvet lapels. I already knew what he looked like in English riding ensembles, so I had been preparing myself to be caught breathless by his appearance.

My dress was made by a designer Ashleigh had introduced me to; her worthy creations were spot-on for historical accuracy, but also blazed a creative trail for fabric and detail artistry. I opted for a radiant, gossamer effect. My gown breathed enchantment through multiple layers of tulle and gold-edged, fine lace; its bell-shaped, golden silhouette endowed with numerous tiers and a satin, pointed bodice with subtle, gathered, ribbon-like accents would incite drama on the dance floor. Delicately shrouded shoulders and Irish lace gloves would draw eyes upward, to my face and single flower in my hair—a fragrant gardenia, Mother's favorite—with coordinated, canary yellow jewelry to accent, not overpower.

I had been advised by Ashleigh that she would be "sporting a rich, auburn updo for the evening, with dress to match," whatever that meant. I was certain that heads would indeed turn, and photographers would be in tow.

Before the front steps of the school, shouting across from our respective swarms of post-graduation well-wishers of family and friends, amidst hugs and plentiful photos, Stewart and I agreed to meet later at the Regents' Ball. That would give me the chance to dine with my parents and return to my dorm to get ready at a leisurely pace, without Dana hovering. As much as I adored how our relationship had blossomed into fairytale grandeur, sometimes a girl doesn't need a second, rather insistent styling opinion from her stepmother.

As I entered the grand hall, the mystique of classical melody was echoing off the high, coffered ceiling and wainscoted walls—their deliberate silence a muted contrast to the volume of timbre. For a few moments, I closed my eyes, absorbing the lilting sounds and lasting presence of the concert piano, colorful imagery settling before my eyelids, making a showy entrance for a future painting concept. Music, as always, offered an inspiration that would never fade.

Ashleigh's swooshing sound of her gown gave advance notice, her thwarted surprise a likeable moment.

"Why, *mon ami*, how dainty are your earrings?" Ashleigh's voice upturned on the last word.

"I don't think that was supposed to be phrased as a question, Ash'," I countered, watching intently as she fluttered her fan in mock delicacy, winking at me. She was seriously lovely, her newly-minted, autumn-hued tresses sculpted into one of the most ornate adornments I had ever seen. Every ringlet, every accoutrement was perfection—and that was just her hair. The dress was spectacular; I proceeded to pontificate on the beauty of her gown. Who knew that persimmon silk with brocade-like texture on the bodice would work so well for formal, evening apparel? Every eye was on my best friend, and why not—she was breathtaking!

"Eliza, you are seriously encroaching on my opportunity to be visually absorbed by others, my friend," Ashleigh complained, in no uncertain terms.

"You've got to be kidding," I objected. "Everyone's watching you!"

"I beg to differ, 'Liza—of course, the eyes that matter the most are certainly zeroing-in as we speak."

I glanced back over my right shoulder, the sparkle of the chandelier above cascading a ray of flattery our way, clearing the view for my handsome escort for the evening. Stewart was striding toward our little tête à tête in the most stately, take-your-breath-away wardrobe of the night. With each step he exuded a confident, deliberate cadence; upon closer inspection, a smart little hint of arrogance, right up to his eyes carried across his face. He had a secret to tell, and he whisked me away to express it.

"What's your little secret you're keeping, Stewart?" I mused, carefully grasping the flounce of my voluminous skirt as we twirled the expanse of the room to Chopin's, *Waltz Number 7 in C Sharp Minor.*

"There's no secret behind these lips—on the contrary—everyone knows who the 'Belle of the Ball' is tonight, myself included. All eyes are directed at you, my lady," his gray-green eyes shimmered a playful, yet unconcealed admiration, as he gently kissed my cheek, now blushed rose from all the now-obvious confirmation of Stewart's deduction.

With another sweep of the hall, we landed back where Ashleigh stood, the "Queen Bee" of her assembled group of admirers.

"See what I mean, Eliza? Don't argue with me about who radiates perfection tonight," Ashleigh chastised in her most motherly tone.

"No offense, Ashleigh, but I heartily concur," Stewart announced with an impish smile, while chivalrously kissing my gloved hand. Suddenly, the aforementioned smirk of pride became crystal clear as to its origins.

A spritely tune with a string ensemble had everyone vacating all corners of the cavernous space, partygoers gathering to the center dance floor. Each partner gave way to the excitement of the future ahead—not a sad, forlorn closure of years of prep school together with years of Professor Blunt's sadistic waltz lessons. A genuine thrill of what was in store for us all, emanated from all present. As Stewart and I danced our way around the crowd, I was reminded of giant schools of sardines swimming in one direction at a childhood, public aquarium exhibit. I let out a chuckle at the comparison.

Still waltzing in grand circles, I looked up at Stewart. His smile was animated as he shared what was clearly not trite, party talk: "I love you Eliza. I know you don't want to think about future particulars at this moment, but I just had to tell you how much you mean to me. I know your parents are supporting you in this, but the idea of you going to France in the autumn for the MFA-Boston Study Abroad Program has me concerned; too many American girls get caught up in the 'Ooh-la-la' of Paris and might forget who's pining away for them, stateside."

"Don't be silly, Stewart," I assured. "Aren't *you* the one leaving first for another round of South American rebuilding this summer, followed by what can only be expected as a rigorous program at Harvard, with likely very little-to-no time for spending with me?"

Round and around we danced, the response clearly ready upon his lips, but not uttered. I closed my eyes, my face turned upward taking in each and every note—the bravado of the melody a deliberate crescendo, ending the dance with a tight cease of sound. The room became a resounding, yet tempered rumble of gloved hands clapping, the musicians taking a bow in unfiltered appreciation.

An intermission was offered by the quartet, with all of the ladies and gentlemen moving about the room for punch and conversation. Strangely, somehow the costumes of the event facilitated a rather astounding example of decorum and refreshing civility, a stark contrast to the usual, expected pettiness and immaturity often demonstrated by teenagers—particularly during a rite of passage as pronounced as graduation. I felt transported right from the pages of a worthy, historical novel. This was not a raucous "Grad Night" by any estimation. This was a society of accomplishment and good manners.

I was reminded of who was the most accomplished of us all—in regard to the pursuit of great causes—when Stewart offered punch from one of the many footmen, for both Ashleigh and me. As we toasted our futures, the three of us regaled with our Hawthorne journeys and triumphs, our hopes and dreams. The mood quickly became solemn, which, true to form, Ashleigh remedied with a witty joke, as it was not the time for serious themes, but rather, a joyful celebration.

On that humorous note, Stewart offered his hand with an invitation for another waltz. This time, Strauss' *Blue Danube* provided the opportunity to shine. Despite it not arriving on the music scene until almost two decades after 1850, it was, regardless, included in the musical repertoire by Professor Blunt, I'm certain, to showcase her students' prowess on the dance floor. The repeated changes in the music, from slow to quick kept everyone on their toes—almost literally. I felt like royalty, like some Austrian princess with her handsome and gallant suitor from another imperial dynasty courting her, majestically, with exuberant showmanship with his footwork and refined self-assurance in front of all of Vienna's high society. I was carried away in the moment—a beautiful, lingering breath of time, and timelessness.

My internal revelry must have passed across my face, as Stewart captured my attention most assuredly, with a poignant whisper that gave me goose bumps, "Eliza, watching your face—your enchanting smile, your graceful, fluid movement to the music, is nothing short of heart-stopping." My smile increased in width and tenure, until my eyes could no longer accommodate the breadth. Just as the intensity of the lighthouse beacon at *Misthaven* shone, the glow from the happiness welling up within me was nearing "super nova" status.

We were all meteors tonight, arcing and shining intensely, catapulting across space freely and onward to our appointed purposes in life, whatever they may be. I had always known my quest in my earthly journey was and would continue to center around creativity, but suddenly, the clarity was overwhelming, like a spiritual awakening: as much as I loved my life here at home, I had to get to France as fast as I could—as fast as my little *jambes* could carry me. I was no longer waiting for fall to say, "bon voyage;" I was going this summer. I was going to experience the luminous beauty of France and paint to my heart's content.

No longer a sidelined, primarily class time-only "hobby," my art had now become much more essential to who I was as a person, to living *and thriving*. I more fully understood the importance of prioritizing for myself as an individual—of knowing that it's okay to expedite things a bit in order to embrace happiness more fully. Most importantly, I now knew that art was as vital to my soul as every microscopic cell of blood coursing through my veins.

At present, my own, handsome beau was staring at me, eyes locked intently in disbelief, as the music had long-since ended. I was still off in another dimension. I laughed nervously, clearly caught off guard, unusually so. Despite the temporary embarrassment, it felt exhilarating to feel such surprise in myself. Suddenly, my Color Theory class was thrust to the forefront of my mind, as I knew that I could instantly create the *exact* shade of rose I was certain my cheeks had blossomed into, and more importantly, that every color on the wheel could not amount to the brilliance of this glorious feeling that exuded from my countenance at this moment. I may have waltzed well tonight, but it was only the beginning of a magical journey into even grander halls of history, substance and emotion. My life was about to become much more focused on *savoir faire*—a more polished and determined certainty in my behavior—to ensure that joy will be forever entwined with every fiber of my being.

Chapter 25

"Eliza, may I come over now to give you your bon voyage gift?" Ashleigh inquired, frustrated that I had postponed her delivery for two weeks prior to leaving for Paris, which I was happy to say was tomorrow. I had wished Stewart farewell for his trip a week ago with a cupcake of my own creation, resembling an Amazon rainforest. As the days grew closer to his departure, his resolve to leave became unconvincing, until Stewart's father somehow ignited a fire from what had previously been withering embers. I have no idea what transpired between them, but it was good to see Stewart engaged in his beloved pursuits again. Based on his almost daily emails, he was having the time of his life.

"Sure Ash', come over anytime!" I eagerly invited, rejoining the conversation. Ashleigh made me commit to an exact time to meet and assure her that I would be there before we hung up the phone. It was so good to return to phone calls when apart, as text messages were too time-consuming, and I detested the tendency of my thumbs going numb.

I looked forward to sending emails and some *par avion* letters smattered with French postage emblems during the next year. I was going to find the most picturesque stamps, ideally ones with the Eiffel Tower emblazoned with a fleur-de-lis, or similar icons of a nation I hoped to learn a great deal about *joie de vivre* from. Although my experience with my chosen study of French language was a bit lacking in execution—as Madame Rousseau felt I spoke the language, *très bien*—at this point, I had to put aside the fear of offending my soon-to-be neighbors and get in more of a state of *c'est la vie*. My goal was to relax and enjoy the imminent change I was about to embark upon. I couldn't wait to leave for France. Childhood would be neatly shelved in safe storage, with ready access for reflection. I was looking forward to opening up the gift that I was certain this art study abroad experience would unveil.

Father gently knocked on the door jamb of my room, of this same townhouse abode we'd laughed and cried in over the years. He entered with trepidation and seemed sincerely melancholy about my impending departure. Dana had already taken me shopping for what felt more like a trousseau in its importance than travel attire, in purchasing several outfits that she felt would allow me to fit in fashion-wise in Paris, until I could add to my wardrobe more fully, once settled overseas. It was nice to have a mother who looked out for me enough to spare me the embarrassment of a fashion faux pas. I had learned to trust her styling judgment and accept her suggestions more fully.

"Eliza, honey, I probably should have given this to you at your graduation, but it seemed much more fitting to present it to you now," Father shared, taking a step back from my doorway. "I thought you'd appreciate the essence of the symbolism here—the magic of the journey," he added with a sparkle in his eye, while wheeling from around the corner a nesting, three-piece set of what I could only assume to be custom luggage.
"I love it!" I marveled, quickly removing the big, blue, white and red bow off of my new prize, in honor of the flag representing my imminent destination, while smiling the most effortless, toothy grin.

Each suitcase had a pebbled finish in an alternating, rich beige and warm gray, supple leather, in a small diamond pattern. The face of the luggage had a black, embossed, illustrated gesture of the icon of the "City of Light" itself: the Eiffel Tower, about two-thirds of the way up. Each, lushly-wrapped handle included a matching, blackened, pewter-like fob of the same emblem, providing an engraved, scripted name and address on its back as a dual purpose. Seeing, *"Eliza Seelye Hales"* scribed in cursive was a thrill. I felt a tangible lightness and my heart skip a beat. The classic elegance of these satchels of exploration was proof of Father's good taste, and once again, in sharing his vision for the use of metaphor as one of life's greatest teachers and intuitive supporters. I received the message loud and clear: *Adventure cannot be stowed away, but rather, seized and taken with me wherever I go, from this point forward.*

It was lovely of Dana to give Father and me this time together, just the two of us, to measure some of our fondest memories through recollection, as well as anticipation of my life on the verge of some very big changes, both creatively and culturally. It's one thing to visit a place on vacation; it's entirely another thing to become a resident, seeking out the best *boulangeries* and becoming habitual in frequenting the locals-only gathering spots. Always appreciative of other lands and traditions, I envisioned a very happy and friendly immersion in the *bon vivant* lifestyle.

A few hours later after reading Stewart's latest email and well into the packing frenzy, Ashleigh arrived, per our predetermined "appointment." Not to be outdone by anyone in the gift department, my best friend on the planet giggled with glee as she put a silver box with lavish, gray mesh bow upon my bed, demanding an immediate release of its imprisoned contents.

"What have we here?" I inquired, moving with turtle-like slowness to incite a wrath of impatience from my lifelong comrade. It worked. "'Liza, at this rate, it will be *last year's fashion* before you even open it! I shudder at the thought!" she screeched, not hiding her disdain for the unthinkable in terms of couture protocol.

Inside the shiny cube were layers upon layers of tissue paper in purple, blue and pink, and a care tag with designer contact information. As I began to separate the paper from the item of interest, Ashleigh ripped the box and paper from me and brusquely handed the opened contents back with no fanfare, whatsoever.

"Here! We don't have all day!" her terse synopsis of the moment provided equal letdown.

Not wishing to suffer any more casualties of war, I moved more swiftly and placed the silken artistry upon my head, swirled it around my neck and secured it in a neat, square knot underneath my chin.
"What an amazing scarf, Ash'!" I beamed, clearly grateful for her ability to choose the most appropriate farewell present. The watercolor-like, broad strokes of cerulean blue, moss green, white, black and more-yellow-than-green chartreuse accents provided a stunning tour map to guide me, once I reached French soil. "Yes!" we both agreed, standing side by side in front of the mirror, gazing at our reflections. We were both feeling the magnitude of the moment of change upon us. I gave her a big hug and thanked her profusely for her vision, but more importantly, for her loyal friendship. *Ah, yes, I was going to miss my Ash'.*

"But that's not all!" she interrupted my moment of nostalgia. "Take another look at the bottom of the box," she instructed with her index finger, allowing me to fish out the business card myself, embellished with the crest from The House of Courbet. This piece of cardstock was the most valued prize in Ashleigh's arsenal of couture bestowals. Nobody had access to The Master of refined tailoring—not even another model, but somehow Ashleigh had the ear of the man who had become the standard by which all other designers worldwide were measured by—and I had his card with his private cell number in Paris, and a date and time for a personal interview to assess my wardrobe needs, all at Ashleigh's expense. I couldn't believe her generosity, nor fathom how someone like me, who was neither a model nor in the fashion business could have access to the man. I was truly stunned.

After several hugs goodbye, Ashleigh was off to a photo shoot and I was left to finish preparing for my early morning flight. I could almost hear the brisk, Parisian accordion music playing while I hurriedly added more clothes to my last suitcase, the zealous expression of its staccato and exaggerated bellows movements a complement to my wish to hasten my departure. This lighthearted music in my head was beckoning all to partake of the mystique of this world famous city.

What was most interesting, is that my American friends would likely never know that I once took private accordion lessons, from ages six to nine. Perhaps in France, my once-closeted musical interest might prove to be a welcome talent, hopefully giving me an opportunity to improve the impression the French have of the typical, American tourist. If I wanted to live like an American, I'd stay home. In France, I would be entirely focused on immersing myself in the culture and welcoming it to become a part of me, so as to affect my perspective, especially on art.

Since school had ended for seniors at graduation at the end of May this year, I would be getting an early start on my trip for summer the first week of June; this meant that I'd be spending June seventh—my birthday—without family in a foreign country. For some, this might be a strange way to celebrate becoming an adult—not the *Paris* part, but the *sans famille* part—but for me, turning eighteen and spending the day at *Le Musée du Louvre* sounded quite "louvrely" to me! It would be a wonderful introduction for my studies for the summer program at The *École Nationale Supérieure des Beaux-arts*, which would begin the following week. I'd also have a few days to settle in at my apartment on *Rue des Chartreux*, about 2.5 kilometers from school. It was an enclave of individual, upscale apartments for women with a "House Mother/Manager" on the first floor. The apartment building offered supervision like a dorm, with the accoutrements of a more lavish setting; they were not your usual, spartan-like accommodations for students. Additionally, two of Father's best friends lived in the next building, a M. and Mme Petit, so I had plenty of people who would notice if I disappeared.

Situated in the *6th Arronndissement*, across the River Seine from the Louvre, the optimal location fulfilled another tactical strategy, since my apartment was only about 4.3 kilometers from this world-class museum. Additionally, Luxembourg Palace and the Gardens were between school and the apartment, so I was certain to linger there often and enjoy the leisurely pace placed before me, instead of regretting not having seized the opportunity later in life. I had listened to too many adults wishing they had, "stopped to smell the roses" and reduced stress in their lives to not learn from their mistakes. A regular stroll through a magnificent park was a must-do on my itinerary while in France.

After dinner, I made sure that I had all of my pertinent documents and hadn't left anything behind. As I zipped up my last suitcase, Father and Dana came by my room to say goodnight. We all felt the impending sting of separation. I would miss them dearly, but I think we all knew that this experience was going to be a momentous delight, and one that was not to be delayed.

Answering my Paris apartment phone, I asked who was calling up-front, as I had been receiving so many wrong numbers. I didn't want to waste any further time with pleasantries. As it turned out, it was Father and Dana, sharing the same land line together. They called me at eleven o'clock at night their time on June sixth, which was five o'clock in the morning, my time on June seventh, so as not to miss me on my birthday. They knew I had plans—plans I couldn't wait to see come to fruition. Thankfully, I was an early riser.

"HAPPY EIGHTEENTH BIRTHDAY, young lady!" they both cheered in unison.
"Thank you both for calling me—and no, you didn't wake me up. I miraculously have adapted quite quickly to the time change, and as you both would know, have accomplished this without any café or other, artificial means," I shared, happy to be maintaining my healthy lifestyle, all on my own.

"Just adequate exercise and a bit of chocolate, eh, Eliza?" Dana quipped. She knew my sweet tooth wouldn't be satisfied until it had been fully drenched in some serious, chocolaty indulgence. Occasional chocolate was my one vice.

Not wanting to waste time talking about dessert, Father interjected with his wish for a happy day for me and inquired about my plans, to see if anything had changed, now that I was actually here in Paris.

"I already mapped-out my tour at the museum, to maximize the experience and preserve my feet, so I'll be ready for school starting next week," I confirmed. The expanse of the Louvre was intimidating, even for the physically fit.

"Well, what works do you plan to see?" Father asked.

"Of course, I must see the *Mona Lisa* and the *Venus de Milo*," I began, "as well as the Renoir and Monet collections—although I've certainly been blessed already with the substantial bounty of their sibling pieces at the MFA," I added, uncertain if I had just "blasphemed" the Louvre's collection or not, by mentioning complementary pieces showcased elsewhere. I decided I was an energetic student, whose love of art was equally sustained on both continents, albeit very different anthologies on grand scales. "Oh, and the *Portrait of Titus* by Rembrandt, Velazquez…and…I just plan to soak it all in, and not worry about seeing 'everything,' because that's impossible."

"By all means, take your time, honey," Dana reassured. "It's your special day; spend it however you'd like."

"That's right, Eliza. You've got an entire year to frequent the place; don't wear yourself out on today's tour," Father added, trying to be helpful. He realized he was spouting the obvious, and was silent for a few moments, while Dana inquired about my wardrobe sitting with *Monsieur Courbet*, and if I'd met any interesting people yet. I knew that I had a lifetime of interesting people to meet, and France was just the beginning.

Chapter 26

Six years later

"You know, this was the perfect way to celebrate the completion of six-plus years of quality, university education and grad school, Ashleigh," I surmised, as I walked the perimeter of the familiar room housing the Renoir collection at the MFA with my BFF, whose youthful beauty was more flawless than ever. "It feels like forever ago that we sought refuge in this place, while students at Hawthorne, eh Ash'?"

"What, no compare and contrast of *Le Louvre*, versus Boston's own solution to bleak and dreary winters, by way of stunning visuals?" Ashleigh baited, clearly looking to spark mock controversy, just like old times.

"My year in France was six years ago, Ash',—*eons ago*. As I recall, you fully enjoyed your two-week stay with me there, didn't you? Don't you want to incite a riot over something more recent—more controversial—like my switch from my rock-solid plan for a BFA in Painting from the School of the Museum of Fine Arts-Boston, with study abroad, and a MFA in Painting from the Rhode Island School of Design, to switching to a double-major of a BFA in Painting and Art History from RISD and Masters in Museum Studies from Harvard? Doesn't *that* sound more palatable for colorful—pun intended—discussion?"

"Ugh. That sure was a mouthful! Now I need a nap!" Ashleigh joked. "Art is art, Eliza; we both know that your rather nonexistent change in majors is not the issue here. I was thinking I would dig a little deeper than that, to the *real* heart of the matter, and that is why you broke off your engagement with Stewart Grey, IV, last year," Ashleigh stated matter-of-factly, knowing full well she just threw me the zinger I had no rebuttal for. "Well, what's your answer, *'Liza?'*" her question still lingered, as she raised her left eyebrow, giving her trademark, *"Hmmm?"* look, for reemphasis.

Following our traditional habit of me leading the way in our cultural excursion, we continued to peruse the French Impressionist collection, admiring the many works by Monet, then meandering over in the direction of my favorite Americans of, Andrew Wyeth, John Singer Sargent, Winslow Homer and John Singleton Copley, hovering deliberately around my old, familiar friend of, *A Boy with a Flying Squirrel*. Not wanting to leave out my newfound heroine of female allegiance in art—whom I bonded with most appropriately in Paris— we moved onward to Mary Cassatt, to her, *Mrs. Duffee Seated on a Striped Sofa, Reading*, while I quickly tried to formulate a response to Ashleigh's inquiry into my love life.

"It just wasn't working, Ash'," I finally answered her ploy to access my emotions, as we continued walking along. "Stewart, as wonderful as he is—and there are no hard feelings, truly—is just not who I am supposed to marry. It became quite clear as time moved on that we were just not meant to be, in any way, shape or form."
"There's got to be more to it than that, Eliza. Spill!" her eyes bored into my soul, knowing that I was not telling it all. She knew me too well.
"Come on, *you know you're not telling me everything,* Eliza…"

I paced about the room, not wanting to reopen old wounds, but Ashleigh was my oldest, most loyal friend—family, even. She was concerned for me, and I needed to include her as I have always done, even if talking about it was painful.

"Stewart is not a self-made man. Okay. I said it. Sure, he can't help that he comes from a wealthy family, but he depends on his parents for far too many things, emotionally. You can get away with it during kindergarten through twelfth grade and shortly after twelfth grade, but when you're turning twenty-two, twenty-three and twenty-four and you're *still* unable to make your own, wise decisions—even if his parents *are* presumably great influences and offer great counsel—shouldn't he be able to come to his *own* conclusions at our age?

"Ash', they talked him out of philanthropy as a career, and steered him right back into their own agenda: Medical School. They were hoping the summer in South America after graduating from Hawthorne would be the end of his interest in it, but when he got back to start at Harvard, he wanted to work toward a Masters in Public Administration and focus on building up his nonprofit organization, and 'III wouldn't have it. They put Stewart on a couple of boards for their own foundations, but it was not a good fit for him," I continued.

"The sad thing, Ash', is that I think Caroline wanted her son to follow his heart, but in the end, Stewart didn't even stand up for his own beliefs, in what he wanted to do with his own life. I saw how passionate he was about his causes and ideas. It was one of the most impressive things about him. In a short span of time, his father snuffed the life right out of him, which, in turn, pulled the plug on our relationship. Don't get me wrong, becoming a physician is a noble profession, but I saw the magic in his eyes whenever he pursued his real dream. It was a vital part of him. I was so sad for Stewart, when he obeyed his father's wishes, at great sacrifice. The light went out; Stewart became a hollow shell at the young age of twenty-three, with what appeared to be an endless, internal echo."

"Wow, Eliza. How sad for both of you, but especially for him, don't you think? You speak of him almost like he died. At least you're living *your* dream, for the most part," Ashleigh's voice offered sincere consolation.

I could tell that Ashleigh wasn't finished, so I waited for her next wave of counsel: "It's a good thing you found this out before you married him, as his parents—or father mostly—would have certainly come between you two, eventually. I would have walked all over him if he

176

was mine and he was unable to come to his own decisions. Who wants a man who can't cut the 'apron strings' from his parents? Tiresome! He had such promise, too—not that being a physician is a bad choice—we both know that—but I agree, he should have stood up for his own vision of a happy life."

"I was so distraught over the change in him, which then, in turn, changed the dynamics of our relationship. I believe I saved myself a lot of future grief though, Ashleigh, by breaking it off. I am most certain of it. What hurts the most is not that we're no longer together— although I did shed my fair share of tears—but my heart truly aches for him and his zest for life. I can only hope that in time he'll find joy again. I also hope that he can someday blend his medical training with nonprofit ideals and find a source of greater happiness. He's far too young to have succumbed to a life that he never wanted."

"So what's next for you, my friend?" Ashleigh inquired in quiet sincerity, as we found our way to the museum café for a bite to eat and sat across from each other at a little bistro table.
"Well, since I'm living in Concord now and considering applying for curatorial jobs—as that is what recent graduates with Masters in Museum Studies do," I said, with a wry smile, "I've been finishing up some of my paintings, with a solo show with simultaneous exhibits across the U.S. happening in the next few weeks. My agent, René Ledoux—a guy, and don't even 'go there,' Ash', as it's strictly business—who I found in Paris years ago, has my works showing in multiple cities."
"Well, do tell which cities you will become a household name in, 'Liza."
"Boston, of course, as well as New York—where the kickoff reception will be held—are key cities. Also, it takes place in Chicago, Honolulu and lastly, in San Francisco, where there will be a concluding reception. I have ten pieces going to each gallery—that's fifty paintings!"

"Wow! You've been *busy!* I have to go with you—to all of them! Can we stay at your great aunt's and uncle's estate in Atherton, just south of San Francisco? As I recall, you had once said that their place is better than any hotel in the city!" Ashleigh mused with zeal, as she pulled out a mirror and put on some pink lip gloss, gently smacking them once together, while we were waiting for our meal. *Why she doesn't wait until* after *we eat to apply lip gloss, I'll never know.*

"I suppose we should stay at Dana's in Manhattan for the New York show, right?" she inquired. We both knew that was a no-brainer; Dana wouldn't have it any other way. I nodded my head after the fact, offering a solid confirmation.

"With Dana's connections, she's been heavily involved with the New York show, helping promote it already. Perhaps I should ditch René and hire her?" I half-joked. "You know, Ash', what a great idea you had, as my Great Aunt Marceline is in quite thick with the art and city government crowd in San Francisco."

"And don't forget, Eliza, her better half—your Uncle James—with his high tech corporation in Silicon Valley he's Chairman of is a certain, heavy-hitter as well. Didn't you say that his corporate stocks have been steadily rising since going public? After all of these years, he's probably a gazillionaire by now. They would both likely have more connections for you than your agent would in the Bay Area," my most devoted supporter and friend surmised, proud of her reminder. By the time Ashleigh turned thirty, I imagine there would be zero degrees of separation between her and anyone of consequence, because if she didn't already know them or were related to them, she'd make it so.

"Oh, before I forget Eliza, I've been dating this young, strapping CEO from Germany I met recently. His name is Wolfgang Fischer—and no, I do NOT call him 'Wolfie!' Anyway, he has the cutest accent and boy is he handsome! So, I told him about you—*of course*—and about *Misthaven*, and you want to know what he said? He said the name of your familial estate is a bit awkward. He means no disrespect, but he advised me to tell you that in German, a very, similar-sounding word of, 'misthaufen' means, 'dung hill or manure pile,' like a *steaming pile of poo!"* she laughed wildly. And with that, I broke down laughing right along with her, so hard that tears were shed.

The next morning, I woke to the rumbling sound of the Town of Concord garbage truck rolling by bright and early at 5:00 a.m. *Ah, yes, it's Tuesday,* my mind murmured, as I reluctantly opened my eyes. After the shock of not waking naturally at a decent hour wore off—as I had made a new habit since I finished school to let myself wake up on my own time, while my schedule still allowed—I decided to make the most of it and take a walk to Author's Ridge, in Sleepy Hollow Cemetery, as soon as it opened. I desperately needed some inspiration, not to mention some exercise. All that talk yesterday with Ashleigh about "hollow shells" made me feel a bit wanting for fresh air.

Walking distance to the Ridge was one of the main reasons I purchased this home last year. My new address was a sweet, historical treat for myself, in the form of a two bedroom plus den, two bath, two-story colonial, approximately 1000 square feet, built in 1810. Its yellow exterior and black shutters complemented my car perfectly—a match made in heaven. When I turned the corner in my car and saw the house for the first time and Sleepy Hollow in the distance, I considered it as a sign. The day I came home from signing the papers and parked my little happy car in the dooryard, I knew this was the place where I could continue to grow.

There was something about this special spot in the cemetery, especially in autumn, where the graves of Ralph Waldo Emerson, Henry David Thoreau, Nathaniel Hawthorne and Louisa May Alcott were buried. These New England writers and authors, products of the transcendentalist era, were champions of sorts, of a new way of thinking and approach to living. They collectively influenced literature, as well as the area I now called home; this influence was an integral part of me now.

Looking out my kitchen window, I saw a flurry of maple leaves begin to swirl about, like an index finger curling inward, beckoning me to come outside to play. I put on my sweats and now-threadbare Red Sox beanie. I covered the worn spot in the knit fabric strategically with my Harvard hoodie and grabbed my small, spiral notebook, pen and keys and stuffed them in my front pocket. Running out the front door for a jog in the neighborhood, I intentionally left my phone at home, to feel a disconnect from the present. In Concord, there were several places where time stood absolutely still; I intended to jettison technology to maximize the pause, just this once.

Being in the middle of the enchantment of fall, the season and locale did not disappoint. The brisk air cleared my head in a hurry, its frigid temperature surging in and out of my lungs, giving a cleansing effect. I ran for three miles around town, coming to a jog in-place at the corner, before heading down to Bedford Street where my partners in story, soundly slept.

Out of respect, I came to a stop in front of the main gate, and took a leisurely stroll up the hill. I had learned reverence at a young age, from all of the visits to my mother's gravesite in Boston. I would always bring her a single, sterling rose from the nearby florist and place it at the base of her headstone. Sometimes I would talk to her; other times, I would just sit or stand silently.

My notepad took up the usual space in my pocket for rose petals brought in tribute to these writers of eloquence. I'd have to remember to bring some blooms next time, although likely I would wait until spring, when I could cut a fresh daffodil for each author from the front path of my house. The hazy, antique mustard exterior of my home, against the foreground of a sea of optimistic daffodils was too much to pass up in the spring; many a tourist would stop and take a cheerful photo, my white, picket fence providing the perfect frame for a memorable image.

As I neared the graves, I gave a nod to each one, then came to a stop, where I leaned up against a tree, letting my mind run free with ideas. Pulling out my notebook, I scribbled a few, random thoughts, including a mini grocery list, then chastised myself for not sticking to the plan of optimizing the effects of time standing still.

Nobody was in the memorial park—and I regarded it as a park of contemplation—its woody expanse a place to consider and commune with nature. Just like the literary giants who rested before me, I pulled out the pages once again and this time, I too, wrote from the heart:

Author's Ridge

Standing 'midst the fallen leaves,
Iron gates twined, wrought surround;
Author's Ridge where their beliefs,
Poets, writers, resting found.

A quiet place in Concord-Town,
Where thinking minds have come to lie;
Words on frayed-edged pages sound,
Their thoughts transcending, to the sky.

Little Women, Walden Pond,
House of Seven Gables—still;
Creations of these authors run,
Whilst standing on this leafy hill.

Headstones mark the final place,
Where history has run its course;
Dwells autumn in this solemn space,
'Twas laid to rest in quiet's source.

Wow! Where did THAT come from? So as not to spoil this incandescent moment of poetic inspiration, particularly in a creative medium that was not customary for me, I put away my tools and partook of the lingering fruits.   I found a bench and sat quietly, giving myself permission to let all of the everyday thoughts in my head dissipate, and rejoice in the beauty of the gift of these words that had been given to me.

The solitude didn't last long, before random thoughts pushed their way to the surface. *Lie, lay, lain, laid? Lie was intentionally reclining in the present tense, laid was intentionally placing autumn in the past in the poem. Okay, I think all could be good in verb-dom,* I analyzed, laughing to myself at the whisperings of word use obsession, bordering on psychosis. My mind had a way of running exhausting circles around opportune moments of peace, but not this time.   I silenced the tiresome thoughts, once and for all.   Now my mind was still, open, *and truly free.*

By the time I returned home from my jaunt, it was nine thirty in the morning.   I found a phone message waiting for me for an interview invitation; it was for the Curatorial Assistant job at the Museum of Fine Arts-Boston I had applied for, three days prior. "Woo-hoo! That was quick!" I triumphed, out loud. *Thanks Mother! It didn't hurt to have that family connection with a potential employer!* I gratefully acknowledged, smiling heavenward.

Working at a world-class art museum like the MFA would be an unbelievable opportunity for me, as well as a way to provide me future options. People waited their entire careers to work for this kind of an organization, and here I was, a new grad, entirely appreciative for this open door.

Still smiling from ear to ear over this unexpected surprise, I promptly called and confirmed my appointment with the museum Director of Human Resources, for Thursday, at 11:00 a.m., while sorting through junk mail with my other free hand. Soon after I hung up, I followed up with the other jobs I had applied for, taking a moment to check my email inbox, to see if anyone had responded in writing first. There, at the top of the list, was a message from the Farnsworth Museum in Rockland, Maine, home of the Wyeth Center, a Mecca for the Wyeth Family art dynasty. *Not Rock-port, but Rock-LAND,* I mentally noted, wondering how many tourists might confuse the two with such similar names, especially since they were quite near to each other along the coast.

At the Farnsworth, I had applied on a whim for an Interim Assistant Curator's position, not thinking I'd even remotely have a chance, especially when interim positions were usually filled in-house, and I hadn't even been a Curatorial Assistant yet. I hadn't even considered logistics, housing or relocation. It was a spontaneous move on my part.

As I read further into the message, the HR Director had offered a rather detailed response. Evidently my published thesis on the contrasts of Andrew Wyeth's creative periods and perspectives, in and around Chadds Ford, Pennsylvania and in Maine, pushed me high up on the list for consideration. My approach, "offered ideas that provoked original thinking, something our members and guests would heartily appreciate," stated the HR Director in her email. This letter was definitely going into my keepsake file, despite whatever the outcome.

The Farnsworth and Wyeth Center environment would certainly be a thrill, for the Wyeth collection alone. The ever-so-slight reduction in commute to *Misthaven* from Rockland, not to mention the beauty of fulltime living in Maine again would be wonderful; however, the idea of relocating, so soon after buying my first home in Concord, for a job that might not be offered to me permanently was a considerable risk. If there was no MFA possibility, perhaps I would jump at the chance. Instead, I decided not to worry about it for the moment. I would confirm for a phone interview and celebrate having a rather substantial success rate in receiving *two responses* already to my résumés sent out!

The job search had definitely progressed. Two weeks later, I was brimming-over with excitement about sharing my news with Father and Dana and accepted their invitation for dinner at the Beacon Hill townhouse. Eugenie—as masterful as ever with cuisine—had prepared the most scrumptious, Mexican feast for us. In between bites of enchiladas, fish tacos and black beans, I shared my interview and art show updates with a captivated audience.

"So, it's the MFA for you, huh?" Father correctly assessed. "Your mother would be proud," he added, with a thoughtful smile across the table.

"Thanks, Father. Yes, after the second interview, I was really hoping I'd get the job, and two days later, they sent me an offer I couldn't refuse," I confirmed. "I start in three weeks, after the San Francisco gallery reception."

"So what is to become of the Farnsworth, then?" Father inquired.

"The initial phone conference with the Farnsworth was more of an informational interview; they made it very clear the position was interim-only, a confirmation of which I appreciated, so things didn't proceed any further. I didn't burn any bridges though, so perhaps in the future, I'll make my way up north; I'm definitely interested in keeping in touch with them."

"And what's the plan for your art show exhibits, Eliza?" Dana asked with a wink, then closed her eyes in a nonverbal, "yum," as she tasted the fish tacos.

"First, I want to thank you for being a one-woman, promotional force to be reckoned with, Dana; your efforts for the New York launch of the show have been phenomenal, truly! I'll have you know that my agent is a bit uncomfortable, though; I think he may wonder if he's soon to be out of a job," I offered, in sincere gratitude. "The show is bound to succeed!" I added, in total confidence.

"I enjoyed myself thoroughly, Eliza, and I can't wait to attend the reception with your father."

"Yes, we'll definitely have to restrain ourselves from being overly enthusiastic as parents, for this monumental triumph of yours, Eliza," Father interjected, wrapping his arm around his bride, squeezing her shoulder in unabashed pride.

"Oh, and I chose the MFA job also, because I've decided that I'm going to get my PhD in History in Art and Architecture at Harvard. The logistics are perfect; the proximity from home, to work and school will expedite the process," I announced, putting into action my commitment to a grueling, two-year schedule ahead of me, if things go as planned.

"Good for you!" Father beamed, raising his glass for a toast and inviting Dana and I to do the same. "*Doctor Eliza Seelye Hales*—that has a nice ring to it, don't you think, Dana?" Father offered with a laugh, clearly overjoyed at the prospect. The smile on Dana's face was as proud as any mother could express. She didn't need to say anything for me to know that she was truly a part of my personal cheering section. I had more of a confidence boost consistently from Father throughout my life than from ten parents, put together—and Dana was clearly, equally supportive.

I took another glance at the press kit I received weeks ago of all of the marketing media for the Manhattan launch of my show, as well as for all of the other locations, including San Francisco. It included both digital and print media. The primary image for the media was of one of my signature pieces from Paris, coupled with one from Boston Common. The graphic designer did a very nice job on the layout. I looked forward to meeting him tonight at my opening reception. I asked René to be sure and invite him as our guest.

The theme of my show was, "Contrasts in Light," and it worked. René was a genius, although I think Dana had some influence on the promotional efforts as well. I had hoped to find out right away just how extensive her involvement was, so that additional, proper credit could be given.

Instead of my usual jog around the immediate neighborhood, I decided to drive over to Walden Pond and peruse the scenery there, while getting in some exercise. I had some nervous jitters about tonight's opening show and needed to shake it off with some meditative hiking and jogging on Walden's trails. After I arrived, I decided to hug the perimeter of the pond, running at a brisk pace. In several spots, bubbles floated up to the surface of the water, indicating some lively fish were out and about. The wooded, musty scent of the damp, fallen leaves was a magnificent diversion from the rigors of fitness.

Enjoying the solitude of this place that Thoreau had made famous through his words, I noticed three cars traveling slowly on the road circling the water. They made the loop several times. By the fourth rotation, I paid close attention to who was in each car, as their presence was starting to creep me out, ruining my chance of a peaceful respite from the world.

Upon further investigation, I noticed that each car had a female driver with one or two, child safety seats in the backseat, with babies clearly on board. I chuckled to myself at this creative image of motherhood in search of a Zen-like moment. It was apparent that each mom was in need of their own measure of tranquility. They needed to drive their babies to sleep in the car, and while they were at it, give themselves the joy of a picturesque view. I marveled at this impressive demonstration, this insightful vantage point; these women were brilliant in finding a creative solution for their families, in finding a way to meditate, replenishing their stores. I made a mental note of this unique display of multitasking. I wondered to myself if these three mothers knew each other and whether they had intentionally made a caravan, or if they were strangers and had each come to this idea and place separately. Regardless, their mutual dedication was inspiring. It was a privilege to witness it.

For the first time in my life, I felt a sustained moment of longing for motherhood. With my future with Stewart dissolved and my desire to create a family requiring a husband, my prospects for bringing children into the world was definitely on hold. I certainly wasn't focused solely on a career; it was just that I was bound and determined to achieve my goals, and education and the arts were but some of them—but so was an abiding commitment in a loving marriage and becoming a mother some day. *Well, where ARE you, my Prince Charming?* I trilled, mentally. With these words still echoing in my mind, I decided to distance my emotions a bit and feel the burn of leaving tracks one more time around the pond.

Ashleigh had told me that she would meet me at the reception tonight at the Gifford Holden Gallery, so that just left Father, Dana and me to travel from the penthouse by ourselves. My flight into La Guardia this afternoon was uneventful, with the exception of the passenger next to me dozing and breathing his ancient breath from a sarcophagus on me during the entire trip. I wasn't sure if it was the stench I endured, or butterflies, but I was not interested in a late lunch, once I arrived at Dana's.

"By the way, Eliza, I neglected to tell you that I took one of your exhibit invitations from Dana and mailed it to Caleb at his office at the *Moore, Houseman and Weintraub* firm, here in the city," Father admitted, looking rather pleased, and not sheepish at all as we stretched our legs for a bit in Dana's Manhattan living room. "I also emailed one to him, just to be thorough. He's local, and I thought he might appreciate the invite," he augmented, intently gauging my reaction.

I wasn't upset; on the contrary, if I was going to see Caleb for the first time in far too many years, this was the place to do it. It was a public place; I would be looking my best; and I had family and the best pit bull in town to defend me, Ashleigh.
"How exciting!" I enthused, causing Father's jaw to drop and Dana to smile that knowing grin she had grown quite adept at, since becoming a part of our family. On that note, I skipped off like a giddy school girl to the guest room to get ready for the main event.

Chapter 27

As we exited the limo, Father took another opportunity to tell me how, "truly breathtaking" I looked. I didn't need recognition or the limelight, but tonight's artist's reception was an incredible honor. As we entered the elevator for the high-rise gallery, I adjusted my black, suede, sling-back shoes and smoothed out my dress. I chose a red, wool, sheath style cocktail dress with matching bolero jacket, trimmed in a crimson braid and accented with a crystal-encrusted buckle on the half-inch, color coordinated, fabric belt. It was an elegant look, but the color brought some serious "pop" to the ensemble. I wore my hair down in loose curls, which framed my face nicely for the photo ops that René had surely strategized.

Swiftly, my bodyguard-of-a-best-friend came and stood by my side, as soon as I entered the gallery. She was visually sweeping the room for any potential obstacles, either emotional or industrial, by the look of her crossed arms, defensive posture and tilt of her head. She took her protector duties seriously, it appeared. I had to laugh just a tiny bit, as it was worth a chuckle—*caring, but funny, that's my Ash'*. I suppose with the update that Caleb might be in attendance, as well as the camera crew that Dana had secured had Ashleigh on "high alert." Sure, they were stress-worthy hurdles, but I was more concerned about how to deal with a more imminent danger: Shane Earhardt, the Senior New York Times Arts Columnist, whose tiptoed, stilettoed feet were clattering in annoying, dainty steps across the marble gallery foyer, heading straight toward me.

My alarm was justified; the last, one-man or one-woman gallery show that Shane covered in her column had ripped to shreds any chance at a successful career for the artist. Like the pampered food critic—who dines on the very best, with chef and waitstaff hovering on pins and needles like a begging dog at the dinner table for the positive review— Shane makes even the most snarky food critics seem like marshmallows. On the flip side, if Shane Earhardt likes your work, you're golden! One good review from her and your career in the art world is set to fly not just high, but soar to the stratosphere.

Thankfully, René appeared out of nowhere and thwarted a most certain, angst-inducing interrogation with "Ms. Wordsmith," by speaking with her on my behalf, paving the way for a more successful interview with me directly, later. I would speak to Shane after an hour or so, after René had worked his magic with his over-the-top French charm and personal tour of the exhibit. In just one, little hour, Shane would be transformed from a potential threat to a much more agreeable and receptive patron of the arts. For this alone, René was worth every penny as an agent.

Later in the reception after introductions, my remarks, conversing with a few guests and the inevitable interview, it became obvious that Caleb wasn't going to show up. Father looked across the room at me, clearly feeling badly that he had opened things up for disappointment. I knew he meant well, so I smiled and immediately got over it, as this was one milestone that was not going to be clouded by past history. Instead, I celebrated a future rich in creative promise.

As the reception ended, I found René and he verbally tallied the sales from the evening; all ten paintings had been sold, and the preview for Shane's next article was surprisingly positive, according to his take on her initial thoughts. Sure, she had some constructive criticism in her observations—which, coming from her would be appreciated— however, the overall tone of the piece was likely to be worth framing, per the heads-up René shared with me, based on an overly chatty Shane.

"What would I do without you, René?" I gushed, in awe of his influence and business know-how. He smiled and winked at the same time, while gracing the room with a chivalrous, one-armed bow, placing his other hand across his heart in one gallant move. Back again at my side, Ashleigh approved, "He's worth every penny." I nodded in agreement at the familiar words, as we headed out the door to go dancing, in commemoration of a most marvelous, artistic debut.

"Eliza, would you please pass me another napkin?" Ashleigh nudged, as we both secured our drop-down tables before us on the plane. We were descending, to make way for our landing at SFO. The San Francisco Bay and many of its bridges were well in view, whitecaps evident, with easily over one hundred sailboats dodging about, below. I had always enjoyed coming to visit Father's relatives in California. Since his parents had died, Marceline and James had become like second parents to him, and grandparents to me. They were going to love meeting Dana, and I was going to enjoy an entirely different dynamic at this concluding, San Francisco gallery reception.

Enough hours before my show to not get delayed in traffic, the parents and relatives, as well as Ashleigh and I drove across the Golden Gate Bridge together in a limousine, as the last time I had driven across had been a distant memory for me. I wanted to have a freshly-minted one, using this architectural icon as a metaphor for this new path in my life. During this happy venture, we managed to take a few, arresting photos upward out of the sunroof as we passed underneath the towers, as well as from the Sausalito side of the steel expanse before the sun set. As the sun was setting to the west, I promised myself that next time I came here I would walk across this bridge and sail the bay below.

Gifford Holden did not disappoint. He was most gracious with Marceline and James, showing them the far corners of his gallery as some of the guests arrived. The show this time was an entirely different feel; my work was of the same, artistic theme as New York, but this gallery was much more open and light. Perhaps having a stand-alone building with vaulted, glass ceilings, as opposed to the closed feel of the high-rise in New York made the biggest, visual difference. The sparkle of the nighttime allure with unique, custom lighting was captivating, placing each piece of my artwork in an optimal, diffused glow, however, also capturing an interesting mix of lightness, shrouded by the darkness of the night sky.

"I'd aim for the cute one, over there," Ashleigh pointed out, interrupting my musings, noting the clothes first—looks second, on the incredibly handsome, charismatic guy across the room. He was definitely working the group he was talking to; all eyes and ears were clearly at attention. We both watched him in profile, with wistful dreaminess, until his date scooped up his arm.

"Well, there goes my hopes right out the window," Ash' announced, looking a bit dejected, as she twisted the ball of her foot on the floor in a symbolic gesture of eliminating the competition. I, on the other hand, stood motionless, as the profiled man and his stunning lady turned and came more into focus, walking straight toward me. At the same time, Aunt Marceline joined us, seemingly well acquainted with the female arm candy on the man who stood before me.

Aunt Marceline began, "Eliza, I'd like to introduce you to Ms. Felicia South, Attorney at Law, and daughter of the Mayor of San Francisco—and her date—"
"—We've met," I interrupted, trying to appear in control, unflustered—just *fine*—about this little, unexpected surprise.

Caleb leaned across the awkward space between us and gently kissed my cheek, breaking free of Ms. South's rock-solid grip for just a moment.
"Hello, Eliza," his feathered words floated near my ear, their downy softness and his memorable scent daring to dance away with my composure.

"Caleb Longfellow!" Ashleigh shouted in an unbelievably high-pitched glee, saving us from a most pregnant pause, giving him a quick hug. *Ms. South was probably thinking of ways she could put Ashleigh and me behind bars; at minimum, she was probably contemplating how she was going to sue us for something, or anything that would release her sweetie from our dastardly clutches,* my mind spouted with no equanimity, whatsoever.

I was normally not the jealous type, but suddenly, my art show was not centered as prominently in my line of sight as much as this haughty opponent. The "crosshairs" in my mind twitched responsively.

To reconfirm my dedication to not stooping beneath me and spoiling the festive mood, I quickly withdrew my gaze from the brunette beauty like I was throwing out the trash, turning my attention instead, back to my oldest friend from Maine, all six-foot two of him. *A friend indeed*, I thought, the irony a bittersweet taste. A small, sarcastic huff of a laugh escaped my lips, thankfully, undetected. I immediately countered with a stifled sigh of disappointment, as the suppressed feelings bubbling just below the surface threatened to make their presence known. I maintained my stalwart posture, rendering any assessment by another of my true feelings ineffective.

The Mayor promptly joined our little group and Aunt Marceline commandeered him, his daughter and the conversation, as Caleb and I just stared at each other for a brief moment in awkward silence. Time had been a flawless benefactor for Caleb. Dressed in a charcoal designer suit with a mesmerizing smile, his sandy blonde hair, now kept shorter than before, was layered with more bronze than gold—a richer palette of hues, I determined in his favor; his brilliant, blue eyes were expressive, but at the same time, entirely enigmatic; his tan face was no longer boyish, but instead, his once-painfully handsome, good looks were now excruciatingly so—straight to my heart did this arrow of pain plunge, deeply and most assuredly.

He was, without question, the most handsome man I had ever laid eyes on. What made this even more poignant, was that I knew that Caleb, as a person, was one of the deepest souls who had ever lived; his evolvement as a human being could only have become *more* caring, *more* interesting, *more* determined than ever. His self-assured nature and quiet confidence was an integral part of him, still. The time that had passed between us did not change these facts—of this I was most certain. This was a fathoms-deep confirmation of truth. *And oh, how I had missed him so. I wanted to talk to him—be near him,* my thoughts raced, but remained entirely private within the confines of my own mind.

With a closed half-smile and a look of resignation, Caleb directed his eyes to the floor, breaking away from my gaze. There was so much I wanted to ask him. There might as well have been an army of people sandwiched by two brick walls between us; I wasn't gaining any access to him tonight. Thankfully, René came and rescued me, so that I could preserve my dignity and prepare for my speech; after all, tonight's gathering was to celebrate art and my small contribution to this effort.

I managed to give an eloquent reception address, sharing some personal anecdotes that only Caleb would have noticed as significant; they were last-minute, extemporaneous additions. My remarks were to the crowd, but my heartfelt message was solely for him. Whether he picked up on any of it remained a mystery.

I didn't let on to our Atherton relatives of the deepness of the connection with Caleb, so I kept it to myself for the remainder of our stay. Two days later, I had a reprieve, in the form of five-plus hours of dedicated, one-on-one time with Ashleigh, on the plane ride back home to Massachusetts. We plotted and schemed and did all of the silly, immature things that women do when they feel slighted or heartbroken, all within the security of our friendship, although we did celebrate my successful art show.

It was a relief to joke about this supernatural coincidence, of seeing Caleb after all this time. It was unanimously agreed that I had been most gracious in my outward conduct at the reception. Nobody knew but us how utterly devastated I was to see him and not receive any explanation of why he had disappeared, or what Felicia was—if anything—to him. The fact that Caleb never traveled much before, but here he was, clear across the country with this lawyer appendage gave us something to consider. Caleb and this fiery brunette were likely an item, and a serious one at that. I did my best to suppress any anger, hurt feelings or jealousy. I was mostly upset at myself for feeling this way.

From Logan International, I sat in total silence all the way home to Concord in the taxi. As soon as I entered my house, I dropped my luggage on the floor, drew myself a hot bath, and within the privacy of the sanctuary of that tiled room, away from prying eyes, I cried what felt like another bathtub-full of tears.

Chapter 28

Three years later

Having fully immersed myself in the rigors of curatorial life at the MFA, along with the arduous task of earning a Harvard PhD, three years had passed me by rather quickly. Ashleigh had set me up for several dates during this time, and I had schlepped my way through more than a few of my own. The writing was on the wall: I was too busy to search for Mr. Right; I also wasn't interested in anyone in my circle of acquaintances as anything beyond friendship. It didn't help that the dating pool within my sphere was tremendously shallow. I needed a change of venue if I was going to find someone to seriously consider.

Despite my busy efforts with my Doctorate, I had been promoted to Assistant Curator of American Paintings after one year at the museum. Now with graduation imminent, rumors had been circulating that I would be invited to become a candidate for the position of Senior Curator within the same collection, as the current one had been considering retirement. It was unheard of for someone so relatively new in the field to have this honor of consideration; I was fully aware of the uniqueness of the situation and grateful, if the opportunity did indeed present itself.

I would be up against three others within the department, but I certainly had a shot. I had also heard another rumor that my dissertation had been read by the Executive Director, as well as the Board, who supposedly, "found it most significant" in their consideration measures. It wasn't a secret to anyone what the topic was, as it had long-since been published. Regardless, not being one to consider rumor as anything but gossip, I ignored the departmental rumblings and focused on the impending graduation ceremony next week and donning my academic regalia, as well as my imminent, three-month sabbatical I had applied for, one year in advance.

I worked hard for nine years of my life to get to this point in my education. While I had been dedicated to being a lifelong learner, I was in great need of a break. This sabbatical was my chance to enjoy some downtime; it would give me an occasion to relax and take a break from academia. After all, who knew when an opportunity such as this would present itself again?

Thankfully, my application for time off was granted. I would use it to focus on the joy of painting, which had sadly taken a backseat for far too long. During this downtime, I promised myself that I wouldn't worry about the Curator job, or those within the department who might be vying for it in my absence. I believed that everything would work out the way it was supposed to. My mother always said, "Everything happens for a reason." Forget about the competition— her words gave me tremendous peace of mind.

Dana had a friend up in Camden, Maine who was considering touring Europe from the end of May to mid-June and needed someone to house-sit in their beautiful, shingle style home. It had a spacious studio and gallery. They needed someone to run their art gallery while they were gone. Dana had emailed me asking if I wanted to consider it. I had put off getting back to her, as I was undecided about staying anywhere other than *Misthaven,* so I would call her tonight and let her know my decision: I would go to Camden.

Camden sounded like the perfect getaway for late May and early June. July and August I would still spend on Hales Island. It had been far too long since I had been there; during the past three years, I had only stayed on the island three times—and two out of the three visits were for funerals. All three trips had been far too brief.

The cheerful isle of my sunny childhood had fast become a place of mourning. That had to be rectified, as *Misthaven* was a place of living and thriving. I vowed that this summer I'd take the time to right this wrong and return things emotionally to their former, happy state.

I received a phone call from Uncle Seth the next day, notifying me he'd be attending my graduation. I hadn't seen him for many years, as he had settled down and finally got married overseas. His new bride wasn't interested in leaving her home country of Tahiti, as her parents were both seriously ill; she and Seth were their primary caregivers, so Seth was physically absent from the family for quite some time. Since his wife's parents had recently passed on, he was now able to travel for extended visits. This one was sure to be a sweet reunion. I couldn't wait to see him!

"Eliza, you *are* wearing that ivory lace dress from Milan I bought you, under your cap and gown, *aren't* you?" Ashleigh's phone interrogation peaked in pitch on the "aren't."
"Yes, Ash', as always, you are the 'Commander of Couture' and I shall not deviate from your profound wisdom of wardrobe—especially for something as important as tomorrow's milestone," I conceded into the phone. I always appreciated our lighthearted banter and didn't mind my being subjected to my best friend's dictatorial ways in this respect, as her opinions were appropriate for just about every clothing circumstance. Even fashion magazine editors sought out her thoughts on many occasions.

Ashleigh would forever be my most trusted friend and confidant. She also had excellent taste, so I would be a fool not to listen to her fashion advice. After all, the "ASH" brand was everywhere. She was one of the, "Thirty Under Thirty" to watch out for. Her fashion, cosmetics and lifestyle empire was exponentially growing.

After we said our goodbyes, I checked my email before I left work for the day. My boss had sent her congratulations on my graduation and a "bon voyage" message from the executive staff and the Board of Directors. This was it: a working, but relaxing vacation in a new locale, meeting new people, as well as returning to my roots in fine art practice and to *Misthaven,* for an *entire* summer! I immediately emailed my boss and thanked her again for the approval and effort on my behalf, as well as for the kind note. In one week, I would be enjoying a new adventure at my favorite place on the globe. As soon as I got to *Misthaven* I was going to take *Eliza's Wake* out for a sail!

"Doctor Hales, I presume?" was Uncle Seth's way of congratulations, as he hugged me, then stepped aside as he introduced me to his wife, Tiare. Ever the joker, he then feigned smoothing the back of my doctoral hood from his imaginary messing it up. Tiare was strikingly beautiful—an exotic portrait of Polynesian magnificence, her warm smile, so friendly. Seth was a doting husband. He exuded a humble pride over his new bride. It was so wonderful to see him so happy; the two of them together made a perfect pair. I could envision the many paintings that included her, lined up along Seth's studio wall, hung throughout his own and in his many patrons' homes. She clearly inspired him.

With the limit of commencement tickets, I was fortunate to have five in attendance: Seth, Tiare, Father, Dana and Ashleigh, of course. Each one was patiently waiting their turn for the many photos I'd be taking with them, as I opted for a professional photographer; everyone was on their best behavior, with zero complaints about the formal documenting of the experience.

After the ceremony we attended the luncheon on campus, but kept our stay brief, as we wanted to save our full-blown celebration for dinner at Thoreau's Inn in Concord. It had become a favorite restaurant for special occasions, and offered a very easy commute home for me!

"I'd like to offer a toast—of bread—to my favorite Doctor in the house," chirped Seth in a snappy voice, while handing me his bread plate with a slice of marbled rye and pat of butter. "You know, if you look closely at the swirls in the rye, Eliza, I think I can see the *Mona Lisa*!" he continued to joke, with a twinkle in both of his oh-so-happy eyes. Tiare was laughing out loud, along with Father and Dana, but Ashleigh chose to sit with her arms folded, and dramatically rolled her eyes first, then smiled knowingly, elbowing Seth in the bicep. She had experienced Uncle Seth's sense of humor and practical jokes since she and I were in first grade; he would take the jab.

The celebration continued for another two hours until I thanked everyone for coming. All present could sense that it had been a full day, and it was time to part ways. For some, it would be a long time before I would see them again; for others, hopefully we would reconnect soon. Regardless, it was an emotional parting. As I hugged Seth and Tiare goodbye, I had a feeling that this may be the last time we saw each other. His resemblance to Mother in his facial expressions warmed my heart, as it gave me a sense of having her there with me on this special day of achievement for the entire family. This day had been a long time in the making—a lifetime in the making, actually.

"Now Eliza—I mean, *Doctor* Hales, be sure you let us know if everything is in order as soon as you arrive in Camden, okay?" Dana urged, in "protective mother" mode, as she and Father were leaving the restaurant.

"And I hope we can hear from you a few times after that, too," Father added, raising his eyebrow with a half smile.

"Doctor, I think I may need a vacation to Maine, to help with my allergies," Ashleigh hinted, as she gave me a hug farewell, the last to leave our little gathering.

"Good art will cure anything that ails ya; that will be my prescription for all," I shot back, with a grin. "As soon as I get settled, I'll be in touch, Ash'——I promise. I'm really hoping to spend some time alone for a bit, perhaps try my hand at dating some lobsterman or lumberjack while I'm there," I offered Ashleigh with a wink.

"No problem. I understand when I am being brushed aside for some coastal hottie," her rebuttal rang, with mock offense. All jokes aside, I really was intent on extending my dating radius, in hope of meeting someone special.

Dana had sent me an email with instructions on where to pick up the house and gallery keys, once I arrived in Camden, which I had printed for safekeeping. It also had the alarm code and contact information for Charles and Eva Beasley, and their Pleasant View Gallery.

As I came into Camden and drove down near the water, its brilliance beckoned me to come out and play. I decided to get settled in at the house before I ventured out, so I continued on to my final destination. Situated right on Route 1, the location was optimal for foot traffic and drive-by tourists alike. *I bet this gallery is going to keep me pretty busy*, I anticipated. I put my car keys in my messenger bag and searched for the Beasley's keys inside the planter by the back door. Easily found, I let myself in and disarmed the alarm.

The house was designed by an architect friend of the Beasley's and could easily have served as a luxurious and substantial, bed and breakfast inn, but its owners wanted to keep things simple. Both Charles and Eva were artists, so they opened up the gallery adjacent to the house in their two-story, charming barn to showcase their own pieces in stained glass and sculpture, plus sell the works of a few others with tremendous talent. As I made my way toward the gallery, I noticed that the red hay loft door with its white "X" was open to the sky. I ignored it, knowing from Dana's details that the loft was sealed from the gallery below, and the alarm would deter any intruders. Once inside, I took a stroll, arcing my path around the room, taking in the scent of glass putty and sawdust, stored nearby.

I was amazed at the artistry. Charles' sculptures in cast metal were meticulously detailed; most were people in wistful, leisurely poses. Eva's glass work was inspiring as well; not your typical church scenes, her pieces were iconic, like a portrait of the natural world in glass. One in particular, in front of one of the windows near the gallery entrance struck my heart, with its primary colors of a puffin near the shore at sunset. The scene was masterful, not tourist kitsch. *This was going to be a wonderful environment*, I determined, as I spied the easel and art table in the back corner.

With Memorial Day weekend starting the next day, I thought it prudent to find where everything was in the gallery—the key to the cash register, log-in to the computer, adjust the lighting, and such. Dana had forwarded copious notes from Charles, so I felt well acquainted to their routine. I'd open up the shop tomorrow morning at ten and see just how hopping this place gets on opening weekend. If it's anything like Dana had shared, I would regret it if I didn't wear comfortable shoes, as I was bound to be on my feet, taking care of customers from ten until four, daily. Thankfully, I would get a reprieve on Sunday, as the Beasley's took the day off, even on holiday weekends.

Before it started to get dark, I grabbed one of the bikes at the house and pedaled down to the water, to sightsee again for a bit. I found a perfect spot overlooking the many boats moored off the shore. It was picture-postcard-perfect, this quaint scene before me. I missed sailing and decided to make my way below to the harbor, to see some of the vessels up close. My eye was drawn immediately to the restored schooner—its floating, nineteenth century history a testament of courage and hardiness. I managed to get permission to come aboard, and was allowed to tour her spacious cabins below deck unaccompanied, noting the fine finishes throughout. Topside, I looked out to the horizon and felt the spirit of her crew, her captains and cargo from centuries past. Surely, this seaworthy maiden had many a story to tell. I stood quietly for a few moments, listening to the soft wind blow and watching the birds gliding on the air currents. The smell of the sea was awakening a part of me that had been silent for far too long.

As I left the ship, the Captain offered me a gift certificate to one of the harbor restaurants, as a "Welcome to the Neighborhood" gesture. Suddenly ravenous, I decided there was no time like the present to use my gift, so I swept my ankle against the kickstand of my bike and was off to dine.

Not wanting to carry home leftovers on the bike, I made sure to finish everything, which was easy to do today, as somehow the salt air revved-up my appetite. I chose a seafood fettuccini and a slice of blueberry pie for dessert. Everything was delicious. As I left to ride back to the Beasley's, tourists were starting to pile into the restaurant parking lot for the holiday weekend. One of the cars with Texas plates stopped me for directions. I did as best as I could and invited them to stop by the gallery while they were in town. Hopefully they'll be my first customers tomorrow.

When I got back from dinner, I took a lingering bath for well over an hour in the Beasley's antique, claw foot tub. The pale blue walls with white enamel trim presented a subdued color palette in which to soak in. The bath salts were scented with lavender and hyacinth—a stirring fragrance that relaxed me into the most pliable mush that ever graced a New England breakfast table. When my fingers looked irreversibly prune-like, I knew it was time to drain the last of the warm, silky water that cradled me into tranquil oblivion. Reluctantly, I eased out, dried off and slipped into my pink, plush robe. Still too chilly for an evening sit on the porch, I opted for a movie, then fell into bed, fast asleep in a matter of minutes.

Chapter 29

Even with an intown location, the morning brought the rapturous sound of birds, who sang and fluttered their way into my heart. It was like a "Good Morning" greeting from the region's wildlife. I was in just too good of a mood to not notice the beautiful and quaint melodies. As I stood by the back door, swallowing the last of my orange juice from today's early morning grocery run, I could hear the wind carrying the sound of the harbor buoys, clanging faintly in the distance on Penobscot Bay. It was a mesmerizing sound that took my memories far away, to an earlier time.

I looked at the clock and saw that it was already nearing 9:30 a.m. I needed to get the gallery ready for opening day, by finishing hanging a few of my own paintings, as well as have my surplus of water and snacks nearby, in case I got held "retail hostage" for too long. Thankfully, they had a restroom in the gallery, but timing would be essential, if customer traffic matched the Beasley's expectations. Memorial Day Weekend was always the beginning of the gallery season in Maine.

René had been steadily selling my paintings in the same U.S. galleries as my opening shows three years ago, but had expanded to new locations overseas. My online gallery presence had also succeeded beyond expectations. I had sold all but a few of my works created since those opening shows, including all of the works in the initial show-run itself—with the exception of one that was not for sale. The watercolor of Caleb's barn, with *Misthaven* off in the distance was for display-only in those initial shows. I had since painted a partner piece—almost identical—so that I could sell it eventually, as many people had inquired about the "Misthaven" painting at the shows, disappointed when they found out that it was not available for purchase.

During one of my rare and somber visits to Hales Island for Mrs. Stanfield's funeral, I felt her spirit was cheering me on to create the matched set. The existence of the twin piece would allow me to retain the original for my personal collection and make some client, somewhere, very happy, plus save me from my business faux pas of showing a piece that was not available.

The subject matter of "Misthaven" was deeply personal—so much so, that even selling the twin was going to be difficult—so I priced it high enough out of reach that it would probably never sell, at least not outside of New York or San Francisco. Having this watercolor partner, "Longfellow's Boathouse" in the Beasley's gallery was like hanging out with an old, familiar friend; it would also either ease me emotionally into preparing myself for someday parting with it, or perhaps would seal the deal for that sale never happening.

As ten o'clock neared, I placed the "OPEN," A-frame sign out front near the street and turned over the hanging, "OPEN" signs in both the front and side windows of the gallery, as the gallery was on the corner, with access from two sides of the property.

It was a good thing I was strategic in gathering my stockpile of edible necessities, as the customers were already coming in a large caravan from the restaurants down the street—the "Breakfast Brigade," was what Dana had said that Eva called them. The Beasley's had a close friendship with many of the other business owners in town, and clearly, these restaurateurs had forwarded their own customers over our way. I would be sure to reciprocate the favor.

The Texas couple from the night before was in the first group of opening day visitors; they bought one of Charles' bronze sculptures, titled, "Penobscot Praise," of a woman looking out to sea. I imagined this feminine figure was yearning to tell her seafaring beau how much she adored him, perhaps sad that she hadn't said so before his long voyage. The emotion of Charles' work reminded me of Andrew Wyeth's and Winslow Homer's similar tales of Maine and the sea in many of their paintings.

The entire holiday weekend had been almost a blur. The constant barrage of customers—many of whom purchased, and not just browsed—was a triumph and exhausting at the same time. Even with Sunday off, I didn't have much time to restock and prepare for the biggest shopping day of the weekend on Monday morning. Being Memorial Day, and despite the inclement weather, Camden offered up a brisk and continuous showing of rather substantial sales. I was proud of the revenue stream for the Beasley's—and even one of my own pieces—but I was looking forward to the day off tomorrow on Tuesday, so that I could paint in the quiet of the morning.

The 3:30 clock bell chimed once in the church nearby, so I started gathering up receipts, as a lull had fallen upon the gallery most surprisingly. I decided I had better take advantage of the downtime, so I could close promptly at 4:00 p.m., and went into the back room to use the restroom. As I finished drying off my hands, I heard a man clear his throat and say, "I think I'll take this one here—the one with the boathouse." I didn't know that someone had been waiting inside. I tightly clamped my lips together and shut my eyes for a second, angry at myself for not pricing the piece higher. He wanted the one painting I had no business hanging up for sale.

As I came around the corner from the back room, the unfiltered sunlight was streaming through the window next to the man, magnifying a shimmer of freshly fallen rain upon him and his tasteful suit jacket. Unaware of my presence, his back was still toward me. He ran his hand through his glistening hair a few times to gently tousle it dry; as he did so, his vigorous physique was barely masked by his apparel, as he casually returned his muscled arm to his side. Even in silhouette I could tell he was incredibly good looking, which made this encounter to thwart this acquisition more of a challenge.

As I strode across the room, I tried to gather my wits about me. Anxiety was clearly written across my face as I reached the halfway point. Again I tried to regain composure, hoping for the right words to talk him out of the purchase, when the man turned around to face me.

"Hello Eliza," was Caleb's relaxed greeting, a peaceful, warm smile stroked the corners of his eyes. Three years had only improved his radiance—what could only be considered a blatant enhancement of what was already perfection. He tilted his head down at me, softening his hopeful gaze, silencing every molecule between us in the room. As he walked slowly toward me, his steps intent, a few, stray raindrops shook from his hair upon the floor. I tried to remember to breathe deeply, but suddenly my lungs felt incredibly shallow and confined. *How did he find me here? Clearly, he knew I was here. He doesn't seem surprised at all!*

In a split-second, my preservation instincts took over: I remembered San Francisco and his female, "appendage." I quickly glanced at his hands—there was no ring, which didn't confirm a thing, as so many sailors preferred not to wear them, so I continued my visual sweep. A fleeting look outside the window determined that his "wife," Felicia and "the newborn twins" were not impatiently waiting out in the "Range Rover" for "Daddy" on their family vacation, stopping by for a quick art acquisition. I had no idea what this visit entailed; however, as I debated in letting my guard down, I ran out of scenarios to race my mind around, so I decided to just stop thinking and try to take in a little more oxygen.

Three years had passed since we had run into each other at the Holden Gallery in San Francisco—an encounter that left me stinging with many, still-unanswered questions; many of the questions were now ten years old, with layers of dust gathering upon them in earnest. Yes, ten years had passed since Caleb and I were face to face, just the two of us. I had thought of that long-ago moment when I dreamed of a future together many, many times; it had become a faded memory, but it was attempting to make a comeback, painfully tugging at the frayed edges of my soul.

When people die, they say their life passes before them instantly, providing a mosaic of events to draw closure from and take with them. For a pivotal moment such as this, my mind chose a painterly approach in gathering up the bracing truths of feelings, bringing them all to the surface in perfect balance, fresh and unvarnished. Each detail emerged like a blade of grass from the earth in slow-motion, developing into a verdant knoll by the water, in which to lie down upon and sleep—as my heart wanted to escape to a deep slumber, to silence the reminders that were becoming louder by the minute in my head.

Ten years had washed over us, but the tide had brought with it a strong remembrance of the hurt and frustration I felt, including the more recent three years ago. I tried to appear disinterested in him at the exhibition, to protect from public display the raw exposure of my wounds. Nobody knew the extent of the anguish Caleb's disappearance had caused me—not even me. Here he was after all these years standing before me, with no obstacles between us. This moment was quickly becoming surreal, a dalliance of my imagination. *Eliza! Remain in control!* I demanded to myself. The internal discourse I was having was a losing battle. It was too late. My availed tears spilled over, betraying everything, unlocking further the secret thoughts that I had kept even from myself all these years.

"Eliza," Caleb's comforting voice assured; his still-familiar fingers reached to tenderly stroke the side of my face, his careful, but penetrating gaze breaking my composure, further still. "I have so much I need to say—to explain—to *apologize* for," he began. "I'm so sorry that it has taken me so long to tell you.

"I'm so, so sorry Eliza that I disappeared after my Dad died. I should have told you what I was going through, but instead, I let my grief carry me away to the farthest place I could get, from reminding me of my life up until that point. I didn't let go of law school, as frankly, the course load helped me keep my mind off of my despair, but I did let go of something infinitely more important: you. As time went on, it became increasingly awkward to even consider trying to reenter your life."

I took a step back and steadied myself, but Caleb was intent on keeping me near. He reached his arms around me and held me close, burying his face into my hair. I could feel him breathing in the fragrance of lavender, one of his favorite scents. Normally after a ten-year separation without a defined, romantic relationship, people wouldn't assume such close proximity, but we weren't very typical— not in the least, apparently, as I still hadn't stepped aside.

My perspective shifted from my own, inner diatribe to empathy for him in one instance. Why was this so seamless? Because I had lived a life full of trust in most regards; my tendencies to care and forgive remained intrinsic. No, there was no purpose in being offended, hurt, or put-off by situations I knew only my side of. As quickly as the floodgates of past hurt had been opened, they were sealed up tight, the discontent quickly becoming a mirage.

I could feel his anguish, as he turned his head from side to side, as if in disbelief himself of this event unfolding before us. He lifted his head, staring off in the distance. I slowly turned the side of my head against his chest; his chest was now heaving, his own emotions on a roll.
He gently pulled me away from him, just a little, so as to see my face and declared, "When I saw you at your gallery show in San Francisco,

Eliza, it broke my heart that I couldn't have a moment alone with you, to tell you how sorry I was and explain things, right then and there. I also didn't want to detract from your big day. I had missed your New York show, because the postal invitation had fallen out of my mailbox at the firm, and the emailed invitation had ended up in the corporate spam folder—I didn't even find out I was invited until long after I returned to New York from San Francisco."

He took a cleansing breath and continued, "It became clear to me at your exhibition that you had moved on and didn't even remember 'us,' really—that perhaps it was a childish thing to consider for you. I was an idiot for thinking I had any business 'explaining' things that were clearly, far-distant, perhaps nonexistent history for you."

Caleb added, with a wince, his baby blues crinkling with distaste, "I made the mistake of dating Felicia for a brief time. I met her at Columbia, but when she invited me to accompany her to a gallery showing with her Dad—the Mayor—I *had* to attend. I should have come alone, as I was already in San Francisco on business for the firm, but her Dad is a pretty persuasive man, and his extended family from New York are longtime, VIP clients. When he also asked me to come with them, I had to oblige, as a professional courtesy. But Felicia, she had other ideas in her head—ideas that I didn't share in. When I found out after I had accepted her invitation that it was *your* show—I couldn't believe it! I had prayed I could have the opportunity to talk to you privately, to put to rest, once and for all, the mistake I had made in not just pushing you away, but removing the purest truth about myself: that I needed you." *Keep breathing,* I reminded myself, as Caleb unconsciously turned his left foot on its outside edge, a reminder that I still knew him.

"Eliza," Caleb continued, "I heard a lot about you from Ashleigh's uncle over the years, and was able to feel a somewhat distant part of your life, but it just wasn't enough for me. That made me angry at myself for feeling so possessive of you—of the beautiful girl *whom-I-*

chose-to-run-away-from," Caleb enunciated, syllable by syllable, clearly still upset with himself. "I was a stupid kid." His eyes were glistening now too.

"I want you to know Eliza that I cheered for your every success, for your every triumph—*always*. I asked myself, 'How was I to ever change a situation that *I* created?' I vowed that someday I would find you again, Eliza, that I would plead for your forgiveness and make it right."

His face full of contrition, his expression changed to one of hope: "I saved your New York exhibition invitation. When I finally got up the nerve to do something about it, I called up your agent, René, to see if the "Boathouse" painting was still available. If I couldn't have you, I at least had to have the painting, as it was a part of you and a memory of us. René told me that you were up here and the painting was, as far as he knew, *still available*." I felt the dual meaning of the words and grateful for René's sense of timing.

Caleb's look deepened. His face leaned in closely and, breathing into my ear, he whispered fervently, "Eliza Hales, I should have never let you out of my sight." I felt goose bumps trailing down my neck, radiating out to my fingertips.

In only a few moments, with Caleb's words, a door had been opened that I could either step through, or turn away from. As I contemplated which direction I should take, the longing returned to the surface at a level I had never experienced before. There was nothing to forgive—nothing whatsoever. He suffered a tremendous loss with the death of his father, and he endured it as best as he knew at the time.

I needed to touch him, to reestablish the connection we once shared, to let him know in no uncertain terms that nothing had changed—and that everything had changed. I lifted his face with both hands, lovingly

212

looked up into his eyes, and with a quiet smile streaming with tears, I offered with much relief, "What took you so long?"

I was overcome with pent-up emotion that had been harbored for a decade—a decade of a full life, but plainly, not as enriching as it could have been. I could see that unmistakably now. The rumbling sound of the rain now driving against the side of the barn could not compete with the beat of my heart. Caleb unfolded a handkerchief from his pocket and gently wiped away my tears. Sensing that he was not alone now in his feelings, his eyes dazzled with an intensity that was effulgent, like a solar flare. I would remember this indelible impression on his face for as long as I lived.

With a look of pure devotion, Caleb gently, but with a deliberate urgency clasped my shoulders, gliding both of his hands up through the back of my hair against my neck and leaned in his face, pausing for just one, brief, moment, that felt like an eternity. The look of love in his eyes pierced clear through to the depths of my soul and bathed me in undiluted light. The compelling force of his exultant expression made my entire body weak—while at the same time, never more alive. From every direction, like a compass guiding my true north, I closed my eyes, in preparation for drinking in the most achingly beautiful moment of my existence.

"Eliza, I've loved you from the first moment you walked into my life," he declared, then his lips found mine, a decadent, but life-essential yearning. As he held me close, he cinched-up his grasp, melding our souls into one, perfect span of time, as each pass between us sealed forevermore: that we belonged together—always.

As if no measure had been lost between us—and yet, we were adults now, with careers and plans—together, we silently locked up the gallery and took a long walk, hand-in-hand into the woods, in the solitude of the conservation land behind the house. Disbelievers who couldn't agree that children and friends once grown up can't still be in love—and clearly, even more so—were sadly mistaken. Thankfully, it was apparent that our trajectories had paralleled all along, moving toward this intersecting point in time.

The sweet smell released from the wet moss under our feet, freshly hydrated from the downpour provided a welcome accent to the serenity of the forest. We hiked for what felt like miles, happy in our contentment, until we came to a log spanning a small brook. Wanting to show off, I sprang across the expanse without even shaking the fallen, heavy limb, baiting Caleb to come across and catch me, which he did; as he captured me, he lifted me in the air and with one, single rotation, returned me to the ground, holding me for several minutes. There was a closeness and shared joy that centrally emanated from us, like the beacon of *Misthaven's* lighthouse.

Finally breaking the quiet of the wood, Caleb proclaimed, "I know you just got your PhD, Eliza—well done, by the way, as I always knew you would," he paused, took a deep breath, then added as he exhaled, "and I know you live in Concord, so I'll just make this perfectly clear: I want to be wherever you are—whether it's Boston, or Concord, or Camden, Calcutta, or Kalamazoo, I want to be with you—*anywhere*."

His kiss still lingering on my lips, Caleb's insistence of his relocation was the real surprise in catching me off guard.
"Would you really wish to leave and practice law elsewhere?" I queried, amazed that Caleb would give up his track to partner so easily, while at the same time, not wishing to whisk in a cloud over our happy clime. Before he answered, we found a trail that led back down, closer to town, and continued to amble through under the shelter of trees.
"Eliza, you and I have always been decisive people," he continued. "I don't believe that has changed in the last ten years, has it?" I shook my head, "no," so he soldiered-on in conversation, trying to frame the magnitude. "None of this advancement in life—if that is what one must call it—ever felt justified, or worth the effort for only myself. I

always felt that I was preparing for something—for a life, a future—with *you*. Making myself a better person—a refinement, if you will—was always in hope of sharing myself with you. I don't know if you feel the same way, but I'm done waiting," he looked with anticipation for a reaction from me.

"Done waiting for what?" I replied, hoping that he and I were both on the same page, emotionally. *Was I getting ahead of myself?*

Two more steps and we were back into town. We made our way across Route 1, over near the harbor. We stood by the railing overlooking the sailboats below, as I gently elbowed Caleb in the arm—the déjà vu of the view was entirely reminiscent of "us."

"I think I know what you mean, Caleb. Yes, I am most certainly done waiting. Now, please tell me if we're talking about the same thing," I urged, as I bit my lip, still wondering, a little hesitant.

Caleb took my hand, and led me down to the showcase of stunning sailboats, many of which were from faraway ports. Pier after pier, we scanned the horizon of vessels, until my eye stopped on the aft of a sailboat peering out from behind the historic schooner from the other day. Occupying the berth that was previously empty, next to this antique lady of the seas, was none other than, *Eliza's Wake—Casco Bay*. "I hope you don't mind my commandeering your boat and taking her for a spin," Caleb's eyes widened, with his grin, a perfectly matched set.

"Once again, yes, I'm *definitely* tired of waiting," I laughed, and grabbed his hand, pulling him aboard my boat, mischief in my eyes. "Let's sail—right *now*," I commanded, and Caleb and I resumed our posts like intricate clockwork, synchronized to the lapping waves against the hull. In a few minutes we were able to make ready for an evening sail, to cap off a most perfect, most unexpected day.

As we passed Cradle Cove and Gilkey Harbor of Islesboro, Caleb went down below, then returned with a picnic basket. It was not my buckled, store-bought one I usually kept on the boat, but a much larger one, handmade by what appeared to be a Passamaquoddy artisan, who truly had honed their craft to flawless precision. Its recognizable, ribbon-like elements of ash, birch and sweetgrass made me utterly homesick for Hales Isle, as both Caleb's and my families collected the Passamaquoddy designs, due to close, personal ties in friendship and understanding. Father had installed a beautiful, open case to display these works of creativity in the library there. It was one of his—and my—favorite additions to the home. It was a conscious decision to not have the display encased in glass, as if the enclosure would somehow stifle the woven art.

"By the way, this basket is for you—an early gift for your birthday," Caleb announced. I realized that my birthday was only a few days away. I would have forgotten all about it, if it wasn't for this pleasant reminder.
"What a beauty, Caleb! Thank you so much. I love it!" I gratefully cheered, then enthusiastically kissed his cheek. My thoughts returned to the many birthdays of his that went unrecognized, due to separation and when we were kids, his aversion to the attention. I intended to remedy that.

As Caleb carefully removed the basket lid, a simple meal of smoked Maine salmon, sliced cheese, grapes, pared apples and crackers was presented, along with sparkling Gewürztraminer grape juice, imported from France. My familiar, dragonfly point blanket now within reach, Caleb wrapped it around my shoulders, staving-off the chill rising from the wind off the water. Taking my eye off the bay at the helm for a second, I watched him move about, having taken his suit jacket off and rolled up the cuffs of his sleeves, as well as putting on his boat shoes, as his feet were bare after boarding.

Even in the cool of late May sailing, Caleb still didn't need outerwear, as always. His arms gestured a supple strength, as he prepared the cockpit table for a most idyllic dining experience. The motion of his body, in combination with the drift of the ocean currents was mesmerizing. Caleb would never be softened from a mostly indoor career. His muscular build was evidence of that. His mind and intellect were equally inspiring. Still captivated, feeling my cheeks start to blush from my blatant gawking and ruminating, I thought it best to set my sights on the horizon, once again. My thoughts circled around the fact that I not only felt pampered, but protected, in our sheltered bay. I felt a direct, tangible line connecting us to the last time the two of us sailed together, and smiled, as Caleb moved by my side, caressed my face, then fed me a slice of apple. I returned the favor and sealed it with a kiss.

Chapter 30

For the next two weeks, Caleb stayed on my boat as my guest in Camden Harbor. Each morning he came to the Beasley's house, where I would have breakfast ready for us to dine together. Each night I would go to bed in my privacy, secretly missing him for all the years we had lost, wondering about expanding on our mutual statements of being, "tired of waiting," a statement that had since been clarified, in some regard. We were both tired of waiting to take up where we had left off. In my heart, I knew that it would not be long before we took off on an entirely new journey, one that would solidify everything we had ever shared together, and enhance our lives a thousand-fold.

During this respite in Camden, we shared in a temporary partnership of running the gallery; he would handle most of the customers, while I would run the register and receipts. Somewhere along the line, he had learned a lot about artistic media. It was a pleasure to listen to him discuss directional movement, center of interest and mood with customers. Like our sailing ventures, we were compatible in each assuming the lead, or falling into a support position in just about every situation, both with clients and in our daily life. There was nothing mundane about our routine; on the contrary, the more I was with him and watched him—especially his charm in interacting with people—the more enamored I became with him, and in dreaming of a lasting future together.

Here was a man who made everything for himself and was now of substantial, financial means. There was nothing to prove; there was no inflated ego. The Boy Scout of long ago was now as universally indispensible in his career and my life as the multipurpose pocket knives of his youth. More importantly, Caleb was entirely generous; he'd be the first person to offer the shirt off of his back, his last dollar, or last meal to a total stranger in need. He would go the extra mile in helping someone with a repair or running an errand for the infirm. This quality was one of the things that I loved most about him—that, and his ability to make me feel joyful every, waking moment we were together, as we fell back into our usual repartee. This familiar, yet new dynamic was intensifying in seriousness.

I wasn't ignorant enough to think that life would not serve up its own smorgasbord of challenges, but I also knew that with Caleb by my side, an interesting and fruitful life, with whatever hurdles may be put in our way would indeed be the life that we would share together. It would be the kind of life that was definitely worth living, a life that by some accounts, was only presented in dreams.

I had heard that the promotion rumblings at the museum began to escalate, from a growing number of emails and text messages from coworkers. It came to a point where I needed to make an appearance, despite my sabbatical, so that I could be included in the Curator candidate screenings. My timing to disappear was a bit off, in this regard. The Executive Director didn't want to have to go outside the organization, but policies in-place made it mandatory; this made it necessary for me to return, to remind the board of my capabilities as soon as possible.

Caleb suggested that he go ahead and sail back to *Misthaven*, while I pleaded my case in Boston. In a week I would join him on the island, where total leisure would be on the agenda. His mother would have him all to herself for a couple of days before my arrival. I knew it would be a blessing for both of them. Father and Dana would arrive shortly after me, for the Fourth of July. They had already been in touch with Mrs. Eddleston, so her preparations for each of our arrivals were already in the works.

Caleb and I agreed it was a stellar plan; however, the idea of being apart made my heart ache, long before we had even separated. It wasn't like me to feel this kind of need, but I did. I came to an understanding that I had felt that need all along, but had unconsciously filed it away for safekeeping—for later, when the time was right to be entirely bold about love, and what matters most in it.

The morning of my meeting with the Board was thankfully, uneventful. I was up on time and took a long shower, back in the routine of my Concord home. I was mentally preparing myself underneath these warm drops of therapy. I made a note in thought to do a deep cleaning of the house before I left for Maine again. After a quick breakfast, I sent Caleb a text message—not wanting to wake him up, but to let him know that I was thinking about him. Surprisingly—or rather, not surprisingly—he responded instantly, with a supportive wish of good luck for my inquisition, sharing an impassioned cheer of confidence in my abilities to "wow" the crowd. He also expressed his reluctance to stay at his mother's home, instead, preferring to sleep on my sailboat—a reminder, he said of, "everything most beautiful" in his life. I closed my eyes in gratitude for the blessing of this journey, and the direction we were headed.

I took the "T" into Boston and was able to arrive early in my office, in time to exchange a few pleasantries with my coworkers, a reminder to those who were competing that I was still very much alive and present. I wasn't arrogant enough to state matter-of-factly to anyone, even myself, that I deserved the promotion, but I was assured that I had given it my all—more so than many—out of honor to my mother, and out of a lifelong pursuit of this as a dream come-true. As my name was called to enter the conference room, I looked up at the skylight at the unveiled sky, smiled and hoped for continued support.

Serving a dual purpose, I had made a date for lunch with Ashleigh while I was back in town. I would give her a much-needed update, as so much had transpired recently. I needed to find out what was new with her, as it was certain to be newsworthy. We met elsewhere in town, instead of the café at the museum for lunch. We agreed upon meeting at Quincy Market for some clam chowder, although Ashleigh chose something less fattening to eat, as she had never appreciated the traditional soup of the City of Boston.

"Eliza, I haven't heard from you in weeks, so I know something has changed—drastically, I have a feeling. I too have something to share, but I want to hear all about you and what you've been up to. I've been in total suspense, so put me out of my misery," Ashleigh begged, as she handed me some oyster crackers to go with my chowder, then resumed pushing her salad around with her fork, picking out croutons along its path.

"I sold the twin painting—the 'Longfellow's Boathouse' watercolor!" I hinted at a much larger announcement, but Ashleigh didn't catch on.

"That's great, Eliza, but how does that keep you out of touch for so long? It makes no sense. What's been going on with you? Have you been okay?" her concerned brow dipped, causing me to feel especially bad for her unease.

Instead of prolonging the ignorance, I blurted it right out, "Ashleigh, I didn't actually sell the painting, but it found its rightful owner: Caleb." Ashleigh's eyes grew wide, her cat-eyeliner looking more pronounced. Sensing her pause to allow me to explain, I proceeded casually, but thoughtfully with, "He came into the Camden Gallery and found me. René had told him where I was. It was on Memorial Day—certainly a memorable one! Anyway, Caleb proceeded to apologize profusely and sincerely, then told me he'd loved me since we first met, and that he would follow me anywhere in the world," I stated triumphantly, then augmented, "—and we also sailed *Eliza's*

Wake that day," I paused, taking a gulp of water. Sensing Ashleigh was preparing to interject, I hurried up and concluded, "We're committed to both of us spending the rest of the summer on Hales Isle, and if he asked me to marry him, I'd do my best to count to ten before I'd say 'yes,' but it would be next to impossible!" I gushed, the love for this man tumbling right out of me, a string of professed adoration in inadequate words. "He's staying with his mother now, and Father and Dana will be arriving for the Fourth, so if he wanted to ask Father's permission for my hand, he'd have easy-access." I even surprised myself with being so presumptuous, but I was optimistic, as I was "tired of waiting" and he was too, I think, for the same thing. I tried to build up confidence that that was the meaning behind his words.

Ashleigh looked stunned, then quickly regrouped. I braced myself for her usual counsel of, "Beware!" disguised as, "sage advice" for the lovesick, but instead, she surprised me with, "Eliza, I couldn't *be happier* for you!" she applauded, a mile-wide smile plastered across her face, a billboard for any dentist seeking to endorse their business in achieving that perfect, dazzling emblem of dental health. Ashleigh added, "Why put off getting married if that's what you both end up wanting? You don't make frivolous decisions, Eliza, that's for certain. As for Caleb cutting you off years ago? He was a grieving kid. You forgave him; I forgive him. Besides, I always knew you still had feelings for him. I knew it the minute you shipped that bracelet to him, 'Return to Sender.' It was such a spiteful thing to do—so *NOT* you, Eliza. If you didn't care, you wouldn't have made such a grand gesture out of that slap in the face, via parcel."

Sensing I still needed more assurance that she meant every word, Ashleigh secured, "You know me; I don't say things I don't mean, so please understand when I tell you that if you don't have your wedding at a place that I can attend, I will be devastated!" she cried out, in all earnestness. "What I mean is, don't have your wedding *on your boat*, Eliza; I will *not* attend without proper, strappy shoes—with *heels*—and you *know* how they are NOT allowed on the *'Wake!"* *Yeah, she got that right.*

I couldn't hold back the laughter any longer. I swallowed my last bit of soup before I spit it out accidentally, from the raw force of the hilarity. "Ash', I promise you, that if—*when*—Caleb proposes, that I will insist on a wedding location where sea legs are not required, okay?" I shook my head, smiling, another giggle reaching my lips and bouncing into the air. "Oh, and one last thing," I quickly added, "I interviewed for the Curator job and I have a good feeling about it; there's a good chance they might offer it to me!"
"Congrats again, 'Liza!" her sincere gesture was sealed with a hug.

"So Ash', you had big news too—what's up?" I redirected the attention, rightfully to her."
"Well, you know how my brand has been primarily in fashion and cosmetics, right?"
"Yes, and don't forget the 'ASH Lifestyle' line," I piped-up, showing I was paying full attention.
"Well, I decided that it's time I put my Marketing and Communications degree to further, good use, Eliza, so I'm founding a media venture!"
"Like an online magazine with all its partnered social media, or are we talking something else?" I was seriously intrigued for her.
"Yes, and much more," she confirmed. "I can't discuss all of the specifics right now, but calling it a media venture in the traditional sense is just the tip of the iceberg!" *Okay, now I was really curious.*
"Oh, and one more thing: Eliza, I'm in love with my business partner."
"Who, Harper Stillwell?" I guessed, realizing by her, 'What? You've got to be kidding!' look that I completely missed the mark—that I was totally clueless who she was talking about.
"No, he was never my business partner; Harper was an investor from an initial venture capital firm, who has long been out of the financial picture. I'm referring to Chase Oshiro. We met in Hawaii, remember?" Ashleigh gave a prodding look. "You may recall, I was

on my way back from a commercial project in Tokyo and he was on my flight, with a stopover in Honolulu. We hit it off and decided to have dinner once we landed."

"Okay, I remember. Sorry about that Ash'."

Clearly reanimated with her exciting news she continued, "He's from the Big Island originally, but he has some serious ties to Japan through his grandfather, who was a high-profile attaché for decades. And Chase is no stranger to fashion, or the media either, Eliza. He founded several global companies in Japan, including a textile endeavor that produces handmade goods—you know, the kind that one could classify as 'art,' more than 'fabric.' He's helping me take my company to the next level," she paused, a big exhale passing through her lips. "What I didn't plan on was falling for him, 'Liza. Mixing business with personal is never a good idea." Ashleigh seemed quite torn about the whole thing, so it was time to help her sharpen her perspective.

"Follow your heart, Ashleigh and don't worry about the business part, or Chase's involvement in that part of your life. You've done just fine on your own with your empire. You've pretty much single-handedly grown a childhood dream into a serious contender in the realm of beauty. You've been too busy to find the love of your life, because you've been doing business, and doing it well. You're only twenty-eight, but you're more of a threat to your competitors than much larger, much more seasoned corporations. Maybe you should consider that business is likely your best opportunity to find someone who is as driven and savvy as you are!" I stared into her eyes, giving my best, "You know I'm right," look.

"I think you're wise, my friend. I don't need to have some life-changing event to slap me in the face to say, 'Hey Ash', time to share your life with someone who really matters.'"

"Then it's settled—a double wedding!" I joked, knowing the reaction I was going to get.

"Eliza, I love you honey, but you and I both know that if I get married, I will *not* be sharing my big day with you. It would be *impossible* to coordinate our color palettes, not to mention, who ties a love knot with a sheet? *My* sheets are 1200-count Egyptian cotton, not rope!"

With that bit of comedy, we rose to say our goodbyes, as I needed to head back to the museum to make another appearance for good measure. We made a promise that we wouldn't let so much time pass between us for our next get-together.

After a couple of days of hanging around Concord, hoping for an invitation for a second interview at the MFA—as I knew they had expedited the selection process—I decided that I had better things I needed to be doing than cleaning house and waiting for an update, like enjoying my paid sabbatical more fully. My house couldn't be any cleaner. I called Caleb and told him that I was on my way, first thing in the morning. His energy transferred most tangibly over the phone, which made my pulse race. *I guess he misses me*, I smiled to myself.

This was a rather different ferry ride. After all of the trips from Portland to Hales Isle before, this time was reconciling a divergence in two people's paths. Like a sturdy branch being grafted into another worthy tree, I was reminded how each tree could have done just fine all on their own, but together, in blended harmony, something truly unique and magical could emerge, and thrive. As I neared the island, the idea of having two months to cultivate my relationship with Caleb flashed before my eyes, effused in dramatic color. Up on the deck, I closed my eyelids and raised my face to the clear sky, the sunlight providing a brilliant shade of dancing red, and warmth that cloaked my eager spirit.

There he was, waiting for me. He wasn't standing motionless, his focus solely on the approaching ferry, but instead, doing what was inherently his nature—what I loved about him; he was down on bended knee, helping a little girl, tying her shoelace. The little girl's mother had her hands full with her other two children, likely readying them for their own, grand reunion, dockside.

As the light breeze blew the little girl's pinwheel in her tiny hand, her joy was effervescent. I could hear her high-pitched giggle traveling toward me on the gentle wind. It was then that Caleb rose and looked up, the smile in his eyes the most welcome greeting of home. It was of a familiar, contented home I had always known, and yet, a remarkable, new adventure, brave and exhilarating.

As I wheeled my suitcase and shouldered my duffle bag down the gangway, before I was even off of the ramp, Caleb reached his fingers through the suitcase handle and strap of my bag, removing them from my care, then placed them aside. There were no words spoken, no trite utterances whatsoever of asking how my trip was, or how he had missed me. Words did not serve a proper purpose for this moment. Instead, he gave it what it rightfully deserved. There, in front of all the other passengers disembarking on the pier, it was just the two of us. Everything and everyone on our periphery were obscured. All I could see were his eyes, transfixed of liquid blue, conveying a message that was pure and undiluted. He was in love with me—madly and passionately.

I jumped into his arms and placed my lips soundly upon his full mouth, a sweet serenity with dizzying effect. Over and over our lips moved together, like a lingering fragrance that tethered emotionally, to a specific instance of heart-stopping, cherished memory—the kind you wanted to replay in your head again and again, savoring the way it made you feel alive.

With a rhapsody of internal music emanating from my heart, I said out loud what had been a part of me always: "With every fiber of my being, *oh, how I love you* Caleb. I've never *not* loved you," I declared ardently, breathlessly, the depth of feeling pulsing through me. He set me down on the dock, and with a slight pause to garner each and every one of his own emotions, it was his turn—this time, he kissed *me* with full intent, and did so with a fervor that caused my entire body to ache. I thought of nothing but him and how he had captured me forever—every part of me. His essence was indisputably powerful. It surrounded me like a misty vapor that whipped up into a mighty storm, then slowly glided, descending, enveloping me until it saturated my every pore. Like the essential requirement of water for survival, I needed him—and he needed me—a complementary pairing of two, independent souls, who weren't afraid of opening themselves up to a new perspective of tandem grace and splendor.

Rusty happened to have his taxi parked nearby, and Caleb spoke to him for a moment, then loaded my things in the car, and the taxi sped off without us.
"Let's walk," his sparkling invitation floated on the wind. I was fully intrigued, happy to bask in the elements of the island and the kiss that had just transported me. This was better than a vacation; this was just the beginning.

We meandered along the shore, weaving our way around driftwood and through the trees. A bird of prey was circling back toward the center of the island, something catching its eye. The beach route bypassed the central artery of transportation, avoiding the dust and crowds, as it was summertime, when tourism was in full swing. At some point we'd have to cut back inland before we got to the point where *Misthaven* resided, as the coastline became too steep. For our immediate future, we were very content in holding hands and offering each other sea shells we thought were worthy of attention.

As we approached the last stretch of shoreline before the craggy rocks, we headed up the familiar, stone steps to the arched, iron gate, patterned with arcs and sea swirls—the gate of my childhood, a symbol of peace and happiness. I had passed through this portal hundreds of times, a gateway to adventure on either side. Caleb reached for my hand and we sprinted up the steps, with me right behind him, our footing sure, despite the mist that had settled in the shade of the fir trees. As we passed through, emerging on the other side, a distinct metaphor of our new life together entered my thoughts, bringing a wide smile to my face, which Caleb noticed immediately, raising his eyebrow inquisitively.

I marveled at the many expressions and mannerisms of Caleb that hadn't changed at all, reminders of so many happy times together, and yet, he was not the same. The talented boy I knew growing up had become a remarkable, and even more multifaceted, man—a man who had just swept me off my feet, literally. He quickly spun me around, set me back on the ground and gently kissed my forehead.

"Beep-beep-beep!" went Caleb's cell phone, an obnoxious, "techno" tone that shattered the magic in an instant. He looked embarrassed that he had forgotten to silence it before, a cute, bashful, "Oops!" expression crossed his face. He checked the caller ID and promptly answered, "Hey Jim, what's up?" Caleb slowly turned around and around in a circle as he spoke, fully engaged in the conversation.

I took a few steps back, not wanting to intrude. Nonspecific information of a case was shared between them, with Caleb's tone becoming more firm as the conversation progressed; he was not pleased with the way things were escalating back at the office, his associate clearly not handling things properly in his absence. The ease with which Caleb always carried himself was rapidly disappearing, his frustration clearly marked by his furrowed brow. I got the sense that his displeasure was not with just this one case, or with this individual coworker, but with his job entirely. As he hung up, it was clear that the phone call definitely knocked the wind out of him.

"Eliza, I can't believe this, but I am going to have to go back to New York for a few days. I will be back in time for the Fourth, I promise.

I have to go put out a fire that I didn't start, but I'm the only one who can. It's nice to be needed, but in this case, it's infuriating that I can't even get away without an emergency erupting, with nobody else capable of taking care of it!" he seethed.

I'd never seen him so angry before. I expect that I missed out on many sour moods over the years, but this was certainly justified. I couldn't help feeling badly for him, especially since he had already been waiting patiently for my arrival on the isle. I tried not to focus on the fact that we'd be apart again, but instead, thought about another joyous reunion. *I could get used to another dockside thrill.*

"Hey, don't forget how wonderful a 'welcome home' gesture can be," I hinted with a knowing grin at our earlier, public display. The islanders certainly had fuel for gossip for months to come, perhaps even for a tourist to write in their travel journal as a, "most, unexpected Maine." Mainers weren't known for Public Displays of Affection. *Glad we could help clear up that fallacy.*

Having already settled in at *Misthaven* while Caleb packed at his mother's, as well as giving a big hug to Mrs. Eddleston, my focus was entirely on these last, few moments with Caleb. We had to rush him to the ferry to make the next boarding. As I waved goodbye to him at the landing as the boat moved away, I blew him a kiss, followed by several more with both hands. I then got a little overly dramatic, feigning being shot in the heart, accompanied by a little stumble, to which Caleb texted me across the fast-growing width of water between us in response: *Me too.* We were certainly in agreement about this sad turn of events. I stood there on the pier until I couldn't see the outline of him anymore, then took off running.

I jogged around the island to clear my head of the doldrums of separation. As I got lost in the mechanics of the fitness, I decided that instead of taking my boat for a sail, I would wait until Caleb's return and resume my original sabbatical plan for painting, building up my portfolio for some new pieces to sell, and one special work to keep, ideally as a future gift of personal significance. I was going to immerse myself in a creative frenzy, as I didn't know when I'd have this much time again to just paint. I anticipated that when Caleb returned we would pick up where we left off, building our relationship.

When I got back to the house, I went up to my room and found all of my art supplies where I had left them, and started refilling my palette with my trusted friends of, cadmium yellow and red, cerulean and ultramarine blue, viridian and hooker's green and alizarin crimson, among others, for the next morning.

I always wondered why white watercolor paint was available, as my instructors taught that if you planned ahead, the white of the paper should suffice. That counsel, along with turning any "mistake" into something else were words to live by, applicable for just about any hardship scenario in life, not just for the challenges of watercolor as a medium.

Caleb called late to let me know that he made it to La Guardia Airport around 11:00 p.m., but I could tell he was exhausted, so I suggested he call when he was rested and had time. I told him I would understand if he was incommunicado for a few days. He didn't need to feel that he had to update me on everything, or check in with me, as I knew he was busy. I'd see him when he returned. I could wait.

After we hung up, I realized that I hadn't checked my email all day. I thought I should see if there was perhaps a message from the HR Department or Executive Director from work, before I went to bed. I had notified them that my postal mail in Concord was temporarily on hold, and gave my forwarding address in Maine before I left, but I knew email was how they primarily structured their offers—or rejections, as it was their environmentally-conscious policy. I hoped that I wouldn't receive the latter.

Sure enough, an email was waiting for me from Susan Santoya, the Executive Director herself. She was a friend of my mother's, but still, it was such a surprise to receive a personal note. *This must be good news!* I skimmed down to the first paragraph and saw the words, "...we've decided to select another candidate for this position who best meets the needs of our organization." *Oh. That's a supreme disappointment.*

I knew it was a long shot, but somewhere along the line I had let myself hope I'd at least make it to the second round of interviews, perhaps even seal the deal and get the promotion. I was certainly disappointed, but I didn't let it put a damper on my mood, as I found I painted more prolifically and freely when I felt more positive.

This career news put me in a frame of mind for considering pursuing other professional avenues, when the time was right. I now had a Doctorate, which, combined with my experience, put me in a different category than I had been in before. I reminded myself to not discount that fact, as well as remember that I already had the qualifications to lead some organizations, even at the executive level. I wasn't going to let this setback ruin my focus for pursuing my dreams. What was exciting, was that I knew my life goals could change to something else at any time, and still be a fantastic opportunity— perhaps even more so than its predecessor. I certainly had options! I liked having the flexibility to pivot, placing emphasis elsewhere, if that's the direction I was drawn to. I had to trust in this path being the right one for me for right now, but at the same time, knew that working toward something is essential if you want to change your life in any regard. Not wanting to lose focus on this precious time to create, I decided that I should just do nothing for the time being other than thoroughly enjoy my sabbatical.

Chapter 31

I was a bit of a hermit for the next week. I didn't visit anyone on the island, entirely focused on finishing up the paintings I had started. One was of my sailboat with the fir trees and ocean in the background, and the other was of a large piece of driftwood against the pebbled shore; its silvered, weathered grain and sharp protrusions erupted a stark contrast next to the rounded elements beneath it. The latter painting reminded me a bit of Andrew Wyeth's work, as I included a similar palette of payne's gray and burnt sienna paint. The more somber colors were a deviation from my usual, more vibrant color schemes, but this change spoke to me. As the linen curtains in my room wafted open in the breeze, the Wyeth-esque moment was too surreal. "Time to go outside and enjoy some sunshine," I announced, to me, myself and I.

It was July third and the perfect time to take a break from my still life, as Father and Dana had just arrived and came in the side door near the kitchen. Mrs. Eddleston was about to offer to help carry in their luggage, but I assumed the role as Bellhop for the day, flexing my muscles, to show that my vacation didn't turn me to mush.

"Something's different," Father observed, wasting no time sharing his analysis as we each put our share of the baggage down, upstairs.
Dana chimed in too, with, "Yes, there's a change in you Eliza. It's subtle, but it's definitely there."
"Well, I've been painting up a storm lately—maybe the joy of creating is spilling over," I shared, my response not quite satisfactory to my tame inquisitors.
"No, that's not it. You've been painting your whole life, Eliza. Now come on and tell us what's got you so rapturously radiant," Father

insisted. "You haven't *met* someone, have you?" he asked with a hopeful gleam in his eyes, taking a sip of his lemonade.
I seem to have some pretty observant parents!

"It's actually quite romantic—serendipitous, really," I began. "My agent, René had been contacted by a buyer who wanted my "Boathouse" painting, and he sent up the customer to Camden, before it sold," they both looked at me, then each other, intrigued. "When the buyer came into the gallery, he asked to buy the painting and told me he would follow me anywhere in the world!" Now they were looking rather bewildered. *This was too much fun!*

"Okay, that's only part of it," I hinted. Their unified breath-holding and concerned looks were evidence that they weren't following me at all. I figured I'd better cease the suspense. "The buyer was Caleb Longfellow. I saw him three years ago in San Francisco, remember? Well, he wanted to apologize then, but was in an awkward relationship and the occasion just didn't allow for proper time to address it. He wanted to do so for ten years, and finally he got up the nerve and did on Memorial Day. Let's just say that I won't forget his apology for as long as I live." My eyes started to look a little dreamy.

Dana caught-on immediately and smiled, but stayed silent. Father still wanted more information.
"So, are you two now dating?" Father got to the point. "You know I always liked him, Eliza. He was always a good young man. I was sorry he left Harvard, but I can only imagine how he must have turned out, if you are so smitten with him—and believe me, you ARE smitten," he stated, matter-of-factly. *That's an understatement!*

Dana finally spoke, and she was the more perceptive of the two: "No, Benjamin, Eliza is not just *dating*, she's already made up her mind. She has chosen the man she is going to marry, and Caleb is the key to her heart. Can't you see it in her eyes?" She reached over and gave me a big squeeze. I smiled a wide smile back at her, remembering her words about the diamond key necklace. Father put his arms around me and looked into my eyes, confirming what Dana had surmised was true. My eyes were harboring tears of joy, now ready to spill.

After a leisurely lunch and another round of questions from my happy parents, I looked up at the clock in the kitchen and realized that Caleb should be arriving any minute on the ferry.
"I've got to run—Caleb's arriving!" and I was out the door at a spirited, all-out run.

Not wanting to be sweating profusely for our reunion, I slowed down my pace as soon as I reached the post office and walked the rest of the way. Surprisingly, fate was on my side; I wasn't late for his arrival, but apparently the ferry was, but only by a few minutes. You could set your watch to their schedules, so something unusual must have happened.

I could see the ship had already passed Big Diamond Island and had come into view, so I tried to spruce up my hair a bit, while I paced around the dock nervously, as I had forgotten to check my face and brush my teeth before I ran out of the house. *Too late now.*

Caleb looked refreshed. Wearing khaki-colored cargo shorts and a faded, "Columbia Law School" blue and white t-shirt, the analogous colors of the ocean framed his brilliant blues on his smiling face. *Father was going to especially love his choice of t-shirt,* I sarcastically mused, kicking a stone off the pier.

Before the ferry had even docked, Caleb had tossed his two, large duffle bags, one by one onto the pier, then leaped over the railing, jumping the six foot span to land without any difficulty. The ferry Captain just shook his head; clearly he had seen this demonstration from him far too many times during his lifetime. Caleb was seriously nimble; his agility was amazing as he continued the trend by sweeping me up into his arms, and showering me with kisses.

"Like my shirt, eh, 'Liza?" he said as he put me down. I offered him a smirk in response. His animation was contagious; his buoyant behavior made me wonder if he was going to start doing cartwheels in a second. I might have to challenge him to a race back to the house.

"What have we here?" Caleb peered to the side of my cheek, as he took out his handkerchief and lovingly wiped the smudge of burnt sienna paint off. "I see you've been on a creative streak," he grinned proudly.
"I missed you Caleb. I hope you're ready for some serious fireworks tomorrow!" my double-edged threat brought a mischievous grin to the man's unshaven face. He sensed my noticing the stubble, so he self-consciously stroked his chin and ran his finger across his upper lip.
"It suits you," I complimented, calling attention to his more casual than usual appearance.
"*You* suit me," he countered, picking me up off the ground and planting a much more determined expression of affection upon my lips. As he pulled his head back to look at me, he was absolutely beaming!

"Well I guess you must have put out some kind of fire, Caleb, as you are utterly triumphant!"
"Yes, Caleb swoops in and saves the day!" he proudly exclaimed, strutting around me in a circle, looking like he was closely evaluating me in some way. I thought at first he was just enjoying the view of my legs, as I had intentionally worn a cute pair of shapely denim shorts, but then I figured out what he was really up to.
"Okay, you want to race?" I challenged him.
"Hold on a sec'—let me hand over my bags to Rusty," which he did in short order, returning to his posturing. I rolled my eyes, putting on my best, "Game-ON" face.

"Okay, you asked for it——" and I was off in a flash, not even giving him a chance for a countdown. Yes, I cheated. He didn't care, as he was in hot pursuit and catching up rather quickly. We both were enjoying the fun of the chase.

We kept to the center island road, the stomping of our racing feet stirring up dust trails behind us. My lungs were thankful to be in the lead. We turned off along a side road and found the trail to the beach, kicking up sand as we continued our sprint. Just when I thought I was gaining distance, my footing started to falter in the instability of the sand. I was caught completely by surprise, as Caleb leaped at me from behind to grab my hand, taking us both for a tumble in the soft, tall grass jutting along the shoreline, his arms cradling my fall. Lying side by side for just a moment, we locked eyes as the force from the stumble provided further momentum. In the end, Caleb had me pinned beneath him, his playful smile, victorious. I smiled up at him to let him know I wasn't hurt, as I expected he would realize the distance we fell in a heap, and worry.

Like the sun's rays on this bright, summer day, Caleb looked at me, joyous. He rolled over onto his back and gently pulled me with him, my body lying off to the side, so as to raise my shoulders and face to a strategic viewing position. His expression was serene.

I took advantage of this new perspective looking down upon his glorious face and slowly drew my finger along his hairline, back across his now-closed eyelids, sweeping down over his lips, where I gently drifted my finger back and forth for a few seconds.
"I'd say we're picking up where we left off rather nicely," my look intent, referring to a prophetic note he once gave me years ago. His eyes showed instant recognition to what I was referring to, and they ignited.
"Kiss me, Eliza," Caleb breathed; his echoed words clung. And I did, with a meaning that could never be construed as anything other than total and complete, euphoria.

Several curious seabirds hopped over to see what we were up to. Our exchange must have been the top news story for the proximate wildlife of the island. Their presence gave a comic pause, ending our blissful moment as we sat up and each laughed a hearty chuckle.

Caleb rose to his feet and offered his hand to help me up, sweetly picking a few blades of grass from my hair, as he quietly hummed a first stanza of an old Welsh melody about one's true love. We stood there for several minutes, as the bell buoy rang in the distance, he caressing my face and I his, basking in the warm glow of each other's countenance.

Arriving at the arched gate at *Misthaven*, after we passed through, Caleb leaned over and kissed me gently, promising to come and find me in two hours.

"Wait a minute, Caleb," I urged, as I tugged his arm to come with me to the house. "I have something I want to give you."
"What is it?" his curiosity was now piqued, running his hand unconsciously through his hair.
"Just wait right there," I pointed nonchalantly with my finger to the Adirondack chair, set on the front lawn off to the side by the lupines. I ran inside and came back out moments later with a wrapped gift of surprise.

"Open it!" The anticipation of his reaction made my heart race.
"Okay, Eliza, this is too much; this is—" and I put my finger to his lips as he held up the revealed painting, made lovingly and especially *for* him.
"It's *Misthaven's* boathouse, with my dinghy in the foreground," he recognized, as his fingers traced the edge of the walnut frame, his eyes hovering on the red boat in particular. "It's beautiful, honey! The shingled detail and the colors—they're so rich and vibrant—especially the sky! It will go perfectly, paired with 'Longfellow's Boathouse,' like a matched set," a knowing smile reached his eyes. "By the way,

when did I last leave that project of a vessel behind here? I don't think it has been on your property for years," he admitted.

"You're right. I painted the red dinghy from memory, but the rest I sketched out and painted it all on the premises, just recently. It's some of my best work, I think.

"There's a deeper meaning in this painting, Caleb. Even when we were apart all those years, you were always there in my heart. You always left that little boat out in the elements, year-round, so it being so casually beached aground in the grass in the painting was a symbol of my connection to you. You always left an indelible impression," I smiled and hugged him, after he set down the artwork. "Oh, and one last thing of note: the sunrise is symbolic of new beginnings. At the time I painted it, it was wishful thinking. Now it's all coming to fruition," I declared, as I wiped each corner of my eye.

Caleb paused awkwardly and looked at his watch, then sheepishly said, "I'm so sorry, Eliza. I don't mean to seem ungrateful—truly I don't, sweetie, but I really do need to take off," Caleb offered with an apologetic look, rising from his chair and hoisting the painting in its wrapper under his arm. "I love you, Eliza," he pledged, his eyes beginning to smolder as he begged his leave. "This really is a truly special gift," and he kissed the top of my head and made his way toward the edge of the front yard. I followed him for a few yards, then waved goodbye.

"I'll see you in two hours!" I called out to him, a sweetness lingering, knowing the presentation was a success.

"Dress for an adventure!" he shouted back to me, smiling as his melodious laugh floated through the trees. I contemplated that strange little mystery for a moment, then jogged the rest of the way back to the house to go take a shower and change.

Chapter 32

"Where's Father?" I asked, arriving freshly showered into the parlor to find Dana curled up in a wingback chair, overlooking the ocean.

"He took a walk a few hours ago. I think he wanted to check on an elderly neighbor," Dana responded, taking another sip of her hibiscus herbal tea. I could smell the zest of the added lemongrass; it was heavenly. I decided to join her, but with a glass of water instead. I needed to hydrate properly, after my earlier jaunt. I was dying of thirst.

"You going out later?" Dana's inquisitive smile curled like a Cheshire cat. "I hear the weather is going to be *glorious* this evening," a sparkle in her eye glimmered, hinting that she knew full-well that romance was on my mind.

"Caleb suggested that I 'dress for adventure,' so I'm not exactly sure what he had in mind. It could be anything, as he *is* a Boy Scout," I winked, walking toward the stairs. "I better go dry my hair before it tweaks," and I gleefully took the steps, two at a time.

As soon as I was ready, I heard Dana's voice come up the stairs. "Eliza? Can you come here please? There's something at the door for you," she called. I wasn't expecting a package, and usually it would never make it from the post office to a home delivery. Curiosity got me, so I arrived at the door to see what was going on.

"What is it?" I asked. Dana handed me a marbled envelope of deepest charcoal gray-on-black, perhaps made by hand, with a black, sheer ribbon wound through its back as a closure. I opened the surprise delivery and found an intriguing note card inside. Trimmed in gold leaf with a red dory, beached aground, with a stand of conifers illustrated off to the left side, the words, "From the Desk of Caleb Daniel Longfellow, Esq." headed what appeared to be an invitation. I couldn't believe the similarity to the painting I had just given Caleb—

astonishing, really. Now I knew the reason behind his lingering gaze on the subject matter of the painting I had just given him. Beneath his name on this custom stationery was a cryptic message:

"Find the tree where I rescued thee and there, My Love is where it be."

"What is *that*, Eliza?" Dana's curiosity was also piqued.
"It appears that my adventure is a *treasure hunt!*" I squealed, and I was off on a most magical journey through the woods.
"I'll see you later!" I shouted to Dana, as I took my letter in hand.

I knew the exact tree, from those many years ago when I had foolishly climbed to its loft above. There, pinned to the trunk at eye level was another beribboned correspondence. I unfastened it and glanced at the contents. It read:

"Further still I see thee sit, upon a rock that seas the shore."

"Marvelous," I remarked aloud with a wide smile, knowing a favorite rock of mine. *This is waxing poetic.* I especially liked the play on words of, "see" and "sea." I headed over to the spot in question and found neatly tucked into one of its crevices, another one of his secret messages, clad in the special, mottled enclosure. This one was more obscure in thought:

"Reel me in like a creature of the sea, and that is where my heart will be."

I pondered the words, trying to remember what he might be alluding to. "Ah yes!" my eyes widened, as the mystery unfolded. I knew just the place!

I arrived at Mrs. Stanfield's cottage momentarily, taking a more thoughtful pace toward the back of her house, where Caleb and I had seen her shark. I paced around the yard for a few minutes, feeling a bit sad that the house still sat empty so long after her passing. The hydrangeas were in bloom and the roses and peonies were spectacular. Thankfully, her beautiful home had remained fully cared for by a kind neighbor. Thinking of her tending her garden, and her famous catch of the day made me smile. *She would have wanted Caleb and me to be together.*

As I turned toward the back of her house, there on the back door was pinned another custom missive. I was getting close; I could feel it. I opened the envelope and read the next clue:

"Here I sit when I wouldst view a wondrous place that shelters you."

Hmmm, this one might take me more time to figure out. "Nope! I know exactly where this place is!" I shouted out loud and off I strode to the Longfellow's boathouse—the spot in question of a most poignant painting—a painting that one could say brought us together again.

As I neared their property, I thought for a brief second about knocking on the front door, to see if Caleb was even around, but I thought better of it; I didn't want to spoil the thrill. Instead, I made a deliberate path to the boathouse where they kept their personal gear; it was near their house, separate from the boat yard further around the point of their land. There on its window sash was another letter, leaning up against the panes of glass, sandwiched by a jasper rock. I picked up the rock and saw the distinctive stripe banding its girth. *A lucky rock—yes, I am the lucky one.* As I opened the covert communication, this time the words jumped right out at me:

"Thou art true and sail the blue, an ocean's breadth, I long for you.
To sea the sky enshroud the sun, my love abounds, my heart is won!"

I didn't even hesitate; I knew exactly where the destination this sonnet was directing me to. I was supposed to go to *Eliza's Wake*. I leaned over and retied my hiking boots, setting off in a straight line to find the deeper meaning behind this quest.

241

With each step, my appreciation grew for the words chosen for my adventure. His poetry was eloquent and stirring. Each clue brought me an additional, pleasant memory of the two of us together, and anticipation for what waited for me in this special journey today.

I looked down the hill toward the dock behind *Misthaven* and could see Caleb was waiting for me on board. I could also see that a new, black, bimini top had been installed on my boat—a complete surprise. I had no idea when or how that was missed in my own backyard. It was another major gift—a very nice plus to have when we could take her out for a sail next time; however, I needed to halt his propensity to spoil me.

When I got close enough to see what he was wearing, it was too late for me to turn around and go back to the house to change, without appearing rude. I was underdressed. Caleb was wearing khaki-colored slacks and a vivid, sky blue dress shirt with the neck casually open. His shirt wasn't tucked in and his feet were bare, which I found incredibly attractive. Despite his easy-care appearance, something about him just shouted, "FORMALITY!" which made me uncomfortable, looking so up-country. As I slipped off my boots to leave them on the dock, I could see something hanging from the boom.

"My lady, let me assist you," Caleb reached down to help me climb aboard. As I got close to him, I could smell cologne—a primal, compelling scent that complemented his own, magnificently. It was one of those fragrances that no matter where or when I were to smell it again, I would be transported right back to him in this very special moment and place, every time.

"Eliza, I knew you'd want to change, so I brought something for you," he gestured to the beautiful, cotton wrap dress with short sleeves—

now hanging off the tip of his finger. "Why don't you go below and change," he suggested. I was completely relieved, as my dusty shorts and hoodie were no match for his choice of attire. For some women, a man buying her a dress, then asking her to "slip into it" might feel too demanding, controlling—perhaps even demeaning. With Caleb, I knew that it was just a kind and thoughtful gesture.

As I thanked him for what was obviously a purchase just for me, I could see that the dress had an effortless periwinkle and pale yellow, large floral pattern on a white background—a very breezy look that was flirty and fun; it was definitely not a, "ditzy Grandma's housedress." Caleb had excellent taste, not to mention he guessed my size 5 correctly.

I climbed below, eager to make a better impression with more appropriate clothing to match his, as something was clearly afoot. Heading to the v-berth, as I passed through the galley, I could smell something wonderful. I decided I better not peek. As I shut the door to change into the dress, I made a mental account of a few amendments to the boat I noticed. In addition to the obvious, black bimini with zippered enclosure, some new electronics were added to the nav station, as well as a framed photo of the two of us when we were teens; it was sitting prominently in the salon, behind the settee. I had forgotten about that photo, as it was one that his mother had taken of us at his house. I also wondered how much all of this sailing gear cost him, as it likely totaled a pretty pricey sum. Without further delay, I let my hair out of its ponytail, bent over and shook my hair, and called it almost done. Finally, I took one quick look in the mirror mounted behind the door, found myself presentable and returned topside, to see what other changes Caleb had made.

He slowly pulled me through to the other side of the companionway and invited me to sit on one of the new cockpit cushions, apparently custom made, with a small, vintage, black, cream and tan Hawaiian print—a stark, exciting complement to the teak and black canvas covers. I decided not to even try to guess why, and stop being so annoyingly curious to all the additions quickly adding up.

I shifted in my seat and turned back toward the companionway, as he had jumped back down below. Moments later, he came up with whatever delicacies had been hiding, smelling so mouthwatering and placed them upon the cockpit table that he had set up when I was changing. He had a feast prepared before us. He handed me a platinum-rimmed, cream-colored china plate with almond-crusted mahi mahi, a mango salsa and what appeared to be wasabi mashed potatoes, which I confirmed with a discreet sniff when he wasn't looking. Next came a linen napkin, which he gently placed across my lap for me. He turned for one second, then came back with imported, sparkling mineral water, pouring it into two, platinum-rimmed, fluted crystal glasses. The silverware appeared to be real silver.

"Caleb, I'm totally impressed," I shared, my words breaking the silence. "Thank you again for my beautiful dress. I feel utterly feminine without feeling like a bee might decide to pay me a visit— and this wonderful meal smells divine! Every detail—impeccable! What a perfectly exquisite surprise!" I looked up at him in gratitude, and mouthed, *I LOVE YOU.*

"Let's have a toast first," he encouraged. "Eliza, I wanted to tell you how stunning you look—always, but here, in that dress with your petite bare feet, you look entirely irresistible." *So we both are attracted to each other's feet—intriguing.* "I wanted to also thank you for playing along with my fun today, but in all seriousness, I wanted to toast you, you incredibly sweet, smart, strikingly beautiful woman and thank you for being in my life again." His eyes lovingly lingered on me from head to toe, then with that, we clanked our glasses and drank.
I then added my own testimony of, "Caleb, being together again is the greatest source of joy in my life. I was content with my life, but I didn't know just how amazing it could be until now. Thank you, my dream come-true," and with that, I took a sip, then leaned over and

kissed him softly on the lips, the trail of his cologne returning with me as I sat back down.

We enjoyed our meal and savored every, last morsel. All the traipsing across the island had me famished, so it was a welcome treat to have such fine cuisine. Caleb poured each of us another glass of mineral water and he came and sat next to me, putting his arm around my shoulder. I leaned closer and put my head on his chest and closed my eyes for a moment, listening to Caleb breathing in and out, in and out. His breathing was even, but his pulse was elevated. I looked up at him and he had his head leaned way back, eyes closed, smiling wide at the sun. When I returned my head to his chest, Caleb was dangling another one of his heathered envelopes between his fingertips before me, within reach.

"What's this?" I asked, looking at his eyes for an answer.
"It's the last clue," he confirmed. His eyes gleamed as he gestured with his chin for me to open it. Inside, there were three, brief phrases. It wasn't a poem this time. It was an ardent declaration:

> *"You chose to seek to find the treasure, Eliza, the treasure of my heart.*
> *My beautiful Eliza, you brought it with you: YOU. I love you."*

I hadn't noticed while I was reading his note that he had slipped out from beside me, as when I looked up he was now right in front of me. Caleb was there, looking straight into my eyes on bended knee, holding up the small, wooden box with pewter clasp from long ago, a profound offering. I remembered the beautiful bracelet, eager to return it to my wrist. A smile crossed over my face in anticipation of seeing it again, and for the added meaning it would represent, now that we were back together.

The look in his eyes continued to grow even more jubilant, his gaze even more intense. Caleb slowly opened the box and vowed, "Eliza, I can't imagine life without you. I have always known you were the

245

only person in the world I wanted to spend my life with. Would you do me the greatest honor of becoming my wife?"

I looked at him with complete surprise, coupled with my feelings of absolute and complete fidelity. He would be mine, always, to have and to hold; and I was his, only his. The idea of this becoming a reality fueled a fire within me that was unquenchable. I had imagined this happening one day, and had even joked about its imminence a couple of times, but to actually be happening, right now, was nothing short of the most beautiful dream I could ever hope for.

There in the box was not just the cherished, green-gemmed bracelet I imagined, but in the center of the same, purple cloth was a ring—not just any ring, but a ring that could only have come from Caleb. This grand gesture had a single, substantial, bezel-set, princess-cut diamond, flanked by eight points of a compass rose element radiating and wrapping seamlessly into the gold shank. The design was not overly-nautical in appearance, but rather a contemporary, artistic design, with an effortless nod to seaworthy origins. It was breathtaking!

Caleb placed the ring upon my left finger—a perfect size 6 ½. He had put much thought into this. It was entirely fitting—a perfect ring to declare our undying love for each other and cherish forever our mutual love of the sea.

My ten seconds had surely passed, and I answered him resolutely, "Caleb, it would be the greatest blessing in my life for you to be my husband. Yes, I will marry you!" and with those words, Caleb gently grabbed my hands and we slowly stood up together. I put my arms around his neck and he cradled my face with his hands. "Eliza—" his voice trailed off, emotion seizing him, and his lips found mine as he wrapped his arms around me, my tears overflowing, our kiss sealing a rapturous concordance of every truth between us, now and forevermore.

246

Our joy encircled this precious moment, marking in time a new journey of a life together. As Caleb pulled his face away and gently turned me to face the sunset, he reached his arms around me from behind, placing his face in the back of my hair. We stood there for a few minutes engrossed in the riot of the colorful sky, with pinks and magentas, dusky plum and blazing orange streaks.

"Caleb, the ring is absolutely beautiful. It's perfect. I can't imagine a more symbolic token of our love for each other," I gushed, smiling, with tears still coursing.

Breathing into my hair, he mumbled, "I love how your hair smells, Eliza." His face still lingering, he added, a little more clearly, "I've had the design sketched for over ten years. I found the best jeweler in Maine and asked to have 'my true north' be created in gold, its radiance guiding me home. You have always been my home, Eliza."

I couldn't believe he used those exact words, "my true north," the very words that I had thought in my head when he kissed me in Camden. *I would tell him this when we were alone on our wedding night,* I thought, smiling contentedly to myself.

"Eliza, I have another ring just like it you know—for me—a wide, gold band with the same compass rose elements overlapping, repeated around the circumference."

"These rings are idyllic for two sailors who love island life and are head over heels in love with each other!" I enthused. I wanted him to know just how perfect this moment was for me, but the words just weren't doing justice, so I cradled his face lovingly, and kissed him fully, no holding back. He understood my meaning.

"Oh, I almost forgot," Caleb turned around and retrieved the bracelet from the box in a flash, clasping it back on my left wrist. "Where it rightfully belongs," he added, kissing the top of my hand, tracing his lips up my arm, then to my jaw line, sealing the return with another kiss, as gentle as a summer rain. I started to apologize for my past, mistaken, bracelet "return to sender" episode, but didn't get very far with, "Caleb, I—"

"Don't. It's in the past. Don't feel anything but happiness, Eliza," Caleb kindly urged, with gentleness in his eyes. He followed up with another kiss, thwarting any further comment on the matter.

We resumed our vantage point for a spectacular finale of a sunset, sitting side by side, our hands clasped, fingers loosely intertwined. I caught Caleb looking at the ring on my finger, and smiled, then nuzzled up next to him more closely.

Breaking the sustained silence, I casually inquired about a wedding date: "When would you like to get married?"

"I think you know how I feel, Eliza. I'm tired of waiting. How about you?" his face beamed, reminding me of our earlier conversation in Camden.

I absolutely concurred, but I wasn't quite sure just how soon he was implying. I tried my best to guess: "How about next spring, right after the thaw? I know the perfect setting! Do you know that little Downeast chapel—you know, the one in Washington County overlooking that little inlet of Cobscook Bay?" my eyes widened, hoping he agreed.

"I know the exact place. I love it! It's perfect; however, I was thinking more along the timeline of August ninth—*this* year; that's *next month*, just in case you were wondering, sweetheart," his toying smirk of arrogance was adorable.

Not leaving any details to chance, Caleb continued, "Oh, and we have the full support of your parents. I already spoke to your father, Eliza, and got his permission. How's *that* for traditional—and expeditious?"

"Wow! I'm impressed, but it wasn't a tough sale—*that's* for certain. Father has always loved you and approved of you—always," I assured, "—but when did you talk to him?"

"I had called him to meet me earlier today over at my mother's house. It seemed like the most private place to meet and the shortest distance. I didn't want to run out of time before the treasure hunt," he grinned, reminding me of the rather involved plan that fell into place perfectly, and why he seemed so torn to leave after I gave him the painting.

"You are quite the architect of perfect proposals, my darling. Oh, and I am in complete agreement on the wedding date. I didn't think you were as tired of waiting as I was, but it appears we are both in complete harmony on the matter!" I smiled up at him and touched his face.

"August ninth it is," Caleb stated proudly. He added, "I really didn't want to have to wait another moment, but to give Dana the proper time to throw something together, thirty days was about all I could spare," he winked. "I wanted to marry you on the ninth, because that was how old you were when we met, remember?"
"How could I forget? You brought me so much happiness then, as you do now. Everyone is going to be so happy for us!" I effused, which reminded me we were not alone in this landmark event. "We better go share the good news," I suggested, then we headed off barefoot up to the house.

Chapter 33

The next morning, I sent Ashleigh a text message with the news. Her response was as effulgent as ever: *Eliza, I KNEW it was coming! BEST WISHES and CONGRATULATIONS to you both! I'm in a meeting with overseas distributors. I'll call you asap!*

I succeeded in keeping Ash' in the loop. I was curious how she would take the news that the wedding was only one month away. *At least it's not on a boat—she should be grateful for that,* I reasoned.

Telling and celebrating with all the parents last night kept Caleb and me up until very late, so I had to wait until today to try and reach Ashleigh. If she didn't call me back in an hour, I would call her. She needed as much advance notice as possible, as she was going to be the best Maid of Honor, and time was required to fulfill her duties properly. The first thing she would put on her "to-do" list would be my trousseau—the clothes specifically, although she would have to share that action item with Dana, if Dana would even consider sharing that motherly tradition. I suspected there would be opinions shared about every aspect of the wedding between those two. I wondered how they were going to get along together for something where they each share such crucial responsibilities. *It was definitely going to be interesting,* I smirked warily to myself.

Dana had already been on the phone with several people this morning, planning, booking, haggling and instructing. She was an essential event coordinator. Father was also involved with something, although he was a bit more discreet about it, choosing to hide out in his study. Dana paced about the room waving her pen in the air like a symphony conductor with her baton; it was a lively demo of grace under pressure.   Thankfully, nobody was mad about the short notice; everyone seemed overjoyed, despite the hastened pace.

As if on cue to protest my thoughts on the short timeframe, Ashleigh called.

"Eliza, so tell me all the details! I'm *so* excited for you and Caleb!" she remembered to pause, waiting for me to answer her.

"First things first: I would be most pleased if you would be my Maid of Honor, Ashleigh. Will you?"

"*'Most pleased?'*" she giggled. "Eliza, is the sky blue? I would no sooner stop breathing than abandon you on your important day. Consider me at your service!" I could feel her support reaching across the miles, but apprehensive about dropping the bomb of a rather abbreviated timeframe.

"Great! Now, here's the tricky part: the date is set for August ninth," I gingerly offered over the phone.

"I assume you mean next month," she nonchalantly replied. "—can't say I'm surprised," was all Ashleigh offered in retort. "I know that you have found your soul mate—or rather, picked up where you left off years ago—and just want to get started on your life together, as soon as possible, 'Liza. It all makes perfect sense to me."

I appreciated her immediate understanding, without question. Resuming my checklist of important, "to-do" items, I reminded her of the most important aspect of color, with, "Don't forget my color palette, Ash'—a chartreuse dress for you in the perfect shade to complement your hair and skin, with matching roses and lily of the valley for your bouquet. For the men, I would like black tuxes for Caleb and his brother Mike. The parents and rest of the family can wear what they want. I'm sure they will match perfectly. For me, I'll have a breathy nosegay of white tulips and roses, with subtle, variegated cabbage. I'd also like a dash of cerulean blue throughout the décor. Take note of the beautiful scarf you bought me for my year in Paris! Remember? Those colors would be the inspiration for the entire event. I know you will balance them perfectly," I stated purposefully.

Ashleigh seemed unfeigned, ready to take care of things. "I *do* love a challenge, though. Prepare to be amazed!" her triumphant voice heralded. And with that note of cheer, I knew our wedding day was going to be idyllic.

After talking with Ashleigh, I went down to the *'Wake* to ready her for a sail, as Caleb and I had vowed last night to take her out today. I assessed that there really wasn't anything needed to be added or repaired, so I took another look around to see what else was new. I saw that there were two new sails added—another jib and a replacement spinnaker. As I closed the sail locker and turned around, Caleb was climbing aboard.

"Perfect timing!" I cheered. "By the way, I've taken inventory of all of the new acquisitions you've made for the *'Wake*. Before yesterday, I would have offered to repay you, but now, since we're about to share in everything, I'll just ask, why all the fuss?"

"I'm glad you asked. I'm making *a fuss*, because I'd like to make a timely suggestion. How about we honeymoon on the *'Wake*? I've been thinking about it for a long while, actually. I've equipped her so that we could take our time in returning to civilization—a very long time, if we should so *desire*," his eyes smoldered for effect.

"Well aren't you the romantic! What a perfect honeymoon sojourn—adventure on the high seas. Brilliant idea! Your ability to plan every, single detail is awe-inspiring, Caleb. I'm starting to feel a bit behind in my own schemes."

"Preparation is my middle name," he winked, and with that statement we were off for a day on the bay, just like old times, but not quite.

Returning later that afternoon, as I was about to step off the boat, I looked back at Caleb still at the helm. As he stared toward the horizon, I said half-jokingly, "You know, after today's sail, I think we really *should* take an extended honeymoon, like, how about we take off for a few months, or maybe even a year?" Looking for a reaction of reason, I didn't expect him to agree with me quite so easily.

"Actually, Eliza, I've been thinking about additional leave from my job in New York. After the recent fiasco I single-handedly thwarted, I can pretty much ask and I shall receive from the partners, even tacking-on more time on top of my current leave, with no ramifications. I could easily ask for more time—seriously, they will say 'yes' to anything I ask—it was *that* important of a save. I'm *golden* at the firm," his eyes flashed with equal brilliance, his confidence reigned supreme.

"I'm thrilled that you have a solid career, Caleb. You've worked hard for it. You mentioned that you wanted to be wherever I am. I am very grateful for your willingness to sacrifice for me, *for us*, but I could just as easily move to New York. Although the competition for jobs in the city art museums and organizations is pretty stiff, I'm certainly game. I don't want you to feel like you have to give up all your hard work for me. You have way more seniority than I do. I'm happy to make the move," I looked into his eyes with warm affection.

"Eliza, don't worry about my options being limited, or me being tethered to New York City. I'm not. I'm licensed to practice law in four states, actually—New York, Massachusetts, Maine and California." I looked at him in astonishment.

"Basically, I made preparations to practice everywhere I thought you might end up someday, Eliza, just in case. If you chose Louisiana, I was in serious trouble," his trademark grin reappeared. "A legal whiz kid can only overextend himself so far," he continued. I was still stunned, just nodding at this new information.

Caleb was now sitting back down in the cockpit and I had joined him. He toyed with the ends of my hair, as he continued his ruminations with, "I've also been doing a lot of thinking about where we might choose to settle down. I don't see myself staying in New York; I never have. It's a lovely city with lots to do and see, but it's just not me. I especially didn't appreciate seeing the love of my life kissing some guy on New Year's Eve in Times Square a few years back," adding a surprise interjection. Getting back to the matter at hand, he went on without skipping a beat. "In fact, it would be very easy to never go back to the firm. I've actually been considering starting my own practice ever since I was a kid. I was thinking Boston, or somewhere along the coast on the mainland in Maine. What do you think?"

My mind had changed direction from making plans with Caleb to wanting to make amends. Of course the situation so long ago was nobody's fault, as Stewart was my boyfriend at the time and Caleb was entirely absent, but I still felt a bit embarrassed. I suddenly felt a little guilty, as I remembered even thinking that I had seen Caleb there and dismissed it readily. I became angry with myself, fidgeting my hands together in my lap.

"Caleb, you saw me and Stewart kissing?" my question strangely came out as a whisper. I had nothing to apologize for, and yet, I continued to feel an explanation was warranted.
"Sure, I saw you two locking lips. Before all the 'PDA' started, I was watching you. I was there with friends and happened to notice you across the Square. You looked so beautiful, Eliza. I wanted to come over and tell you how I felt—how I'd always felt, but then you became a bit preoccupied," he smiled reluctantly.

I realized that my guilt was not from kissing someone else and Caleb seeing it. My guilt was from feeling like I betrayed the memory of Caleb and me, by not believing that I saw him there across the Square.

I considered the weather and the crowd at the time, and tried to put it to rest, by offering up a simple apology for the circumstance.

"I'm sorry you had to see that. I'm even more sorry that I didn't believe I saw you there. I actually thought I had seen you there Caleb, yet I didn't believe my own eyes. I had felt your presence with me every time I was in New York. When I was gazing at the tree in Rockefeller Center, I felt you with me. I thought of you often Caleb, wondering what you were doing, how you were doing. Being in the same city as you and not being able to see you felt entirely wrong. I tried very hard to forget you and stop caring, but it never stuck."

"Hey, I wasn't trying to make you feel guilty," his voice was gentle. "I was just mentioning that I was jealous, that's all—incredibly jealous, actually," the gleam in his eye gave away his sweet sense of humor, as well as confirmed the sincerity of his candid words.

"Who knew Caleb Longfellow was the jealous type?" I joked, trying to lighten the mood.

"Hey, I can be honorable; we can invite Stewart to the wedding, if you'd like," his competitive streak emerged.

"Thanks for the gesture, but no thanks. I don't think that would be a good idea. We were engaged once," I admitted awkwardly, wishing this conversation had not opened up to put a damper on the celebratory mood.

"I know, Eliza. You were living your life—sadly, without me, but hey, I finally swallowed my pride and made things right, didn't I? Now I get to marry the most loving, capable and most exquisite bride in the world!" His smile was triumphant.

"Caleb, I knew the minute I said 'yes' to Stewart that we were doomed," I admitted. "He wasn't the right man for me. I was a puzzle missing the most important piece: you. Thankfully, I didn't make that mistake with Stewart and instead, went on living my life, subconsciously hoping you and I would find each other again, although the idea stayed under emotional, 'lock and key' until you walked through that gallery door. Thank you for unlocking my heart to the limitless possibilities of happiness, as they were finite without you; with you, infinity seems like an understatement." With that declaration, we sat facing each other for a very long time basking in each other's warm smile, caressing each other's face, tracing locks of each other's hair with a free fingertip, while our other hands remained intertwined. It was a deeply intimate moment of togetherness, securing that our love knew no bounds.

Chapter 34

I didn't get much painting done over the next few weeks leading up to the big day, other than finishing my works in progress, but I rejoiced in the knowledge of having a lifetime to be inspired for creativity. Caleb would be a huge contributor to that endeavor. In fact, we had discussed and refined our immediate plans and decided upon a two-month cruise for our honeymoon aboard *Eliza's Wake*, returning to *Misthaven* for October, for the foliage. To add more chaos to our already overburdened wedding schedule, we were going to both move our individual households to *Misthaven* and reside there after our honeymoon, compliments of Father, to execute our future plans on the island that brought us together in the first place.

Being equally productive people, even with our blissful honeymoon on the seas, I fully expected us to have preliminary business plans drafted before we returned to dry land, as we both decided our future as husband and wife and partners in life did not involve remaining in Boston or New York; we were both going to give our employers our resignation notice. We both had money saved. We would rent out my house in Concord. Not many people had the blessing of a strategic vision as a couple, who also had the foresight to know that sometimes the best plans are the ones that travel by and come to you by way of the wind.

"Please hold still Eliza, while I fix your veil," my Maid of Honor chastened me in the back room off of the chapel. Ashleigh and Dana had both been busy bees since we announced we were saying, "I do." Now they were still doting, arranging and perfecting every last detail of this most special day. "From the bottom of my heart, thank you both for everything. You two need to find your places," I said, with absolute and tender endearment as I was about to walk down the aisle.

As I stood there in my quiet moment alone, I was picturing in my mind the look on Caleb's face, my heart fluttering, knowing in just a few minutes I would be enveloped in this most precious of moments. *We were getting married!* We were about to embark on the most magical of voyages together: matrimony.

I took another turn in front of the full-length mirror, admiring the gown that had been worn by my mother. Even with all of Ashleigh's fashion connections, she knew not to even mention any other dress. My mother's dress and veil had been carefully preserved for me, housed at *Misthaven* for all these years.

Mother had a tasteful sense of simple, timeless style, thankfully, so that I could share in this special day with her, this way. Even though I was alone in this room, I could feel her presence. There was an acknowledgement between us, that she too was blessing our marriage.

The stunning, white dress was of the perfect color—not too cool and stark, and not bordering on cream. My gown had fitted, long sleeves and a form-fitting bodice, with princess seams in smooth satin. The scoop neckline nicely accented my collar bones, along with the six carat, teardrop, single diamond pendant and matching earrings Dana let me borrow, per tradition. The Basque waistline formed to a crisp point, flowing elegantly into the full and ethereal, tulle, ballerina-style skirt that hovered along the floor with sheer grace. Every twelve inches along the bottom edge of the skirt, exquisite lace peeked from behind the mounds of its partnered fabric. The back of the gown had diminutive, pearl buttons forming a fluid, vertical line, continuing the neatness of the design.

My hair was in a sleek updo, in a clean chignon with a smooth bang, pasted off to the side, allowing the flounce of my elbow length veil to billow over my head and shroud in elegance. I pivoted on the balls of both my feet, then pointed each toe out from under my dress to see the satin bow on each, white, sling-back, peep-toe shoe, hand-carried from Milan, a gift from Ashleigh to me. The expected blue I chose to wear was a tiny secret, an embellishment on a garment for my husband's eyes only.

My emotions were holding steadily to preserve my makeup, but they were also circling the possibilities that lay before us. We were about to declare our love and commitment in front of one hundred of our closest family and friends. We would be solidifying our love by a much higher degree—lofty even, my mind reeling in the headiness of this reality. I was not afraid. *No, indeed not.* I was overcome with joy and hope. I was considering the reverence of this monumental occasion on this beautiful morning of August ninth.

"Eliza, my dear, it's time for me to take you to your perfect match," Father quietly entered the room, gesturing with his bent arm for me to grab on. "He is worthy of you in every way," he added in hushed tones. "The many things you two are going to create in your life together will be nothing short of remarkable," he concluded, smiling proudly at me.
"I would say a most definite, 'interesting and fruitful' life lay ahead of us, Father. Caleb has always been the man by whom all others have been measured. I am the most fortunate one to be able to occupy his heart. And *my* heart? My heart is full—to overflowing." I grabbed my bridal nosegay, as I candidly insisted, "Let's get me down the aisle before my tears give way to an abundant display."

The dressing room we were in had no direct access to the interior of the cozy chapel, so we walked outside to enter through the front, double doors. Looking up from the entrance steps, I made a mental impression of the milk white, clapboard siding and high steeple, its diamond shingle pattern and bell a perfect complement to a coastal, New England wedding.

As Father and I entered the narthex, I could see the light streaming in through the memorial stained glass window behind Caleb at the altar, casting deliberate dimensions of harmonious glory, celebrating the joy that effused from both of us. As my eyes were drawn to Caleb's, we each witnessed our mutual exhilaration of this journey we were about to endeavor upon.

Even from this distance, I noticed immediately that Caleb had an extra-close shave. I understood his conscientiousness, and smiled in anticipation of what was soon to be intimately ours as husband and wife. The excitement in his eyes was equal to the magnitude of his smile. He wore a black, two-button, notch lapel, designer tuxedo in light wool, with a white silk vest and necktie, and white, silk, pocket scarf. As stunning as his formal attire was, the man clearly dressed the suit.

Like a film camera shot where the center of interest is locked in-place and all other aspects surrounding him are catapulted forward in the blink of an eye, I too held this same perspective of *absolute proximity*—a nearness that was beyond quantifying. Our eyes met and were fixed and riveted, like the gravitational pull of the sun. The brilliance of the moment was equally luminous.

The traditional *Wedding March* melody was not part of the ceremony. Instead, a classical, string quartet occupied the nonexistent corner of the compact chapel, their prelude music a combination of Chopin's Nocturnes, playing his *Nocturne in E Flat Major* as Father walked me down the aisle, toward my soon-to-be husband. The brief distance to where Caleb stood proved necessary for an abbreviated version of the composition.

As the room quieted, all eyes were upon us as we exchanged our vows. They were simple, sacred words that hung closely in the air, a lasting nourishment for eager souls enlightened with the rapturous music of fidelity and promise.

As he looked at me, I could see everything that we could be together in his eyes, and the assurance that our road together on this passage would be most abundant in both richness and fulfillment. As I looked at him, I conveyed my life and my truth in a prolonged gaze of majesty of this elevated state of being—of absolute togetherness. There was no more waiting. There was no beginning or end, just the eternal circle of two lives soaring together in union, like the rings we now wore, reflecting the very same.

"I love you Eliza," Caleb whispered, and his entire being poured into mine through our kiss, an expression completely our own, signifying we were husband and wife—a blended bliss stirred to perfection, funneled into the outlying reaches of my existence and back again, running in-place along with the beat of my heart.

To offer a hearty thank you and proclaim the honeymoon commenced, Caleb encouraged, "Everyone, I'd like to extend our sincere gratitude to all of you for coming to celebrate with us today. My beautiful wife and I—and I *LOVE* saying, *'my wife'*—would like to ask for your help in this metaphorical gesture of helping us launch our voyage together in life, by pushing the boat away from the pier." Father, Dana, Seth, Mary, Ashleigh and Caleb's brothers closed in on the assignment at the deep water pier at the end of Leighton Point, just a mile down the road from the chapel, as all of our friends and extended family looked on. The steeple bell still ringing, it segued nicely for a farewell wish.

"Don't worry about us," I added. "We'll check in when we get a free moment. For the time being, just know that *we know* you're wishing you were us, taking off from worldly obligations and just skirting the wind for a leisurely, delicious moment in time." Everyone laughed, in full agreement. And with the cheers and hollers from our loved ones, we were indeed launched into this new life full of wonder, *together*.

Coming Soon

The Sequel:
Misthaven of Maine: Journey to Beyond

About the Author

Debut American author, Loretta Boyer McClellan sees the art of the novel as an exciting medium and source of abundant joy in the creative process. With a degree in Art, her multilayered career in executive marketing and communications, and as a journalist, published poet and lyricist, designer and artist, "sized the canvas," so to speak, for fiction writing.

Ms. McClellan is a San Francisco Bay Area native and resident, and part-time resident of coastal Maine. She has lived and worked in many parts of the United States, drawing from these many experiences for her writing.

Loretta Boyer McClellan's greatest delight is her family. She and her husband are the parents of four sons.

She is currently working on her next novel, a sequel to *Misthaven of Maine.*

Media

For publishing updates and author contact information, please visit:

MisthavenofMaine.com
LorettaBoyerMcClellan.com
Facebook.com/LorettaBoyerMcClellan
Twitter.com/lbmcclellan
McClellanCreative.com

Thank you for reading, *Misthaven of Maine!*

www.ingramcontent.com/pod-product-compliance
Lightning Source LLC
Chambersburg PA
CBHW070858180626
46817CB00003B/812